ASH

HIVE TRILOGY BOOK ONE

JAYMIN EVE

LEIA STONE

COPYRIGHT

For information on reproducing sections of this book or sales of this book go to www.leiastone.com or www.Jaymineve.com

leiastonebooks@gmail.com

DEDICATION

To our fans, this one is for you.

ONE

Rounding the corner of the path, I pushed myself harder, red and gold fall trees blurring in my peripherals as my legs demolished the last mile of my run. I was totally going to break my record. My best time so far was five miles in thirty minutes. I was so beating that today.

I breathed deeply, finishing the last few yards at a slow jog, and as I glanced down at my watch, I had to stop for a second before looking closer.

Twenty-five minutes ... *Okay, that's ridiculous.*

I'd only started running a year ago ... after that night, the night when everything in my world changed. Since then – running, self-defense, gun training – I wouldn't be a victim again, that was for damn sure. But to be smashing out five miles in twenty-five minutes – I wasn't even breathing hard. *Not exactly normal.*

As I jogged up the steps into my dorm building, a breeze ruffled my long black hair, refreshing against the light sweat I'd worked up. It was late September; the fall days were beautiful and it was just starting to get cool at night.

Pushing open the door, I crossed the common room quickly and hopped up the three sets of stairs to reach my room. My university, Portland State (PSU), was in northwest Portland, which happened to be my home town. I would have loved to have gone to college in New York or LA, but we couldn't afford it and I couldn't leave my mom. I was almost finished now though; this was my last year – four years of majoring in marketing. God knows why I chose that. I was twenty-one and still had no clue what I really wanted to be when I grew up. Everyone else I knew had the next ten to twenty years of their lives mapped out. Me? I had nothing. So for now, marketing seemed like a good ticket to an interesting job.

"...totally an ash. They were fucking gorgeous."

Two girls pushed past me going in the opposite direction, their voices loud and excited as they chatted about the newest batch of ashes at our university. Personally, the vampire/human hybrids didn't do it for me, but I was in the minority there. The blond girl giggled, and I kind of wanted to bitch-slap her. "Yeah, they must have been on their way back to the Hive," she twittered away.

It made my blood boil the way humans got all crazy over the Hive compound, like they'd do anything to make their way inside. I'd been inside those gates one time, and there was absolutely nothing good there for any human. We were nothing to those creatures, lower than animals, just food, plain and simple. I was lucky I got out with my life and my blood intact.

I shook off those thoughts as I removed the key from my sports bra and opened the door to the apartment I shared with my best friend Tessa. We'd grown up together, both of us from single parents, and we were as close as sisters. I stepped into the semi-dark room, slamming the door behind me.

"There is something seriously wrong with you, Charlie." Tessa was leaning across our small, round, piece-of-shit dining table, her blond curls mussed everywhere. She wasn't exactly a morning person. "No sane person gets up and jogs, it's just not done. Plus, you're not even sweating. Why the crap don't you get all red and blotchy like the rest of us?"

She rubbed at her eyes, before downing the rest of the tar she called coffee. "I'm still betting you just run around the corner and sit in Starbucks checking out hotties for thirty minutes."

I laughed, crossing to the fridge to grab a bottle of water. I took my first swallow, but strangely the water didn't seem to quench the non-stop thirst I'd had the last few days.

"I don't know what's up with me," I said, taking the seat next to her. "You remember what I was like when I first started jogging. I almost had a heart attack and nearly had to be resuscitated."

Tessa snorted. "Oh, I remember. You limped along for about half a mile before collapsing in a heap and declared that the next person who suggested jogging as a way to relieve bad memories was going to get cut."

I hadn't been kidding about that either. Running was like torture to me back then, but it did help chase the mental demons away. "Yeah, and not even twelve months later I'm running five miles in twenty-five minutes and I barely even break a sweat."

Actually, it was really only in the last month I found this whole exercise and defense thing easier. Maybe I was just starting to get it. My muscles knew what to do.

"Come on," I said, jumping to my feet and hauling her up after me. "Comm skills is in thirty minutes, and it's gonna take you half of that just to fix that rat's nest."

She flipped me off but didn't argue. I waited to make sure she actually made it into her bedroom before I dashed across and entered my domain. I had time for a super-quick shower, then I'd have to haul ass to get dressed and out the door in time to jog across campus.

WE MADE it to class just in time. I'd only managed to drag on some jeans and a tank-top, but lately my hair and skin had been doing some awesome stuff on its own, which was very useful during those late rushes to class. Tessa was next to me, propped up on her elbow. Her desk was empty of anything but her takeaway cup of sludge. Unlike me, she'd managed to style an outfit, fix her hair, and smooth out any flaws with her perfectly applied makeup. I had on lip gloss and mascara and that was an achievement.

"Do you think they'll be in class today?" Tessa said as she turned her head toward the doorway.

I shrugged, trying to pretend I wasn't also watching the door, but for a completely different reason. Two ash were normally in this class. They sat near the front, kept to themselves, and probably tried to ignore the fact that ninety percent of the females spent the hour staring at them. The ash were pretty much physical perfection. That's of course if you ignored that fact that they were part bloodsucker. I watched the door hoping like hell they had been hit by a car today and would never make it to class again.

Two perfect heads of golden brown stepped through the door and moved toward their special seating. *Fuck.* A chorus of feminine sighs echoed through the room and I tried my best not to roll my eyes. *Smug, gorgeous assholes.* No car accident and the Hive hadn't burned to the ground last night. *Oh well, there's always tomorrow.* I'm pretty sure I was the only one in the room who hated the beautiful bastards.

"Settle down." The graying professor stepped up to his lecture stand, dropping a bunch of paperwork onto the table. "Okay, so we'll be picking up from chapter eight today..."

"I swear to God, Charlie, I would totally blood-whore myself for one of those Ash." Tessa's hazel eyes were hooded as she ran her gaze along the two elegant males.

"I seriously wish you would stop saying that. They're animals, Tess. Who knows what they do to their donors."

As if he'd heard me, the golden ash closest to us turned his head and fixed his dark eyes on me. All of them had the same eye color, black with a ring of silver right around the pupil. It was just one of the many things which set them apart from us. From humans. I refused to lower my gaze, sensing mainly curiosity from him, before he dismissed me and turned back to the professor.

I shuddered, counting slowly in my head to calm down. Those eyes reminded me of that night. When the nightmares came, it was always black with rings of silver. Tessa knew some of what had happened to me, but I hadn't wanted to go into detail about the attack. Let's just say the nightmare stories about vampires were not all fiction.

"You know, Charlie, we should be thanking the gods. They gave us a race of perfection and every single one is male."

Tessa's lecture was getting old. "Yep, they're all male. Yep, they're all gorgeous. Yep, they use humans as nothing more than living, breathing blood donors. The gods totally love us."

Tessa rolled her eyes and finally shut up. It was a tired debate with us and she knew I was sick to death of hearing about them. Why the human government let those gorgeous freaks walk among us was lost on me. At least they kept the vampires secluded away. I shuddered at the thought of the creatures who walked the night. Ash might be gorgeous and strong and fast, but in my personal opinion, for pure freak-me-outness, they had nothing on the full-fledged vamps that sired them. It was weird to call them vampires; sometimes I felt like I was living in a fantasy movie. Of course, *Anima Mortem Virus* just didn't have the same ring.

We all knew the history. A few centuries ago some rabid bats bit some villagers and gave them a virus that increased longevity, increased strength, improved skin elasticity – among other things – and depleted blood platelet count in the process. The virus allowed the host to live forever, but a constant influx of blood was required for the renewal of cells. It also killed the female reproductive system but not the males. Of course sperm would survive. Friggin' men, they had it easy.

Tessa nudged me and I shook off my thoughts. The professor was glaring at me.

"I'm going to guess you don't have the answer. Moving on." He went back to rambling about how certain colors made you want to buy certain products. Ugh. Damn this class was boring. I stood up and slowly walked down the aisle to go to the bathroom, which would hopefully kill at least five minutes of his lecture. As I passed one of the golden-haired freaks, I noticed his body stiffen and his nostrils flare. His hand snaked out and grabbed my arm.

"What the crap!" I muttered, trying to wrench myself free, but he held on. He stared up at me, pupils pulsing, black and silver eyes flickering. He was taking in deep breaths, his jaw clenched.

You're not allowed to touch me, shit-head.

"Mr. Daniels!" the professor shouted, and the ash

released me right before I was about to clock him one in the jaw.

Holy hell. I bolted to the bathroom, rubbing my arm.

They weren't allowed to do that. They couldn't touch a human without an invitation. Dammit, he had looked ready to eat me or something. Maybe it was feeding time and he'd zoned out. They weren't supposed to be around us unless they had recently fed. But of course rules were made to be broken. I didn't trust ash. They weren't natural.

I shivered, washing my shaking hands. Tessa was crazy if she thought they were something to be desired. Those pulsing eyes were animalistic. I shook myself; I didn't want to think about it anymore. Returning to class, I was totally ready to glare at that asshole and let him know who was boss. But the ash were gone. My face turned beet red as all eyes rested on me. The professor paid no mind and kept rambling. Reaching my seat, I sank low into it, wanting to disappear.

"WHAT THE HELL was that all about in class?" Tessa crooned as we walked to lunch. "What did it feel like? Did you orgasm – I heard that when they touch you it's like a mini orgasm."

I snorted. "You're flippin' crazy, Tessa. You believe everything you hear about them. Did I look like I had a mini orgasm? I was a second away from smashing him in the jaw."

Tessa sighed again. I was going to have to start thinning out her peroxide. She was losing brain cells far too rapidly.

"So did Professor Jennings kick them out or what?" I chewed my lip. I wanted to go for another run. I was starting to crave it, the pull on my muscles, the wind in my hair, the pumping of my heart. It was an adrenaline rush.

"Nope. The two ash shared a look and then they got up and left." Her eyes were wide like she was telling me a horror story.

I shrugged. "Good, he broke a rule by touching me without permission. The other one probably went to take his ass back to the Hive, where I hope he'll stay forever."

I grabbed an apple and water bottle from the snack cart and sat with Tessa on the lawn outside.

She eyed my food. "You're joking with the rabbit food, right? Where's my best friend and what did you do with her?"

I snorted. She had a point. I was a total foodie, but lately my appetite wasn't there.

"Hey, bitches!"

I forced myself not to roll my eyes, but that overly high-pitched voice belonged to Valarie. She bounded across the lawn, her best friend Amber in tow. Tessa and I shared a look. There was definitely a bitch here but it wasn't us. Amber was okay, but Valarie was like a mosquito, constantly buzzing around with an ulterior motive.

I finally managed to stop rolling my eyes and turned to

the girls. They looked similar, long straight bottle blond hair, big blue eyes, fake tanned to the shit, and plastic parts from their rich families.

"Hey, Val ... Amber," I said.

Valarie threw me one of her famous glares. She hated being called Val. And even though Tessa was friends with them, she still grinned at my attempt to annoy the princess. Valarie sat down next to us, smoothing her short skirt over her toned legs. Bitch was perfect but so plastic. No one's boobs were that perky.

"In honor of my birthday tonight, I'm renting out a large part of Stag. You guys should come."

I whistled low. Stag was the hottest club in Portland. "That must be costing daddy a pretty penny." That wasn't exactly what I wanted to say. That was the nice version.

She glared at me and jumped to her feet. "At least I have a daddy."

Ouch, the bitch strikes again. Valarie and I barely tolerated each other. I had no idea why Tessa liked her, but it was only because of my friend that I didn't dropkick Valarie in her perfect teeth.

Tessa elbowed me in the ribs. "We'll be there. Thanks."

I glanced at my watch and jumped to my feet. "I have a stats class, so I'll meet you after and you can talk my ear off about all of the ash you hope to see at the club tonight."

Tessa also stood, then gave me a wink. "You know me too well."

I really did. She was an open book, but absolutely solid as a best friend.

I jogged off in the opposite direction, dreading the thought of tonight, but knowing that Tessa definitely needed me to keep her level of stupid to a minimum. One thing was for sure: if there were ash at the club, and one of them grabbed my arm again, I was ripping it off. That was for damn sure.

TWO

Tessa and I hopped on the MAX and took the train downtown. She put a hand on her hip and gave me a sultry look. "How do I look?"

She was wearing a short black fuck-me dress and bright red lipstick.

"Like you want to become a blood whore," I said with a shake of my head. She'd made me leave my hair down tonight. It curled across my shoulders and down my back in waves.

She laughed. "Good."

I gave her a WTF look as she eyed my skintight jeans, black ass-kicking boots and tight red tank. I was showing all the goods, because Tessa wouldn't have let me leave the house otherwise. She was always pissed I didn't let her dress me like her own personal doll.

She gave an exaggerated sigh. "I have long given up on trying to give you better fashion sense."

I flipped her off, which had her throwing up her hands. "Seriously, we're supposed to be looking to get laid, not kicking someone's ass."

I grinned. My outfit was perfect. You never knew when some ass-kicking would be required. Especially on the streets of Portland. That's what all my training was about now. And speaking of ... my eyes fell onto the large, dramatically lettered, laminated poster that permanently marred the train walls.

Are you an Ash?
*Increased stamina
*Lack of appetite
*Anger outbursts
*Insatiable thirst
*Beauty & Strength
*Male
Call the hotline if these symptoms come on suddenly!

IT WENT on to list the risks and dangers an ash posed to society, and urged them to call for free testing. I shook my head. What bullshit. One fine day you were walking along thinking life was awesome and you were a human and not a bloodsucking creep, and then bam, your body started to change and there was no way to stop the slow transition to an ash. All because twenty something years before, your mom couldn't keep it in her pants and gave it up to some lusty vampire. It was illegal of course to procreate with vamps, but sometimes rules are broken. Repeatedly.

"Why do you think all ash are male?" I asked Tessa. She was obsessed enough with them, she should know.

A cheeky grin quirked up the corner of her lips. "Who cares? I don't question a good thing. Besides, that means less competition for us."

Okay, apparently she was obsessed *and* stupidly uneducated about ash. Great combo there. The vampires and ash were unnaturally beautiful, the exact sort of weapon which came in handy for the luring of stupid, horny women. There were vampire females of course – for the luring of stupid, horny men – but no female ash. For some reason the union of male vampire and female human only ever resulted in male offspring. Male offspring who appeared to be completely human until their early twenties. The virus slept dormant inside their brain until the time their frontal lobe finished development. Then they slowly began to change, and soon figured out that their mama had had some fun with the undead. Some ash knew before their transformation, others were kept in the dark until the last moment.

Familiar landmarks zoomed past; we were almost at our stop. Tessa and I moved closer to the door and waited for the train to come to a halt. There were plenty of students from PSU with the same plan as us tonight, so when the doors opened we just flowed along with the crowd.

It was after 11pm by the time we walked the three blocks. Music washed across the streets, heavy with a strong bass.

"Holy shit, looks like Stag is pumping tonight," Tessa said, practically shrieking my ear off as she dragged me through.

I followed, comforting myself with the fact that at least no ash should be here now. Vampires and ash were not allowed out in public places unless by special permission, such as college classes. Vampires couldn't handle the sun, so the humans were given a curfew of 1am. After that, the night in Portland, and many other major American cities, was ruled by the Hive, and it wasn't in a human's best interest to be caught out after curfew. Unless you were a blood whore. Of course, Tessa never cared for these rules. I'd had to drag her home more than once after lock-out.

The bouncers checked us off the list and then we were inside. Lights strobed across the industrial styled club, bouncing off polished cement floors, steel, and bronze décor.

"Drinks first?" Tessa bopped along as we pushed through the already crowded space. The distinct smell of pot wafted in from the balcony and I chuckled. All of Portland was out tonight.

I caught a glimpse of Valarie's peroxide hair up in the VIP section and realized she'd slightly exaggerated how much of the club she had exclusive for tonight. Still, even though it was small, the elevated zone was a wicked area. She'd love lording it over the rest of the people stuck down here on the main floor. If I pointed her out, I knew Tessa would want to head straight up there. So of course I steered her in the opposite direction.

"Yep," I said, "let's hit the main bar." I desperately needed something wet and preferably ninety percent alcohol.

Tessa immediately put her skills into play and started shoving her way through the crowd. She was small enough to fit into some questionable gaps, her blond curls smacking into the people around her. I wasn't huge myself, but at five feet seven I was half a head taller than my bestie. Which meant I couldn't always follow her path. I lost sight of her for a second, but we caught up again at the bar.

"Four tequila shooters and two strawberry daiquiris," she was saying as I sidled in beside her.

The tired, not-particularly-happy-to-be-alive female bartender scurried off to fill the drinks.

"Four shots?" I snickered. "Girl, we're going to be hammered before we even leave this damn bar."

I wasn't a huge drinker. Mostly I liked a few glasses of wine with dinner. But generally it was impossible to hit a club with Tessa and not leave shitfaced. Looked like tonight was going to be no exception.

"I don't know what you're worried about," Tessa said, grinning as she swayed to the dance music. Her black dress was riding very high on her thigh, and more than one group of dudes had noticed. "You could out-drink me every night of the week and twice on Sunday."

Right. I'd forgotten about my newfound super ability to down a bottle of wine and only get a light buzz. "Maybe tonight we should test this theory," I said. I had to shout a little when the beat changed to something much heavier.

"Hells to the yeah," she shouted, before turning to stare along the long metal bench. "Hey, can you make that eight tequilas..."

THIRTY MINUTES LATER, Tessa and I were still at the bar. I was currently in a drinking contest with two head-shaven, muscle-bound beefcakes who had been pretty sure they could take my hundred and twenty pounds.

They were wrong.

Shot glasses littered the bench in front of me and I could tell that the bar-chick was hoping we'd move this shit along soon. Beefy #1 and #2 were glassy-eyed as they tried to share the last of their bottle. They didn't make it though, slumping down and passing out before they managed to finish.

"I win!" I shouted, swaying a little.

Tessa grabbed my arm. "Come on, babe. Time for us to go and find Valarie."

The nice pleasant fuzz in my head dissipated almost immediately. "Do we have to? I might actually kill myself if I have to spend more than ten minutes in her company."

Apparently all the booze had done was loosen my tongue.

"She's texted me eight times," Tessa said, almost

falling off her heels as she tried to drag me away from the bar. "You've already drank a week's worth of shots. Let's go find our friends and dance."

I reluctantly let her lead me from the main floor. I knew if Tessa wasn't so sloshed herself, she'd be questioning how I managed to finish an entire bottle of tequila and still walk and talk. I was sort of questioning it myself. The alcohol couldn't be weak or watered down, those guys had crashed out trying to finish a bottle between the two of them.

My metabolism was on fire at the moment. Must be all the jogging.

"Tess!" Valarie was all over my best friend, completely ignoring me. I left the pair of them discussing whatever shit drunk chicks talked about, and wandered over to crash onto one of the huge sofas. Tessa was used to me doing this. She'd find me soon and drag me out to dance.

As I settled back, I liked that the shots had my mind all nice and mellow. I felt like I could finally relax and not think about all the scars and shit that littered my life. Still, as the multitude of couples started to surround me, I couldn't fight the pangs of loneliness. I hadn't had a relationship since that night, not even of the casual kind. I just couldn't let my walls down long enough to trust, but I was starting to improve. I was out tonight, I was drinking. There had to be some healing going on.

I shifted to slouch further into the couch. The VIP area wasn't as packed as the main dance floor, so I had the entire thing to myself. Valarie couldn't even pay for enough friends to fill the space. I snagged two glasses of champagne off a waiter as he strolled by, and settled back to enjoy my free bubbly.

After finishing the first, I was sipping at the second when a tingly sensation trickled up my spine. I lifted myself, legs straightening, leather boots shining in the lights as I twisted myself to see the entire area. Tessa was on the dance floor, grinding up against some tall blond guy with cool-nerd glasses. Valarie and the rest of her goons were close by, but none of them were paying attention to me.

But I could swear I was being watched. I tried to tamp down the paranoid feeling, knowing that it was probably just my overactive imagination. Still ... the feeling persisted.

Tessa distracted me then by hauling her butt off the dance floor and running – as fast as she could in her hooker heels – over to me, screaming the entire way.

"Shit, Charlie, you'll never believe it." Her eyes were wide and full of excitement.

I pulled myself up, dropping the half-full glass of bubbles onto the table.

"What," I said, laughing as she grabbed my arm and bounced agitatedly.

"They're here – holy fuck, they actually came out before curfew and are downstairs right now."

My breath caught in my throat. I tried to swallow down the flash of nausea assaulting me. I wanted to believe she was talking about One Direction or the Biebs, but since there wasn't actually a rule about them being out after curfew, I knew it was not any humans that had her panties in a twist. It was the ash.

I dropped my eyes to my wrist. My slender gold watch was telling me that it was far too early for those creepers to be out. So what the hell? Even though I wasn't hammered, I was regretting the heavy alcohol choice by now. I wanted a clear head if I was going to be around the ash. They got the drop on me once.

Never again.

I realized I was clenching my fists, so I relaxed them and let Tessa drag me across to the dance floor to get a closer view. Sure as shit, there they stood, two tall, gorgeous men. One had dark hair and gave off a creepy vibe; the other was a yellow blond and looked like a bad guy's sidekick. The women surged closer to them, some practically dry humping their legs. I shook my head. Suddenly, Tessa ripped her hand from my grip and bee-lined it in their direction. Oh hell no! She must be hammered. She wasn't that stupid was she? Completely sober now, I pushed my way through the gaggle of girls until I reached the front.

I arrived in time to hear: "Tessa! With a T," my best friend slurred.

Then I realized that she was sitting on dark-haired creeper's lap. Anger flooded my chest. It was before curfew and she was drunk – this was so wrong.

"Tessa!" I said in my best mom voice, gripping her arm and yanking her off his lap.

Now that I was closer, my nose was assaulted with scents of copper and musk. Bad boy glared at me with those goddamn black and silver eyes. The eyes that haunted my nightmares.

"Hey, relax, honey, we're just having some fun. Right, Jessa?" His voice was all smooth and low.

"It's Tessa," I ground out. "And fun's over." I held Tessa against me. She felt like a dead weight and I wondered if the alcohol was getting the better of her.

As I went to turn around, his arm snaked out and grabbed my wrist, holding tight enough to cut my watch into my skin.

What the actual fuck? Twice in one day.

My vision went a little red then, thoughts flashing across my mind in rapid succession. You know how you kind of wonder if you're capable of murder? Everyone has the wild thought on occasion. I had definitely wondered before.

Well, this moment gave me my answer.

I pushed Tessa behind me with my free arm, thankful that she managed to stay on her feet long enough to stumble away. I turned back to the owner of the hand gripping my arm.

"Let. Go!" The sound of my own voice scared me. It was raw and animalistic.

His eyes started to pulse then, like with the ash in class, and he licked his lips as he looked me up and down. He did not let me go; he started to yank me closer.

Wrong answer.

My free hand flew out, my palm straight, and smashed into his nose. I felt the crack of cartilage, and almost immediately blood covered my palm. His grip loosened and I wrenched myself from his hold, before doing a quick pivot, prepared to grab Tessa and flee. A hard grip landed on my shoulder, dashing those plans. Fear was taking hold of me, saturating my movements and sending my thoughts into a tizzy. I tried to focus, forcing my defense instructor's words through the fear. *Deep breaths, don't panic.* In one swift movement I spun, prepared to kick the guy who was holding me right where it counted. Ash or not, a knee to the nuts hurt every man alive.

I did not hesitate, going straight for the shot, but of course no human stood a chance against an ash. He moved quicker than my eye could track. Somehow he managed to step outside my range but still fill the space with his presence. Sucking in a ragged breath, I halted my attack, watching him with caution. It was a new ash standing before me, not the creeper or his sidekick. Somehow I knew immediately that this one was not like the other two. They had been annoying d-bags, but just normal run-of-the-mill ash. This new ash was different. Everything about him screamed dangerous. Pure and simple.

The longer I stared, the more I felt compelled to examine him. Every single one of these creeps were beautiful, designed as first class chick magnets and killing machines. But I had been right the first time; this ash was so much more.

Holy gods of everything sexy, what have you created here?

If I was completely honest with myself, at one point in my life – around my mid-teens – I had found ash and vampires fascinating. I'd never been in Tessa's league of obsession, but I'd acknowledged their beauty. Never since that night though ... but this stranger was doing all sorts of things to my body and blood. Something about the way he wore a caged lethalness like a second coat, his movements so smooth and contained. He was scary – scariest male I'd ever seen, and yet he created a sense of calm and security inside me. And he was drop dead gorgeous.

"Are you okay?" His strong baritone voice cut through my hormones. A scuffle behind him drew my attention before I could answer. There were two black-clad ash behind him. They had the pair of original ash d-bags laid out on the ground, hands zip-tied behind their backs.

Unable to help myself, my eyes slid back to the lethal male. He was at least 6'2 and all muscle. His unruly chestnut hair hung in loose waves across his forehead. He wore black military fatigues, and everything about him screamed danger. It might have been the glint in his black eyes, or the way the silver seemed to be larger and more distinct than other ash, but he was definitely not a man to be fucked with.

I needed to pull myself together. I didn't bother to answer his question. I started moving away from them, grabbing Tessa, who must have at some point passed out on the floor. The tequila was finally kicking in for her. As I sidled close by the hardass ash in the fatigues, the silver of his eyes started to swirl and his features hardened even further as he looked me up and down.

I put my hands up. "Don't get any ideas. This blood is your buddy's."

What was with their eyes? Did the swirl of colors mean it was feeding time? I didn't want to stay and find out.

The ash didn't stop me, but his gaze never left my face. There was something hidden there in those black depths. Something calculating. He was assessing me and I was not okay with that.

"Ryder! We got another call," one of the other ash said. The ash – Ryder – flicked his eyes away for a moment, his clenched hands loosening enough to reach up and hook onto the comm device on his belt.

I took the opportunity while I could. I needed to escape the presence of these dominating males. Reaching down, I practically yanked Tessa into my arms, barely even feeling her weight as I booked it out of the club. The entire time one word was running through my head – the scary-ass gorgeous ash's name: Ryder. I sighed.

Perfect. Why couldn't I meet a normal guy?

THREE

It took me forever to get home, mainly because Tessa was a dead weight. I ended up catching a cab and putting it on her credit card. She might only be from a one parent family too, but unlike mine, hers had lots of old money. Tessa had a fat trust fund and she wouldn't mind me charging the cab to her card.

After managing to finagle her shoes off, I dropped her onto her bed. And then, finally, I got to wash that creeper's blood from my hands, and then remove my makeup before getting into bed myself. Stretching out, I tried my best not to think about all the strange shit that was happening to me lately. Including but not limited to the pull I'd felt to that ash tonight. Ryder. I had no explanation. Maybe, if I'd been a dude, I'd be worried that mom had done the down and dirty with a vampire. I certainly had some of the "poster" symptoms. But there was no such thing as a female ash, and my father had been a human soldier, killed in the line of duty.

Maybe I was just going through a hormone imbalance or some crap. I should probably get to the campus clinic and have my blood work run. Just to be safe.

I drifted off, and for the first part of the night slept like the dead. It must have been in the early hours that a vivid dream engulfed me.

The world was washed in blood. I swam in rivers of crimson, swept downstream as I struggled to quench the insatiable thirst inside of me. No matter how much I drank, it was never enough. I thrashed around, trying to free myself from the nightmare, but I couldn't wake. Hands grabbed me and I was yanked from the river. The thick, tacky blood coated my body and I swear I could even taste the metallic tang on my tongue. The copper scent assaulted my nose. It was odd ... but so good. I was carried, and the world started to cry, and it felt as if my soul were crying with it. I lifted my face to feel the drops, only to realize they were blood also. The world wasn't crying, it was bleeding.

I startled awake, my chest rising as I gasped, trying to fill my heavy lungs with air. *Dream.* Holy shit, that dream had felt so real. And so goddamn creepy. A splash of wetness landed on my face, and almost in slow motion I raised my hand and touched my cheek. My heart rate slowed a little when I realized that it was really rain this time, not blood. A second drop landed, and within a blink of an eye I was up off the ground and on my feet. *Rain?*

Off the ground? My head swiveled rapidly, eyes

darting left and right as I tried to figure out what the crap was going on. Was I still dreaming? How the hell did I get outside during my sleep? I knew I had been safely in my dorm room, and now I seemed to be ... my eyes alighted on a series of warning signs which were scattered around a tall chain-link fence. Sweet love of the gods, I was halfway across town, outside the gated compound surrounding the Hive.

I blinked more than once, trying to wrap my head around what had happened. I looked down at myself to see I was still clothed. I was either losing my mind or something really serious was wrong. I used to sleepwalk when I was younger, but never got further than the living room. One thing I did know was that I needed to haul ass immediately. I could not be caught after curfew in this area. I'd pretty much be signing my own death warrant. I looked up at the moon high in the sky, and hugged my arms across my chest against the bite of the cold. September seemed to be up and down lately with cold. Tonight, with the rain, I could feel the iciness of winter around the corner.

I didn't think, I just ran, my bare feet smashing against the gravel road, not even caring that they were getting all cut up. I was still in my sleep shirt, but that didn't seem to be the most pressing issue right now. Somehow, despite my shock, my body knew what to do. I had never run so swiftly, but within moments I was out of the danger zone and back in familiar territory. I hadn't consciously made the decision to head this way, but something drove me toward my family home. Toward my mom. Sometimes a girl just needs her mom, especially if she might possibly be losing her mind.

I turned onto my street, large trees lining it. I hadn't grown up in the best neighborhood, but it was perfect, middle class suburbia, and I needed some normalcy. As I dashed up the steps to my front porch, I didn't bother to contemplate on the fact that I'd just sprinted across town in under ten minutes. The trip should have taken me thirty at a brisk pace. I ran a shaky hand through my long, tangled hair, and tried to calm my frantic thoughts. My feet stung from my barefooted haul-ass run, and I saw smudges of bloody footprints dotting the porch.

My mom was a surgical nurse and worked a lot of shift hours. My muddled brain couldn't quite remember what shift she was on right now, so instead of disturbing her I reached down and scrambled beneath the potted plant to find the hidden key. It clicked quietly in the lock and I let myself into the cool, familiar front hall and locked the door behind me.

Padding through the parlor, I ended up at the kitchen. Instinct drove me forward. I was so, so, thirsty. Opening up the single door fridge, I knew Mom would have plenty of goodness inside. She was the best cook around. But as I stared at the contents, not even the peach and pecan pie tempted me.

I grabbed a sports drink, wondering if I needed a kick of electrolytes. Flipping it open, I took a large gulp, but before I could swallow it I found myself spitting it all back out. It was disgusting. Tasted like chemicals and salt. I read the label in the dull light of the open fridge. Date was fine, so what the hell was wrong with it?

I sensed a presence just seconds before she spoke: "Charlie baby, what are you doing here?"

Spinning around, drink still clutched in my hands, I held back a sob and threw myself into my mom's arms. "I don't know what's wrong with me."

Words poured from me. I was all out of whack. My thoughts seemed to be going a million miles an hour, and yet I was barely comprehending the simplest of things.

I pulled back a little to stare at my mom. She was still young and beautiful, despite the fact she'd done double duty and raised me by herself. Truth was, I couldn't have asked for a better parent. And I needed her calm mom words more than anything.

"What happened? Did you run here in your night-gown? Barefoot?" Her gaze roamed over me, the dim lighting enough for me to see concern in her dark brown eyes. We shared the same eye color and general build, but my mom was very blond and I had quite dark hair. Same as my father. Who I only knew from the two or three scattered photos of him around the place.

"Shit, I'm probably bleeding all over your kitchen floor." I lifted my feet to inspect the cuts. My stomach dropped. *No!* They were pretty much healed. Just slight pink lines remained.

I couldn't say anymore; the nausea and dizziness was

starting to crowd in on me. Darkness pressed at the edge of my consciousness and weakness invaded my limbs.

"I'm so thirsty, Mom." Those were not the words I intended to say. I was going to tell her that I'd had a dream and sleepwalked. But the thirst was driving me crazy. If I was so thirsty, why the hell did everything taste like shit?

"Charlie!" Her exclamation was muffled. She sounded like she was miles away from me. I shook my head a few times, fighting back the darkness, but eventually I couldn't any longer. I slumped forward, knowing at least tonight my mom would be there to catch me when I fell. My last thought was about the plump vein throbbing on her neck.

LOUD VOICES BROKE through the fuzzy static in my head. I groaned, trying to remember what had happened last night. Images filtered through slowly. I'd gone out with Tessa, and ... drank a lot. Was that why I had this crap-tastic static in my head?

"Charlie, can you hear me, sweetheart?"

That voice was familiar. What was Mom doing in my dorm? I tried to pry open my eyes. It took more than one attempt for me to crack them a sliver.

"Mom..." I croaked out. "What's going on?"

I felt her cool hands on my face, and I groaned as pain shot through me. I felt like I was burning up. I was sick. Sicker than I'd ever remembered being. This was so not a simple hangover.

"I need you to listen to me, Charlene Anne Bennett. I

love you more than anything in this world, and it doesn't matter what anyone says to you in the next few days, that will never change. Do you understand me?" Her voice was strong and didn't waver.

Holy shit, she was scaring me.

Fear gave me the boost of adrenalin I needed to pry my lids fully open, and my mother's worried face came into view. She wasn't the only one either. Standing behind her, one on either side, were two ash. Both of them had those eerie black eyes with the silver rings locked on me. I realized then I wasn't in my dorm. I was lying on my mother's kitchen floor. Why was I in my mother's house? Actually, more importantly, why were ash in my mother's house?

"Mom..."

I needed to get her out of here. Ash were dangerous, especially in a private residence with no one around to help us.

"I'm so sorry, Charlie. I tried to tell you so many times. But ... I didn't think it could ever happen. You were a girl, so you had to be John's."

I struggled to get up, and with assistance from my mom I managed to get into a sitting position. From this angle, I was suddenly mesmerized by the pulsing vein in the side of her neck. I opened and closed my eyes a few times, but still, when I looked again, the vein was definitely pulsing with blood.

One of the ash picked up his phone, and pressing a button lifted it to his ear. He muttered three words:

"We need Ryder."

And just like that I passed out again.

THIS TIME when I awoke my mom wasn't there, and unlike the fuzziness from before, I had all of my memories and they were crystal clear. *Holy shit.* There had been ash in my mom's house. My feet had healed in seconds. The bloody dream. The vein in my mom's neck. What the actual hell was wrong with me? Was my drink spiked last night with something ... some sort of hallucinogen? A human growth hormone that made my body go nuts? There had to be a medical explanation.

I looked down. I was clothed in a starched, white hospital gown. Mom must have brought me here after I spazzed out on her and lost consciousness twice. But a glance around only raised my confusion. This didn't look like any room I'd ever seen at Legacy Hospital. For one thing, it was way too big and teched out, and it had a huge glass window, like an observation station, dominating the entire right wall. A shadow darted across the window and I jerked my head a little, trying to see what was there. Was it a doctor creeping around? Or was there some awesome stalker in my life?

A throat cleared behind me. Standing three feet from my hospital bed was him, the gorgeous, deadly-looking ash from the club last night. Ryder. Had he been standing there the entire time? *What the hell was in my drinks last night?*

My focus locked on him again and the air almost sizzled between us. That strange pull was still there, a connection I sure as shit did not want with an ash. Speaking of ... what the fuck was he doing in my hospital room?

There was very little expression on his face; his jaw was clenched. I swallowed hard, my tongue swollen. I was so goddamn thirsty it felt like my head was going to explode. I lifted my arm to adjust my position and found that I was chained to the bed.

Oh hell no. It was becoming startlingly clear that my initial instinct had been correct. This wasn't a freakin' hospital.

Ryder hadn't moved. His dark eyes seemed to be locked on mine. Finally, he shook his head. "It can't be." His words were low and muttered, not really intended for my ears.

I pulled against the chains. "Where the hell am I? What have you done with my mom? You need to let me go right now. This is all kinds of jacked up and against the law."

My tongue stuck to the roof of my mouth, making the words garbled. Ryder moved then, in that preternatural way which suggested speed far greater than a human. He grabbed a small mirror off a side table and approached me slowly.

"Charlie, I need you to stay calm. Your mom phoned the hotline number when you passed out. She saw your eyes, and knew that ... well, it's damned impossible ... but we think you're an ash."

My mouth dropped open. What did he just say? Before I could verbally react, he was holding the mirror out and shoving it in front of my face.

I froze as my reflection shimmered back at me.

"No!"

I howled. It was low and animalistic. My eyes...

Gone was the dark brown so like my mother's. In its place was a black iris with a ring around it. The ring was a silvery green, dancing like it contained bolts of lightning. I wanted to tear my gaze from those alien eyes. But I couldn't stop looking.

Holy fuck! I had ash eyes.

Even in my distressed state, I noticed that something about my eyes seemed a little different from the male ash eyes I had seen. But there was no mistaking the fact that I had the very distinct eyes of a human vampire hybrid. My mother's words floated back to me. She had been trying to tell me something, to prepare me for this moment. My chest heaved as I fought back the panic that was coming. Ryder held the mirror in place, as if he was trying to force me to stare longer, to acknowledge all of the things I had conveniently ignored over the last few months. It wasn't just the eyes. There was no denying how flawless my skin was; it had a light glow, and my hair shone like in a Pantene commercial. Not to mention I could run like an Olympic athlete and was thirsty for something no liquid I drank could quench. But still, even with all of that, the eyes were the worst.

I was a freak. How had this happened?

As Ryder lowered the mirror, the dry burning need in my throat and mouth roared to life. Everything was starting to make sense now. If I was an ash, I needed...

Ryder produced a small bag of blood.

No! Not blood. I couldn't be like them. I wouldn't.

The moment I had that thought, he pricked the plastic bag, and as the metallic tang filtered into the air, some sort of instinct knocked into me. I jerked hard against the chains and was relieved to hear them snap. There was the slightest burn in my gums, near the canine areas, and I could actually feel the lengthening of my fangs.

But I was too far gone in the blood haze to care about that.

I popped up on two feet and stood on the bed looking down at Ryder. He looked only mildly surprised by my rapid movement as he tossed me the bag. He then reached for a long stick which had been resting near the end of my bed, with some type of metal electrodes at the end.

The blood bag was cool to touch, and as my eyes zeroed in on the dark red within, my stomach churned. This was gross. I was not doing this. No, no, no...

Before I could stop myself, the thirst within roared harder and I lifted the pouch, bringing it to my mouth. The fangs, over which I had no control, slid out again and punctured the plastic. I began sucking the glorious blood into my mouth and down my throat. Pleasure exploded on my tongue and I moaned. I had a fleeting thought of Tessa. I would have to tell her that touching an ash had not done shit, but drinking blood was most definitely a mini orgasm. Even though my head was still saying gross, the rest of me was in heaven. For the first time in forever, my thirst was contained. Vitality poured into my body. My heart pounded in my ears and my muscles tightened. All too soon the bag was empty.

"More," I growled at Ryder.

He slowly pulled a walkie-talkie from his belt clip. "We need to put the south ward on lockdown."

What the fuck? He wasn't producing the blood I wanted fast enough, so I leapt down from the bed, ready to rip his pockets open in search of more of that liquid orgasm. But before I could get within two feet of him, his arm snaked out, grabbing me by the neck and slamming me back down on the bed.

I froze as both shock and arousal poured through my newly sensitized body. He leaned down close to my ear and I could smell him – cedarwood and other spices, not to mention that something decidedly male and enticing. Of course he would smell yummy too. I could not catch a break. His breath tickled my ear.

"I don't want to hurt you."

My thoughts of Ryder were distracted by a heady scent of metallic deliciousness wafting toward me. That smell – someone had more blood nearby. My leg kicked out hard, launching Ryder off of me. I got two steps to the door when I felt a massive surge of electricity rock my body and I fell backward.

Strong arms wrapped around me just as the blackness took me.

IT FELT as if the jolt knocked me out for only seconds, but it must have been longer. I awoke in a different room, and even though I should have had the mother of all headaches after taking that much electrical pulse, I felt amazing. My senses seemed to be on overdrive, and it took me only moments to catalogue the area. I had expected to be chained to the bed again, but in this room there were no chains. A tugging sensation had me focusing on the IV in my arm. I followed the cord to find a large bag of blood slowly dripping into my vein. I ran my tongue over my teeth. The canines were short again, and for the first time in days my mouth felt wet and hydrated.

Movement and a scraping sound caught my attention – two figures stepped into view. The pair, who had not realized I was awake yet, were across the other side of the large room, but I could hear them perfectly.

"She needs more blood than most ash. Nearly the same amount as a vampire in the midst of the change. If you keep her hydrated, you shouldn't have any more outbursts." A short-haired, strawberry-blond woman wearing a white lab coat was speaking to Ryder. On instinct I inhaled. Her scent was different to the male ash and humans. She was a vampire. Somehow I knew this already, like I had an inbuilt radar that told me human, ash, or vampire.

My eyes fell then to the stick Ryder still held in his hands. I had a distinct flash of burning pain as I recalled how that bastard had electrocuted me.

I was an ash. Shit. I knew newly-turned ash could be dangerous. Something about needing large influxes of blood for the cells to adjust to the virus as it finally released and took root in your body. I could have killed my mom. Maybe I should be a little more grateful to be here and not out there hurting someone I loved. Though what I really needed was an explanation. How could this even happen? A female ash. I always wanted to be unique, but this was not exactly what I'd had in mind.

I stared down at my hands, only to find that they looked slightly different, the skin tighter, paler, baby soft. Holy hell on wheels, I did not know how to process this. I was legit a damned ash. What did this even mean for me? Would I ever see my mom again? Tessa? What about college? I was not ready to give my life up and live in the Hive.

My tumultuous thoughts were cut off as the lab-coat woman left the room and suddenly Ryder was back by my side. His eyes locked in on me as he stopped about three feet from my bed. He didn't seem surprised to see me awake. Probably he'd known the entire time.

I cleared my throat, unsure of what to say. "I'm a woman," I blurted out stupidly.

His cheeks lifted then, the sides of his mouth quirking

into a sexy smile, full of dimples and straight white teeth. Until this point I had not seen the man crack even so much as a smirk, and now I was assaulted with that much sexiness all in one go. He was lethal in more ways than one.

The gods hated me today. I did not want to be attracted to an ash. I couldn't be.

His smile faded then, morphing into an expression that was part heat and part curiosity. His eyes drifted down my body. "Yes, I see that."

Well, eff me. "No, I mean ... how can a woman be an ash?"

He took another slow step toward me, his hand still gripping his torture stick. Whether I deserved it or not, I really wanted to get him back for that one. Although, as I scanned his huge arms and graceful stalk toward me, I doubted I could take him on.

"We're all a little mystified at your presence here. But there's no doubt ... you're an ash."

As fear flooded me, so did anger. "So I just give everything up and join your bloodsucker gang?" I spat the words out. There was nothing I hated more than losing my freedom, my choices. Sure, I probably wouldn't have found the cure for cancer, but that wasn't the point. The point was I could have, and now that chance was gone.

He lowered the stick to his side and I noticed his ankle was in a walking boot, like he had recently been injured.

"You will have to abide by our rules and live here in the Hive, yes."

I had guessed I was in the Hive, but now it was confirmed. *Wait!* I was in the mother-effing Hive! Of course I was. My skin crawled at the realization of how many ash and vampires were around me right then. Thousands. I forced myself not to think about the only other time I'd been on these grounds. This time would be different. *Yeah, sure.* This time I'd probably have hundreds of the bastards trying to hurt me.

My eyes darted again to his firm grip on the torture stick. "You can put that thing down. I think I've had my weekly intake of electric shock, thanks." I glared.

He didn't budge. "My broken ankle would seem to disagree with you."

My mouth dropped slightly. I did that? *Shit.* "Oh. Whoops."

He shrugged like it was no big deal. "It will heal in a few hours."

I leaned back on the pillow. Maybe for now I needed to just shut the hell up and do what this guy told me. I clearly didn't know anything about this place, and there was no returning to the human world for me. My entire life was going to change. No more Tessa, no more Mom. Curfew, blood thirst, fighting. *Shit ...* I had forgotten about that part. The fighting. The rumors of the fighting match required to earn your place here. I felt the heat behind my eyes then, the pressure which had me pressing my tongue to the roof of my mouth. But there was no stopping it. Big hot girly tears tumbled down my cheeks and I rolled over and faced the wall as sobs wracked my body.

I heard the soft click of the door as Ryder left to give me privacy and I let it all out. I needed to process this shit and get over it, because if the rumors were true, I would soon be fighting for my life. The Hive was overpopulated. If you wanted to live, you had to earn that right.

AFTER CRYING IT ALL OUT, I pulled myself together. That was my one moment to fall apart. Now I would deal with this shit the same way I had dealt with every bad thing in my life – by fighting back. I got out of bed, wincing as I pulled out my IV and the tape which had held it down. Noticing a pile of clothes on a nearby chair, I crossed over to pick up the first item. I felt my brows draw together as I stared at the shiny material. I wasn't happy about wearing something of theirs, but I had no choice. I also noticed boots and underwear, which surprisingly enough looked to be my size. I slipped into the cotton underwear and followed this with the skintight black jumpsuit, which had silver panels on the side. Everything fit me like a glove. The back and front right pocket of my suit had "#46" on it.

Had they custom made this outfit for me or something? How long had I been out of it? Surely not long enough for them to measure and fit me with an outfit. Ugh, did those creeps take my measurements while I was unconscious? I really shouldn't even be surprised by that.

Dressed and nervous, I was just deciding whether or

not to try and open the door when I heard voices on the other side. I pressed my ear against it.

"There has never been a female ash. She's special. The rules are not the same for her and we shouldn't have her fight with the others. What if she's killed?" Ryder's voice was low, controlled, but I could hear undercurrents which made me nervous. I couldn't tell how far away he was, but I could hear him as if he was right next to me. Ash perk.

A cold, hard voice cut him off. "There are eleven open beds left in this hive and forty-six new ash. She will fight with the others and earn her place like everyone else."

"Sir, I respect your position, but—"

"But you're not in my position, so do your job and follow orders. Find her a trainer and a sponsor and be done with it!" Loud footsteps retreated.

"Dick," Ryder muttered, and I smirked.

The door opened suddenly, cracking me in the side of the face.

"Ow!" I rubbed my cheek as Ryder stood before me.

He let out an exasperated sigh. "Do you make it a habit to listen behind closed doors?"

His eyes locked in on me and I was struck by the notion that, like my own, his were a little different than the others. More silver.

I stepped back a few feet. "I might be guilty of doing that on occasion."

He had no cast on his leg now. He hadn't been kidding about the quick healing. And, thankfully, he no longer carried the torture stick. He gestured for me to follow him.

"If you can keep from attacking everyone, I can allow you to join the rest of the new ash."

"No promises." I pursed my lips. I wasn't kidding either.

The smallest hint of a smile crossed his face as if he'd heard the extra thoughts I didn't add. He picked up his walkie-talkie. "I'm taking new initiate number forty-six out into general population. Be advised."

My eyebrows shot up. *Seriously?* What else had I done in my blood craze?

I followed him out of the long hall. We passed a dozen doors. My pretty cool, black ass-kicking boots clanked against the black and white checkered linoleum floors. At the end of the hall, Ryder opened two double doors which led into a nice waiting room. A beautiful, extremely well-coiffed female vampire sat a reception desk, talking on the phone. There were closed-door offices scattered to the left and right.

Ryder led me to a door marked "Orientation."

He opened it and I glanced inside. It was empty of people. Just a few desks.

His expression was unreadable as he gestured for me to step inside. "This is where I leave you," he said. "I will send Jose along to get you acquainted and give you a tour."

Oh. I tried to school my immediate disappointment. Ryder was the only somewhat familiar person I knew here. Along with disappointment, there also panic and nerves fighting to spill from me. Guess I couldn't rely on Ryder any longer. It was probably best he left anyway. It would just make things easier all round if I didn't go all Stockholm on this ash, and start falling for my captor. He was lethal in more ways than one.

"Thanks for..." *Not letting me kill my mom.* And so many other things.

He stared into my eyes again and I saw him inhale deeply, the silver of his eyes pulsing. Clearing his throat, he nodded. "Welcome to the Hive, number forty-six. Try to stay alive."

He turned on his heels and left. *Number forty-six?* Asshole. I let the door slam behind me before turning to sink into the closest chair.

AN HOUR later and I was still getting the tour of this crazy place. Jose, the Hispanic ash who had been my guide thus far, was like a robot on crack. He spoke rapidly, mostly about all the Hive facts I was supposed to give a shit about.

"So, like I said, the Hive is a master of ingenuity. Eighty stories. Twenty are dug deep into the earth. The other sixty tower high above, as you have seen from the city. There are shutters on all the upper levels so the vamps don't burn up. They stay closed at all times during daylight hours. As soon as night hits, then the entire Hive opens up and comes to life."

I was following him aimlessly, trying to ignore the crazy stares I was getting. Apparently the rumor mill was already in full swing. They all knew a freakin' unicorn mythical ash creature was amongst them and they all wanted to get a look. A few full-fledged vampires had passed us – and I'm not gonna lie – when their strange energy brushed against me, my heart started hammering in my chest. Those bastards were so creepy. They barely walked – more like floated.

"This is the floor." Jose stopped and I walked into his back.

"Ooof." Whoops.

He glared at me and then went back to robot mode.

"This is the most important floor of the Hive. Level eleven, feeder and blood storage level. Every vampire and ash has a feeding schedule and a preferred feeder. Or if you like the bottled stuff, that's fine too."

He pulled out a tablet and looked down. "You're O-negative. I'd suggest for pure taste you stick with that blood type, but you can drink any sort. Hmm, I see here you have been cleared for six feedings a day. That's a lot." His brow creased. I craned my neck to try and see what else the tablet said about me. He shifted it out of sight, turning it off and slipping it away.

He straightened, and continued the tour. As he opened the doors on the feeder room, the distinct copper scent assaulted my nose and I felt that burn in my gums again. Somehow I knew my fangs had lengthened. It felt like when my chocolate addiction kicked it. Blood now smelled as delicious as melted chocolate, the kind humans dipped their strawberries in.

Humans. Oh man. I was already drooling over blood

and separating myself from humans. *Not good.*

Jose checked me in with the ash receptionist, a large, beefy, black-haired male, with really dark caramel skin. Beautiful like all ash.

"Well, this is the end of the tour. By the time your feeding session is done, I will have your room assignment ready."

I was trying not to salivate as I looked at the open glass refrigerated cases behind the guy at the desk.

"Feeding session?" Shit, just hand me a few of those bottles and I was good. No session required.

"Your requested feeder is waiting in room seven," front desk ash told me.

Requested feeder? Had Ryder set something up for me already? No way was I actually ready to feed from a human – I wasn't sure I was ever going to actually bite into a person like they were a freakin' apple. I was just opening my mouth to give a definite "Hell no" to the guy behind the desk when it hit me, a familiar scent. Under all the liquid chocolate was my bestie. Right ... my requested feeder. Tessa, you crazy bitch.

"Thanks!" I opened the fridge, moving along the shelves until I found the O-negative shelf and grabbed a bottle.

"For later," I said, before bolting down the hall. The doors were all numbered, and as I dashed toward number seven, I lifted the blood bottle and inserted my fangs into the two holes perfectly placed in the lid. The burn in my mouth increased as the canines fully extended, piercing through the seals. It was like they could sense the blood. I chugged the liquid down as fast as I could. I wouldn't talk to Tessa thirsty. She would not heal like Ryder. As the splash of deliciousness coated my tongue, I tried not to moan. Moans were strictly for chocolate and orgasms. Not blood.

I slowed as door number seven appeared, and after removing the bottle and making sure all the blood was gone from my mouth, I burst through. My body immediately gravitated toward the warmth in the room – I was a damned predator now, and already my body was attuned to stupid blood – but I forced myself to focus on the fact that this was my best friend. I drank in the sight of her. Finally, something that felt familiar and like the old Charlie.

Tessa looked like shit. Her makeup was smudged, her blond curls wild.

She stood as I ran to embrace her, but when we were about two feet apart her eyes widened and a rich, cloying scent wafted from her. I halted a foot from her. I'd smelt this heavy scent before, when I had been afraid. Tessa was scared of me.

Her eyes scanned over me rapidly. She was cataloguing all the changes. The blood I'd just downed was working its magic, and I knew my eyes would be shooting out all kinds of swirly ash vibes.

The smile slid off my face. I wasn't sure what to do. You know shit's real when your best friend for most of your life is afraid of you.

"Hey," I finally said. My eyes fell. I stared at my shiny boots. I really, really needed Tess to be my normal and annoying best friend right now. I was pretty sure I couldn't handle one more disappointment this week.

As if she'd sensed that need, I felt a hand touch my cheek, and as I raised my head, a smile spread across her haggard features. This time she didn't hesitate to pull me into a bone-crushing hug.

"Sorry, your eyes freaked me out. They're kind of really fucked up, Charlie."

I relished the brutal honesty this girl could dish out. "You don't look so hot yourself," I countered.

She pulled away. "Yeah, that's what happens when your best friend turns into an ash and gets taken to the Hive."

I sat down and took a deep breath. "Tess, I am so, so happy I got to see you this one time, but that's all this can be. It's not safe here. If you sign up as a feeder, others could use you."

She sat next to me and threw across her biggest bitch game-face. "I'm coming here every week. Every. Single. Week. If I get fed on, then so be it."

She was daring me to counter her. I couldn't. I was selfish enough to know I needed her.

"I might not last a week," I whispered, thinking of the rumors.

She put an arm around me and said, "Tell me everything."

And I did.

FOUR

After talking with Tessa, I reluctantly pulled myself from her side and returned to being an ash. I got my bunk assignment from the receptionist. I was feeling all kinds of tired after this shit storm, and was pleased to find out that ashes still slept. At least I might have an escape from my newly discovered life during sleep. The receptionist had passed on a message from Jose, telling me how to find my room. Apparently I now had no escort. Which was fine with me. I found the right hallway no problem, level forty-four, room twelve. My card swiped open the door, and after seeing the room was empty, I collapsed into what was hopefully my bed and passed out.

A scratching, thud noise had my eyes flying open. Instinct pushed me to sit bolt upright, frantic.

Standing on the other side of the room was a gorgeous, tall, buff guy with dark espresso skin. We locked gazes for a few extended moments. I was awake enough then to hate on him a little for his ridiculously long eyelashes – wasted on a man, for sure – before deciding to speak and break the silence.

"Hi," I squeaked. I should have realized I'd be sharing a room with a guy. There were no girl ashes.

He didn't hesitate to cross the room and extend his hand. "I'm Jayden, hottest chocolate ash up in this bitch." He did a flamboyant hand gesture for added measure and I cracked a smile. I had impeccable gaydar, which was definitely not required with Jayden. I instantly liked him and realized that those eyelashes were probably very much appreciated by this particular guy.

Shaking his hand, I introduced myself. "I'm Charlie."

"Girl, you have the entire Hive in a frenzy. Female ash. Crazy stuff."

I cleared my throat. I was thirsty and not for water. "Yeah, well, no one is more surprised than me."

He stiffened then, his rippling muscles freezing in place. "Your eyes look a little hungry."

Breaking his statue-like pose, he crossed the small room and opened a little refrigerator before tossing me a cold bottle of blood. "It takes a while to get the guts to feed from a human. I'm assuming you still like blood of the bottled variety."

I caught the bottle midair and nodded, wasting no time popping my fangs into the lid. I was able to contain my excitement better. It wasn't that the blood was less orgasmic – it was all kinds of amazing – but I was gaining a little control over my reactions.

"Thanks."

He nodded and took a seat across from me on his bed. Our room was tiny. Like closet small.

"Wow, they really roll out the red carpet for us, huh?" I gestured to the room, which held two beds, the refrigerator, and a door to what I assumed was an adjoining bathroom.

Jayden smiled. "This is shitty temp housing for the newbies. If we survive the culling, we get proper cribs."

My face went slack. Okay, yes, I had heard rumors, but here it was confirmed, the *culling*. Defined in the Webster's dictionary as "Killing a bunch of motherfuckers off."

Jayden noticed my shock. "Oh my God, honey. They didn't tell you?"

They hadn't told me shit, but I wasn't going to tell him that yet. He moved and sat next to me, his warmth strangely comforting. I barely knew this guy, but for some reason I was getting legit and genuine vibes off him. There was a sense of nurturing about him, and that made me trust him.

"Tell me everything about this culling," I said, letting my eyes fall on his pretty face.

His huge arms nearly ripped the seams of his shirt as he shifted back to lean on them. He cleared his throat. "Should have known those bastards would keep you in the dark. Look, I really don't want to be the one to tell you this. Basically, vampire-human sexual relations are illegal, so we technically shouldn't be allowed to live at all."

That much I did know. And something told me the worst news was still to come. Come on, don't draw it out. Hit me with it.

"But the vamps allow a small number of ash to integrate into the Hive each year. In two weeks there will be a culling ... a series of fights to the death, all of which takes place over seven days. First we fight individually, and then when the initial weak are weeded out, it moves on to team fights. All of the new ash must fight, and if you survive, you get to become a member of the Hive. Yay." He ended the last part with fake bravado.

I released the breath I had been holding. Well, I'll be damned, the rumors were true.

Jayden went on: "There're lots of rules and traditions that go along with it. There're sponsors that pay for training, and a ranking system that says whether or not you fight first or last, and who you'll team with if you make it that far. All of which can be the difference between life and death. You might be happy to know that rumor has it you caught the eye of Lucas. He's on the Quorum. I haven't figured out yet if..."

He trailed off and I was wondering more about who the hell this Lucas was. How many freakin' vamps had I encountered in my bloodthirsty crazed days here?

My stomach growled. Odd. I didn't feel thirsty, it was actual hunger that panged me. This felt much more like my old days of being a food whore.

Jayden's smile quirked even higher. "Believe it or not, we still need to eat one human food meal a day, especially when healing." He jumped up. "How you doing with this? Wanna curl up and die or are you ready to give this a try?" Those ash eyes sparkled at me. "The way I see it, you have two options right now: try to commit suicide, or come grab some food with me." There was barely any silver in the black of his eyes. "I know which option I'd prefer. I'm not much for blood on my clothes, and I would hate to clean up your dead ass."

I laughed, an actual real laugh. If I did need to be in this shithole and fight for my life, I might as well keep my spirits up.

"Food," I said, and stood. "I'm not one for giving up. I'm the life and lemons sort. As long as there is tequila too."

"Amen to that, sister."

I hadn't been kidding, I was not one to give up. I would push all the information down to my deep dark place and pull it up later when needed.

AFTER TAKING a quick shower and slipping into a new jumpsuit – I had like ten #46 suits in my side of the box cupboard – we left our room and went down a long hallway. I memorized the route as we pushed through two double doors and into a huge cafeteria. As we stepped inside, the noise hit me first, followed closely by the multitude of scents. My senses were kicking into overdrive, and it actually took me several long moments to deal with the overwhelming stimulation to my body, filtering it all out, compartmentalizing so I didn't start freaking out.

There must have been over a thousand ashes in there. And at some point after my entrance, the noise started filtering away, until every single one of them had stopped what they were doing and was staring at me.

Holy cracking ash babies. I was frozen in the doorway. Unable to move, but at least finally not drowning in the sea of sensations.

Jayden broke the tension by giving me a push forward. "Hurry, or all the good food will be gone." His tone was all casual and relaxed, despite the fact there were still thousands of eyes locked on us. Jayden was one cool gay dude.

I took a tentative step into the room. My olfactory sense was smashing me with information, like it knew somehow how to catalogue the smells. I knew one thing for sure: they were all ashes. I scanned the crowd, trying not to linger too long on any one group. There were scary faces in here. But all beautiful. It's like any human or offspring affected by the vampire virus were smoothed out or something. All flaws just kind of sculpted away. Don't get me wrong, each still had completely individual features, all unique, but the flaws were non-existent.

I took a tentative step after Jayden, and it was then my eyes locked onto a familiar dark head. Ryder. He was sitting on the left side of the large cafeteria-style room with a group of big, badass-looking ashes. I noted that his table seemed a little different from the others. They were sat further apart than the rest of the tables; there were six of them, silently watching me; they all wore black clothing, army style, and all had identical cold and menacing expressions. They were the sort of ashes I would never want to find myself in a dark alley with. Ryder was no exception, except ... there was just something else a little more about him. Or maybe I was actually developing some sort of weird Stockholm syndrome since he had saved my ass, twice.

Deciding there was no place in this room to act like a weak ash, especially since the newest culling participants would be looking for kinks in my armor, I just jutted my chin high, showing no fear. I thought I saw a flash of something in Ryder's eyes, but all he did was give me the slightest of nods. I tore my eyes away and continued to follow Jayden into the room. Then, just like that, everyone went back to what they were doing.

The food was set up in a low row of serving trays. Jayden hurried along first, and I followed slower, grabbing a few bits before settling on a black bean burrito. Hurrying to catch up with my roommate, I noticed his plate and I arched an eyebrow at him.

"Christ, are you feeding the entire Hive?"

His plate was piled high with hummus, chocolate cake, nachos, bacon – everything just on top of the other and smashed together in some disgusting concoction of flavors.

Jayden laughed, his black eyes twinkling. "I like you." He hip bumped me.

We found our way to a section in the back that was marked off behind a velvet rope.

"What's with the special seating?" I asked, sitting down.

Jayden glanced back at the main part of the room. A serious look came over his face. "No one wants to become friends with us until they know who is going to survive."

Right. Awesome. I suddenly wasn't hungry. Depression settled over me like a thick blanket.

"You don't have anything to worry about," he said. "The shit you pulled with Ryder, you're probably a top pick."

Ryder ... was he talking about me breaking his ankle? How was that special? All new ash were strong, weren't they?

"Top pick?" I mused aloud.

He popped a piece of bacon in his mouth and moaned. I gave him an odd look.

"Like I said in the room, the night before the culling starts we get ranked. The top picks fight less. They get to sit out a lot, and some of them only fight once or twice before the team event. The vamps like the weak to get killed off first."

"Well, shit, that's depressing." I took a bite of my burrito. A flavor explosion played over my tongue and I moaned. He burst out laughing at my expression.

"Your taste buds are enhanced. Every meal is like sex in your mouth," he told me.

Someone slammed down their tray across the table,

glaring at us. "Quit acting like best friends," the new guy spat. "You're all going to be at each others' throats in two weeks."

Jayden threw a chip at him as my stomach sank. "Calm down, meathead," he said.

Maybe this new guy was right, I shouldn't be making friends. I glanced at Jayden and he smiled. Shit. Too late. I kinda already went and liked my roomie. I'd just have to worry about it if and when Jayden and I fought. For now, Jayden and I were on the same team.

I ate half of my burrito. The conversations had dried up in this section of the ash hall. Mostly everyone just stuck to themselves and threw around lots of glares. After thirty minutes of this, I dropped my plate onto the return tray and said goodbye to Jayden. I needed some alone time, and if I remembered robot Jose's tour correctly, he had said the roof had a jogging track.

My room hadn't had any jogging clothes, just the jumpsuits, so I decided to just head up and hope for the best. Luckily, as I made my way upstairs, there was a supply room just outside the gym and running area. A female vampire, who was not very friendly at all, hooked me up with some running shoes and clothes. Probably didn't want to get attached to an ash who was most likely going to be killed in the first round of the culling. Or she was a bitch. Either one.

Fifteen minutes later I was running on top of the world. Sixty stories in the air, it was glorious. The freezing wind slid through my hair and my feet pounded on the track. I could see the whole city from up here! The Columbia River divided Oregon from Washington. I had officially found my new favorite place. If my entire world had to fall apart, then this was something in the glass half full part of my life now. I pushed harder into the run in awe of my new speed and strength. As I angled myself for the turn, someone whipped by me on my left.

"Number forty-six..." Ryder's voice sailed by as he blurred past. He was doing the seamless graceful thing, his movements controlled and strong.

Asshole was still calling me number forty-six. I picked up my speed, my lungs increasing as my legs blurred underneath me. What can I say? I was competitive. As I caught up to him, I was assaulted by the beautiful network of muscles that made up his back. He was wearing a tank, but I still had plenty to perv on. Pushing myself harder, I grinned as I stepped in beside him, matching pace. Yes! I was an unicorn-ash-badass.

Ryder side-glanced at me.

"Getting slow, ash," I said.

At first his expression didn't change, but then, as he leaned forward a little and took off at some sort of super speed, I swear the slightest of smiles lifted his lips. Dammit! I was never going to catch him now, so I decided to slow my pace so I wouldn't fall on my face. No reason to give him any more reason to think I was a clumsy idiot.

As we did another round of the track, I noticed a newcomer was standing next to one of bench chairs, far back under the cover, out of the light. It was a gorgeous vampire with bright blond hair and fair skin. He had not been on the track when I started, but there was no missing him now in his very white trench coat. He was watching me, gaze locked on with intensity, and I found my pace slowing as my curiosity was piqued. He was tall and well-built, his distinct silver vampire eyes swirling as they continued to track my movements. He was momentarily distracted when Ryder stopped in front of him and gave a military salute. Words were exchanged; their demeanor was friendlyish. Then the vampire pointed at me. *Oh shit.* I stopped about twenty yards away, cautious as the blond started to wave me over. Ryder spared me a quick glance before turning his back and taking off down the track again.

This guy looked about twenty-five and was watching me with an intensity that made me swallow hard.

I couldn't exactly ignore him. The vamps ran this world, so even though I really didn't need any new drama in my first real day in the Hive, I found myself slowly crossing the outer lanes, stopping an arm's distance away.

"Hi," I said.

The vampire gave me what seemed like a genuine smile. "Hello, Charlene. May I call you Charlene?"

Hell no, you're not my mom. "Sure." I needed to play nice. I had no friends here.

He extended his hand. "I'm Lucas Belcroft."

Lucas. This was the dude Jayden had said was interested in me. Looks like I was about to find out why. He held out a hand for me shake. I hesitated briefly, but the sense of otherness which kind of freaked me out about vampires was not as strong with Lucas. I took his strong, firm hand, and instead of repulsion I was met with a light flutter in my stomach. I let go as soon as Lucas's silver eyes began to swirl.

"I wanted to make your acquaintance for many reasons. And I am reaching out as a member of the Quorum, the vampire council. We are all very intrigued by you."

Yeah, no shit. Female ash. Didn't happen. Got the freakin' memo loud and clear. "Yeah, I'm a little shocked myself." I noticed Ryder was eyeing us while running.

Lucas' eyes dropped to my chest for a fraction of a second, but then rested on my lips. Men, vamps or ash, were all the same. "We have been in discussions since you were ... discovered. The rules and traditions stand for a reason, and there are no exceptions. You do have to participate in the culling, but I will do everything in my power to make sure you survive."

There was a possessiveness in his voice. Homeboy wanted this ash-unicorn bad, for what I didn't know. I was struck with an uncomfortable thought then, one which I really should have had earlier but there had been already quite a bit going on in my head.

My father was a vampire.

Not John, the soldier Mom spoke of, who had bravely saved his men from a landmine. Nope, I had been sired by a virus-infected bloodsucker. *Crap!* What if Lucas was my dad? That would be super weird, because he was really hot and I had been checking him out. Note to self: no more checking out vampires until I knew which one was my daddy-o.

Seemed I needed to have a chat with my mom. I wasn't sure if that was allowed or not, but I was damn sure asking the first chance I got. I focused on Lucas again.

"And why would you want me to survive?"

He smiled again. Dude was quite cheery for the undead. "I'm your sponsor. We all want our initiates to survive."

Okay, not exactly the detailed answer I was looking for, but it sounded like the sponsor thing was set. I wondered how it was decided. Did they just draw names out of a hat, or had this Lucas specifically requested me?

"Well ... thanks." What the hell else was I supposed to say? He wasn't breathing or moving much and it was starting to freak me out.

"Well, I just wanted to introduce myself. Enjoy your run. Stay in shape, it will help with the training." Then he left, white coat trailing behind him. It was sort of abrupt, his departure, but I was okay with that.

After this weirdness I didn't feel much like running, unless it was back to my mom's and away from the Hive. I took one last glance at the perfection that was Ryder and left to go back to my room. After showering and changing into a new jumpsuit – not a lot of options in here – I came out to find Jayden suited up and sitting on the bed lacing his sneakers.

"It's training time. You should be paired with a trainer

by now, right?" My roommate was nice. He was trying to help me through this, even knowing we might have to fight each other. The thought of having to kill him to survive made me sick.

"Right," I lied. Lucas hadn't mentioned a trainer.

Suddenly Jayden inhaled and his eyes did that weird little pulse thing. I froze. That freaky shit needed to stop.

Jayden swallowed. "Can I tell you something?" He was practically salivating.

Fear knotted my belly. I could only nod, my high ponytail bobbing up and down.

He paused. "There's something about you. Your blood, your smell, it's ... irresistible."

What the...? "That's not normal?" I squeaked.

His eyes pulsed again and he shook his head. "No. Ashes don't feed on other ashes, even ones like me that like boys."

I laughed. "Well, maybe it's because I'm the first female. The boys want my *special* blood." I winked.

He swallowed hard. "No, it's more than that. I just thought you should know. Watch your back. Anyone with less self-discipline is going to have a hard time restraining themselves." He stood suddenly and crossed the room to the fridge, whipping out a bottle of blood and chugging it in one fast go.

Well, shit. Couldn't a girl catch a break?

I FOLLOWED Jayden through the barrage of halls and

thoroughfares. The Hive was a lot like the way I pictured an anthill, tunnels zigzagging through the building and down into the ground. There were these huge industrial sized elevators at the end of each corridor which zoomed up and down the levels.

Training was on sublevel eight, which meant we were going underground.

There were five other ash in the elevator with us; they varied in size and shape. We all looked to be in our early twenties, the prime time for the ash gene to be triggered and the change to occur. No one spoke. Jayden nudged my arm in a comforting manner, but even he was quiet for once. When we were on the right level, it was a simple matter of traversing along the hall to reach the large double doors at the end.

My heart was pretty much lodged in my throat as I tried to imagine what the hell this training was going to entail. The males around me looked like they were being marched to the executioner or something.

I had so many unanswered questions. I had never much been interested in the Hive or any of its inhabitants, even before the attack. There were classes in school on the virus and the resulting vampires. It had been a long time since the very first case, and the human race was used to the bloodsuckers now; they were an integrated part of our history. But I purposely avoided those high school and college subjects. What did I care about the social structure of the Hive? Or the hierarchy of a race I was determined to avoid.

Fate, however, seemed to have a different plan for me, and now it was time to start information gathering. "Tell me about this Quorum," I said to Jayden, startling him out of whatever eye-screw he was trying to do with a vampire who'd crossed paths with us. *Flirt.*

He turned those eyes with their sinfully long lashes on to me. "Girl, you are so fucked, and not in the fun way. You don't know about the Quorum?"

I didn't say anything, just kept my eyes locked on him and let my annoyance seep out. He held up both hands. "Got it, you're a badass. Okay, so the Quorum is the council of vampires which lead the Hive and each Hive has their own Quorum. They are the strongest members of the ten houses."

I did remember hearing about this. It had been a crazy time when the first strains of the virus emerged. Humans were falling ill, some dying and others becoming vampires. To save the population, the world leaders banded together, and went on a mass culling. They wiped out the infected animals and humans, but a small group of vampires managed to escape and hide away. They became the ten Originals. The founding lineage behind each clan, discretely turning humans and fathering ash.

"Are they still alive, the Originals?" I asked.

Jayden shook his head. "None of the Originals survived the first war with humans, but their lines live on. Each of the vampires, and ash, fall under one of the ten groups. A DNA test can tell which group you're in, but they don't waste money on that until you survive the culling. Each group has an elder vampire which leads, maintains order, and disciplines. These ten form the Quorum. Plus the token ash."

"Token ash?" I was surprised about this.

Jayden's shit-eating grin increased. "Are you telling me that the most delectable, scrumptious piece of ash you'll ever lay your eyes on sat by your bedside for two days while you were all blood-crazed, and you didn't even go so far as to find out a single thing about him?"

I let out a breath. He had to be talking about Ryder. "Ryder is the ash representative on the Quorum?"

"Technically he is. Ryder heads up the enforcers, and he is the scariest, sexiest, piece of—"

"I get the point," I interrupted him. And I also seconded his point, but one couldn't forget that he'd electrocuted, shoved, and dismissed me on more than one occasion. Ryder might be a badass, but he was also mainly just an ass.

"Right, well, he is as strong, fast, and lethal as a full-blooded vampire. Some say he might be a direct descendant of an Original, not a watered down mutt like us. He is feared and respected. He was an automatic vote for the ash Quorum seat. Although I heard he almost never bothers to go to meetings. Too busy keeping the streets safe from us crazy ashes."

That's what he'd been doing that night in the club, keeping humans safe. Kind of raised my opinion of him a little.

"Number forty-six..."

It took me a few moments to realize the high-pitched voice was calling my number. I swiveled to see a female vampire striding with our group along the hall and toward the training facility.

She had long, very dark red hair. It was dead straight and rested against the curve of her butt. Her eyes were silver of course, and she had them heavily lined in kohl, which only enhanced the elfin beauty of her fine features.

"Yes..." I said with caution. I wasn't really keen on being separated out from Jayden right now.

"You have a visitor in the Quorum chambers. This is not normally allowed before the culling, but Lucas ... he wanted an exception to be made for you today." Her voice held a tinge of something ... sort of a mix of anger and jealousy.

My eyes flicked across to Jayden, who shrugged as if to say "No idea, babe." Was my mom here? Maybe Tessa? With a flick of her head, the vamp chick spun on her heels and started to stride the other way. She wasn't tall, but she moved preternaturally fast, and I hurried to catch up. There was no small talk as we crossed the hall and took the elevator even deeper into the underground. Red wasn't really clueing me in on where these Quorum chambers were, but I swear the dial read Sub20. We were deep underground, and I was going to have to work really hard to not think about the amount of rock which was above me.

Stepping off, the halls in this area were lit with fire lanterns up high in the smooth, rock walls.

"Stay close," Red told me, before marching off again.

I was starting to get nervous. I should have stopped for a second and wondered if her words were truthful before just blindly following her down here. For all I knew, she was here to kill me and wanted to go somewhere a little less populated. Jayden hadn't seemed nervous or worried by her, but he was new to the Hive too, and probably didn't understand the politics that well.

I had just about convinced myself that she was leading me toward a fire-breathing dragon, or a pack of pissed-off vampires who would eat the flesh from my bones while I was alive, when she paused outside a large, ornate double door. There was an emblem engraved into the door, and words written beneath, but in no language I'd seen. Maybe some type of secret vamp language.

Red seemed to be waiting for something. Finally, she tapped out a weird pattern and the doors silently slid open.

"They're waiting for you," she cryptically said, before fading off into the dimly lit tunnel.

Great...

I placed my hand against the cool stone, and taking a few fortifying breaths, shoving the door back with a hard push. If I was going down, I wouldn't cower out here, I'd march in with my head held high and confidence in my ash eyes. Never let them see your fear, right?

It took me a few seconds to adjust to the brighter room. More fire lanterns were scattered around. Maybe it was hard to get electricity to run down here. There was also a massive fireplace with a heavy mantel, which had a huge fire burning inside. The room was circular, and in the center stood a heavy wooden table. It looked to have been carved from the largest tree in existence, because it was a single piece spanning at least twenty feet in diameter.

The room appeared to be empty, no dragons or gang of crazy vampires, or so I thought until a familiar head of very blond hair came into view.

My feet were moving, stray tears rimming my eyelids as I dashed across the space.

"Mom!" I threw myself at her, forgetting for a moment that she was much more breakable than I was.

She held me tightly, no hesitation in her grip. It was the same as it had always been. Unconditional love.

She still smelled like lilac and spearmint, her favorite gum flavor, and despite the fact that I had to push down my urges when I was this close to her neck, I managed to control my desires and just enjoy having my mom here.

I pulled back, and we both sank into one of the large chairs. I rested against the heavy wooden back, which was intricately carved with an array of roses, that towered high into the air.

"How are you here?" I couldn't tear my eyes from her, a little slice of normal in the last few crazy days of my life. I had no idea how much I needed this. Seeing Tessa was one thing, but my mom was everything.

"I needed to speak with you, sweetheart." Her face was serious; I didn't like it. "I have to explain why I never spoke to you of this. But I didn't want you blindsided during the culling." Her voice wavered a little on that, but she plowed ahead. "You never were very interested in this world, no matter how many times I tried to broach it with you. There are so many things you don't know, but the first one is that I never married the man in the war photo, John. He was just a boyfriend, and for a long time I thought he was your true father because girl ash don't exist."

I leaned forward in my chair, wondering where this story was going.

"I don't like to speak ill of the dead, but John was an alcoholic, and abusive." She looked down timidly at her hands.

Oh hell no. With that one sentence, part of my world and soul came crashing down. That asshole in the photo that I had always adored and loved had hurt my mother.

She went on: "When he was deployed in the war I thought it was a good clean break-away for us. I would write him a letter and end things. We were intimate the night before he left, and afterwards he hit me again. This time there was no alcohol. This time his excuses fell on deaf ears. I was done with being a victim."

Okay, TMI. But still, go mom.

"The next day he was deployed and it was the perfect time to make the break. I felt so free, so glad to be out of that destructive relationship. Of course, in an ironic twist of fate, it was that very night I almost lost my life and all sense of freedom with it." Her brows drew together, a shine of tears at the memory glistened in her brown eyes.

"On my way home from class I was attacked by a rogue vampire. Rogues were a little more common back then. The enforcers weren't quite as concerned about public opinion."

Even though all of this had happened a long time ago, my breath still caught in my throat. How was she still alive?

"What happened?"

Those brown eyes softened then, as if some wonderful memory had superseded the horror of her attack. "Carter happened. He came out of nowhere and saved me. He fought the vampire, and despite killing him, ended up quite injured himself." She brushed back her mess of hair. "I couldn't leave him like that, no matter what the rules said, so I took him home and patched him up."

Mom was a nurse, and would never ignore the plea of an injured person. What was she talking about rules though?

"Carter was so different than any man I ever knew. He was gentle with me. Caring."

Shit, I was starting to see where this was going.

She finished in her soft voice. "That night, passion was high, and, well, you know how these things go."

TMI times two. Thanks, Mom.

"Carter and I were inseparable for the next few days, and I realized that for the first time I was in love. We'd already broken so many rules. What was one more?"

The pieces sort of came together for me then. What

human could have fought off a vampire and just ended up injured? None. So that meant...

"Mom, are you saying...?"

She nodded. "Carter was a vampire."

Holy shit. Holy, holy shit. Well, at least I knew my father wasn't Lucas. 'Cause that would have been whacked out.

I heard a sniffle and knew this story hadn't been easy for my mom to share with me. But I was really glad she had. I reached for her hand.

"It's okay. I'm so sorry you were with the Army asshole. I'm actually more grateful to know that my father is a vampire than an abusive drunk."

Tears sparkled in her eyes.

"When I fell pregnant, I wasn't sure whose it was. Carter wasn't able to visit me often. He said some internal politics were shaking up the Hive and he might need to go into hiding. He was special in the vampire world but he never told me why. Then I found out it was a girl and I knew you were John's daughter. I told Carter and he promised to be around either way, but then one day ... I never heard from him again. Days after this, I got a letter from the Army saying John died in battle and, well ... I knew that it was just going to be you and me."

One of those tears slid down her cheek. Shit, this was heartbreaking. Carter was almost as big an asshole as Army dude. Who left a woman he loved, even if she was pregnant with another guy's baby? It wasn't like she cheated on him or anything.

"He's probably dead," I stated.

But my mother shook her head, her blond hair rippling in the firelights. "No."

She said that with such surety. There was definitely something else she wasn't telling me. Before I could press her harder, she reached forward and tucked a chunk of my hair behind my ear. For a second the closeness between us and the distinct and delicious smell of her blood distracted me. She pressed that same hand to my cheek, and I knew she was about to drop something else big on me.

"Carter is not dead. Every year on Christmas, since your birth, I get ten thousand dollars wired to my bank account."

I blinked a few times, trying to remember if there had ever been any indication of these secrets that littered my mom's life. How could you know and love a person so much, and yet not really know them at all?

"Forgive me for not telling you all of this," she choked out.

"Mom, of course I forgive you. It's okay." Yeah, it wasn't really okay, she'd kind of effed-up my world, but there was no point mentioning that now. The past couldn't be changed and I would never stop loving her. We hugged for a long time before I finally pulled away. She looked into my eyes and chuckled.

"You have his eyes now. The crazy dancing green-silver."

That was interesting. I was already curious about the difference in my eyes to the other ash, so much more silver.

And she was right, this weird dancing green, like an arc of electricity, zagged through it.

My mom leaned in very close. "We could run away. I could give you blood. I don't want you going through the culling."

My heart pinched at her words, her so very tempting words. But I knew there was no way. I needed blood six times a day. Not to mention my crazy eyes. Humans would flip the hell out and my mom would die of blood loss. "Mom, that's sweet, but I don't think we would last very long on the run."

I had already scoped the plump throbbing vein in her neck more than once. My mom sighed. "Well, this Lucas person seems to care about you. He sought me out and snuck me in here to see you." She raised an eyebrow. "Maybe you could use your *female gifts* to make sure he takes care of you."

Oh my God. She did not just said that. "Female gifts? Are you whoring me out?"

She laughed, and just like that some of the heavy emotional stuff lifted and we were back to making jokes. "I'm saying he's in a place of power and you're a good looking young lady."

I plugged my ears. "La la la. Oh my God, Mom."

She shrugged. "That's all I got. Those were the only two plans I had." Her voice shook.

I sat up straighter and grasped her hands in a strong grip. "Well, I have a plan."

She looked hopeful.

"I'm going to get some big, buff, scary looking ash to teach me how to be a badass, murdering fighter, and I'm going to survive the culling with my own two hands."

My mom smiled weakly as if she didn't believe that was possible. Great. Team Charlie, party of one. A knock at the door jarred us from the moment. The stone barrier swung open. Red was back. Her graceful catlike poise had me instinctively leaning in front of my mother in a protective gesture. Home-girl looked ready to pounce at any moment.

"Number forty-six, your time is up. The human must leave the Hive now. No more visitors until after the culling, when you have earned the right, like everyone else." She practically spat out the last words.

My mother and I shared a look. *Bitch*. And the next person to call me number forty-six was getting a fat lip.

I hugged my mom and took one last sniff of her lilac and spearmint scent. If I closed my eyes I could almost pretend for a moment I was back home. Then, with my heart heavy and my eyes aching, I stood and followed Red. I turned back to meet my mom's eyes one more time, as another vampire appeared out of nowhere to escort her away.

I struggled to get my emotions under control the entire time I followed Red. Vamp-bitch dropped me back off at the double doors on level eight, the training room. The only sound in the space was her high heels clicking off back down the hallway. I took a moment to gather myself, to focus.

Training. Right. I was going to train to fight for my life. Everything about this felt wrong. One moment I was an upstanding human citizen and the next I was being booted to bloodsucker-ville to fend for my life. Effed up. Well, maybe I wasn't exactly upstanding, but I wasn't a complete drain on society. Now I felt discarded. Where the hell were the police? Couldn't I call 911 and get bailed out of this? Hah! Yeah right. I was infected, no one wanted me.

"Are you going to stand out here all day or do you actually plan on learning something."

I tried not to jump as Ryder's deep voice broke through my thoughts. Dammit, he'd snuck up on me again. I turned to glare at him, startled to see he was with another ash, tall and pale with short, military-style dark blond hair. God these men were gorgeous. I wasn't sure how long my hormones could be stemmed here and have no release. My fear and distrust used to keep the interest at bay, but I was slowly becoming desensitized to their freak ways and now only seemed to zero in on their hotness. Plus, I was starting to see that blaming an entire race for the actions of two assholes, was pretty darn unfair.

When I didn't answer, Ryder introduced blondie. "This is Zeke, your trainer."

I scanned Zeke up and down. He looked buff, like he might be a deadly weapon, but nothing like Ryder. "Hi, I'm number forty-six." I shook his hand, giving Ryder a bright smile. Laced with venom of course.

The corners of Ryder's lips curled slightly.

Zeke nodded as he released my hand. "Do you have any training at all?"

I stood taller. "Yes, women's self-defense, shooting range, and I'm a runner."

Zeke huffed as if that was nothing. "Well then, let's see what you got."

He opened the double doors and I was assaulted by the smell of leather, blood, and sweat. For the first time, the noises from within were audible. The room was sound-proofed. There was a lot of grunting going on, especially as most of the ash were being slammed onto the mats that littered the open gym floor. Looking up, there were huge exposed rafters and a forty-foot ceiling. Surrounding the fight-zone were a few spectators sitting in bleachers suspended above the gym on some upper floor viewing area. Great, a crowd.

I followed Zeke to an open area. Ryder took a spot leaning against the wall to watch.

Zeke planted his big frame in front of me. "Okay, attack."

"Like, for real?" I scratched my arm nervously. Damn, he wasted no time.

"Like, totally for real," he said in a valley girl voice. Asshole. I put my hands in front of me in a boxer's stance and heard Ryder and a few of the other trainers chuckle behind me. Bastards, all of them.

I decided to act like the airhead they clearly thought I was, stumbling forward and pretending I was going to clock Zeke in the face. He acted as I expected – his arms lifted to block my pathetic attempts at a swing. Then, instead of throwing the punch, I whipped my leg up and kneed him in the groin, connecting solidly. The air whooshed out of him. This was followed by a groan as he curled in on himself.

I forced myself not to smile, but that was perfect. And would hopefully teach him not to treat me like a Barbie doll. My celebration was short-lived though. He recovered quicker than I expected and threw himself forward, taking me down to the ground.

Shit. Being underneath your attacker was the worst possible position to be in. He straddled me, his bulk securing my limbs, and in seconds he had an elbow to my throat. I squirmed, trying to breathe. Ash needed to breathe or they died, right? I tried to pull both knees up, but he was too strong.

As I struggled, he continued to stare at me, those black eyes piercing and strangely empty. "You're dead," he said. "If this were the culling, you'd have been gone in five seconds."

He released my neck and I rolled over gasping and coughing. I popped up quickly and placed my hands up again, sucking in huge lungfuls of air. Mothereffer was going down.

"Yes!" Zeke said. "Use anger, come on. Show me what you've got!"

Once I managed to breathe freely again, I was up and bouncing on the tips of my feet, trying to remember that I was an ash. I was stronger and faster than my human self.

With a battle cry I ran at him, spinning and delivering a roundhouse kick to the side of his head. He fell backward, but used his long legs to snake out and trip me.

I landed on my right elbow, but was able to prop myself up before he could pounce on me again. He was too big and strong; I couldn't allow him to take me to the ground. I kicked out and smashed him in the stomach with my heel. He winced as I jumped back up into standing position.

"She's scrappy," Ryder called out to Zeke. Damn straight. Scrappy Charlie. Bring it on, you beautiful bastard.

Zeke lifted a brow at Ryder. "She'd scrappy, but also slow and weak."

Before I could track his movements, his arm snaked out lightning-quick and karate-chopped me in the throat. I bent over gasping as his knee came out of nowhere and cracked me in the skull. Then it was lights out.

FIVE

I came to groaning; the throbbing in my skull was awful. What the hell had happened to me now? It took a few seconds, but the training hall and Zeke slowly started to come back to me. What the freak? Where were my awesome ash healing powers?

I cracked open one eyelid to see Jayden peering at me. His dark eyes flashed and he looked worried.

I sighed. "I feel like shit." My thirst knocked into me as Jayden handed me a bottle of blood from our refrigerator.

His full lips straightened as he frowned at me. "Yeah, skull fractures take a while to heal."

My eyes widened as I sat and chugged the glorious blood, moaning a little. I couldn't help it, blood was so damn good now. But seriously ... I had a skull fracture? I thought I was supposed be training, not getting completely broken beyond repair.

After downing the bottle, I looked at Jayden. "Did everyone see? Did all those assholes laugh?"

He chewed his bottom lip. "Not really."

I could already tell when he was lying. His luscious lashes fluttered around like they were butterfly wings trying to take flight.

"Liar," I said, wanting to roll my eyes, but figuring it would probably increase the ache in my head.

He leaned into me a little more. "Well, they might have at first, but Ryder put a stop to that fast. He threw one of the trainers across the room and into the stadium."

Well, that was interesting.

The blood started to work its magic and I was already feeling a bit better. I sat up, ignoring the faint throbbing in my skull.

"So I'm definitely a dead person once the culling begins. Awesome." I gave two thumbs up.

Jayden shot me a weak smile. "I don't think so. I heard that after seeing you get your ass kicked, and throwing around a few members of the Hive, a certain scrumptious badass offered to train you himself."

I swallowed hard, my heart picking up. "Ryder is going to train me?"

Jayden nodded.

I was sort of intrigued about that. Why would Ryder offer to train me? And did I even want him to? I was slowly starting to forget that electrocuting me thing he'd done. I was falling victim to that chiseled jaw and those damn elusive dimples.

Jayden extended his hand. "Come on. I have something to make you feel better."

I took it and let him help me up. The room spun for a minute.

"A margarita?" I asked, and he chuckled.

I followed him out of our room and into the long hallway. We journeyed along the corridor and got into the elevator. When he pressed the ground floor button, I had a burst of insight, and excitement started to tingle in my blood. Were we going outside? Please oh please, I missed the sun, trees, air...

He saw my face and chuckled. "Just because the vamp bitches can't handle sunlight doesn't mean we should stay cooped inside." He was as flamboyant as ever.

"Yay!" I hung onto his big bicep, giving him a side hug. I was so used to the outdoors. Oregon had so many gorgeous lakes and rivers and trees, it was impossible to stay inside when that beauty beckoned you. The Hive was nice, but there were no windows. Everything was closed except at night. It made me feel stifled and I wanted some freedom. Just for a while.

Jayden led me out of the elevator near where another ash sat as receptionist. Guess vampires couldn't be this close to possible sun exposure. My roomie signed some type of log. I leaned over his shoulder and saw that he had put our numbers, twenty-one and forty-six, and the time and date.

The receptionist raised a perfectly shaped eyebrow. "Be back in an hour," he said.

We nodded and I wondered what happened if we weren't back in an hour. The windows near the outside had the roll-down shutters like the rest of the Hive, so when Jayden opened the door and the sunlight hit me, I was temporarily blinded. Raising my arm up to shield my eyes, I walked outside.

Within moments my eyes adjusted and I almost cried. A large strip of forest lay before us, thick tall trees with green moss growing up the trunks. Bushy green ferns and fallen logs littered the forest floor. Even though it was cold, the scents were still strong ... the rich soil and earthy foliage. I sighed. Home.

Jayden began to walk and I silently followed him. I noticed a few other ash sprinkled around. Glancing over my shoulder, I was blindsided for a moment by the high wire fence that surrounded the Hive, and on the other side a human guard station. No one came in or out of the Hive without a record of it. Of course, the fence reminded me of that night. I remembered gripping it as I was wrenched past the empty guard station. No one had been around to hear me scream.

I cut those thoughts off again. I would not live in the past any longer. Somehow I had this moment to enjoy the feel of the life-giving sun on my skin, and I was taking it without regret. Twigs and branches snapped under my feet as I followed Jayden. My headache was gone. The sunlight and fresh air had finished up the healing which the blood had started.

Jayden walked to a huge fallen tree trunk and sat

down as I took a seat next to him.

We sat in comfortable silence. "Thank you," I whispered. "This was just what I needed." He rested a hand on my knee and smiled, but didn't say anything else. My heart swelled and also sank at the same time. There was no way I could fight Jayden in the culling. Even to save my own life. This whole culling situation was bullshit.

"Spit it out, girl." Jayden must have seen that I was wrestling with something.

I chuckled. "Why are you being so nice to me?"

He nodded as if he understood. "I had a really hard time in middle school when it was apparent that I was different."

God, middle school was awful. I had braces, weird boobs, and a fascination for rap music. I couldn't imagine being gay on top of all that.

He winked at me. "Right, so I guess I understand the position you're in. You're very different. It makes me think of myself when I had no friends and no one to understand."

My throat tightened with emotion. I wasn't prepared for Jayden's honest reply. I squeezed his hand, but before I could respond, a loud snap of a twig behind us caught my attention. Just as we were spinning to see what was up, a steely voice cut through the tranquility. "Well, well, if it isn't the queen and the unicorn."

Jayden and I jumped up. Three large ash were stomping towards us. I scanned their jumpsuits, able to make out the smaller numbers which were stitched into the upper right side of their chests. Numbers eleven, three, and thirty-seven. Two had black hair, and number three was a redhead.

Jayden turned to me. "Am I the unicorn?"

I nodded. "Of course you are, you have magical eyelashes. Besides, I've always thought I was a queen."

One of the black-haired boys bent and scooped up a thick, sharp branch. Straightening, he glared at us. "You know it's common practice to thin out the weak ash before the culling."

I very much doubted that. The vampires wouldn't like to lose their special type of fight club entertainment. Still, as they advanced on us, it didn't seem like these ash cared much. I swallowed hard, knowing that any hopes I had of us not getting jumped had just went up in flames.

Jayden bent over and pulled a knife from his boot. Damn son!

"Who you calling weak, bitch?" Jayden's voice had lost all gayness and was pure deep hardass. I decided he was my new BAFF. Best ash friend forever.

Jayden positioned himself in front of me as I grabbed a big a rock with a sharp point. I was more likely to injure myself with it, but I had to have something.

The redhead scanned me with droopy eyes and a sloppy grin. "Let's kill him first and then have some fun with her."

Fear ran through me as my grip on the rock tightened. I was feeling seriously pissed at my mom for gallivanting around with Carter right about now. I should be with

Tessa scoping hotties at Starbucks, not this. Jayden lunged as two of the black-haired ash went for him.

The redhead snaked around him and came right for me. I was ready. I used the self-defense technique of "never let them get their hands on you," skirting quickly to avoid his grasp, before managing to fling the rock straight at his forehead. It hit with a dull thud, and my strength was more than I expected as the skin split across his browline. His features hardened.

"Bitch!" he roared, stumbling for me.

His hands grasped my shoulders and he hauled me up and slammed me back against the tree. I cried out as I felt a crack in my side. It felt a lot like a broken rib or two.

Number three's eyes were pulsing as he stared at me, his fangs lengthened. I remembered what Jayden said about my blood being irresistible. I didn't know what happened when an ash bit another ash, and I didn't want to find out.

Falling back on the best defense women have had since the dawn of time, I kicked him in the balls, hard, and he let me go briefly. I slid down to the ground, groans escaping as my entire body protested. This was definitely too soon since my fractured skull. I fought through the pain, knowing I had to get to my feet. This redhead dick would be coming at me again. And sure enough, his snarling face was lunging toward me when suddenly his body stopped and like ... disappeared. *What the hell?* My side and head screaming in pain, I dragged myself up and came face to face with Ryder. Wearing a cold, menacing look, he pointed a sleek black gun at the redhead's face and pulled the trigger. The snapping of the bullet made me jerk. Holy shit. Right between the eyes. Ryder had just killed someone like it was no big deal. I averted my eyes from the body. I knew that red had just tried to kill me, but still, his dead body was not something I wanted to see.

Holstering his gun, Ryder stepped toward me, arms scooping me up to hoist against his body. I struggled against him, wanting to walk on my own. I didn't like to be carried around like a damsel. Plus I would not look any weaker in front of the other ash. Ryder stared down at me for a few extended beats, his breathing deep, eyes full silver. Eventually he settled for looping an arm around my waist and letting me use him as a very muscular crutch. My ribs and head continued to protest as we stepped away from the tree. Once I was out in the open, I looked around for Jayden. Fear for my friend was pushing down all other emotions.

"He's fine," Ryder said, directing my gaze to where Jayden was holding his right arm. Blood seeped out from under his fingers and I could see a long, shallow gash in his shoulder.

The pair of black-haired ash were face down on the ground, hands zip-tied behind their backs, two of Ryder's teammates, dressed in black military fatigues, standing above them, each resting a boot on their backs. Through Jayden's constant chatter about the delicious core group of enforcers, I knew them by sight now.

One was Markus. He was Scottish, with thick red hair

which he wore man-bun style, and a beard to match. Dude was pretty suave. From the small amounts I'd heard of him, his accent was quite delicious. The other was Oliver, who was Latino and hot as hell. He had that dark and mysterious thing down, and I wasn't surprised to see my bestie Jayden giving him more than a single glance. The boy might be injured, but he wasn't dead. If you included Ryder, we were currently surrounded by three members of the "sexy-six" – Jayden's name for their group.

Ryder drew my attention – not that I was ever not paying attention to him – when he quickly scanned up and down my body. His expression was clinical, like he was looking for injuries. But his eyes were still all silver.

My cheeks reddened and I lowered my face a little. Together we crossed to the two ash on the ground, Ryder's arm and heat plastered firmly to my uninjured side. When we reached the dicks on the ground, the enforcer's hand tightened and he kept me close as he crouched near their messed-up faces. Someone had beat on them badly.

His voice was chilling. "Let this be a message to anyone else who wants to disobey the rules. You save the fighting for the culling. Understood?"

"Yes, sir," the ash ground out, barely able to breathe with the other big boys standing on them.

"Okay, boss, what should we do with them?" Markus asked in that rolling brogue. Noticing my stare, he gave me a wink.

Ryder readjusted my position, taking more of my weight. How had he known I was starting to falter again?

He threw Markus a slight grin. "Throw them in the pit for a night. Let's see how tough they really are."

Markus and Oliver both whistled low, before reaching down to hoist the boys up by the underarms. Ryder turned to face me, his chestnut hair flickering with streaks of gold in the sunlight. Behind him, the now silent and broken douchebuckets were being led away to this mysterious "pit."

Ryder leaned in closer. "From now on, you're my problem. Get a lot of blood and rest tonight, then tomorrow report to the training gym first thing in the morning – and also right after lunch, and after dinner. Understood?"

Problem? I gritted back my retort. He'd quite possibly just saved my life. "Yes, sir, ash, sir."

He heaved out a breath, before leaving me in Jayden's care. "See you in the morning, number forty-six."

"Leave your torture stick at home," I reminded him.

I looked up to see Jayden smiling at me, relieved to see that his wound was pretty much closed up now. "What?"

He shook his head. "Nothing." And we walked back to the front of the Hive.

THAT NIGHT my dreams were the most vivid I could remember. Again with the red blood rain, with the constant thirst. But there was a new addition: Ryder and Lucas, both half-naked, both trying to teach me to fight. Or teach me something anyways. The half-naked thing was sort of distracting, even in a dream. As the dreams faded away, I awoke to see Jayden on his bed, slowly rotating his shoulder. I sat up and rubbed my eyes a few times, before reaching for my hair-tie and twisting my hair into a top knot.

"How's your arm?" I croaked out through my scratchy morning throat.

Jayden flicked me a small smile. "I'm almost fully healed. Took a fair amount of blood. His knife sliced through something important."

I winced at the memory and my hand went instinctively to my head. I could already tell I was a million times healthier today. Which was fantastic. Just in time for someone else to kick the crap out of me.

"Yesterday made shit real," I said to my roomie, my nerves shaking my voice. "Like, those ash were prepared to off us just like that. And in two weeks you and I are legit going to go on a legal killing spree."

Jayden gave me a half smile. "Yeah, those boys could have stopped the party before it started. Thank God Ryder showed up."

Ryder. I had mixed feelings about that man. On one hand, he was clearly lethal as eff, and had saved me more than once in here. On the other hand, he annoyed the heck out of me with his "number forty-six" dismissiveness. Still … I couldn't suppress the tingling of anticipation in my stomach. If he wanted to see me three times a day, we were going to be training together a lot over the next two weeks. Which was both something I wanted and dreaded.

Truthfully, I wasn't harboring the same level of hate toward ash any longer. It's hard to hate what you are. But I wasn't sure I was ready to start crushing on them either. I just couldn't figure out why Ryder drew me in so much. It was almost like ... I knew him from a long time ago, which was crazy talk – I would definitely remember meeting someone as hot as Ryder.

I snapped out of my haze and focused on Jayden. "So, since I never got the welcome packet, tell me ... what are the best ways to kill an ash?"

Ryder had snapped a bullet between red's eyes and he was gone. So even though we were harder to kill than humans, a bullet definitely worked. Still, I needed to know all the other ways.

Jayden handed me a bottle of blood and I drank while he talked.

"We're hybrids, so we can regenerate like full-fledged vampires, but we are also still living, like humans." He was slowly drawling this out and I needed the information faster.

"Hit me with it." I hurried him on.

He shook a finger at me. "I hope you aren't this impatient in the bedroom." I flipped him off but we both smiled. We had officially reached BAFF status.

"We heal really quickly, so you need to inflict a lot of damage, masses of blood loss or major organ failure. Blow us up, light us on fire, put a bullet in the brain, rip out the heart, or decapitation."

My mouth hung open. "Jesus."

He winked. "You asked, sweet cheeks."

I shivered. "So the culling?"

He frowned. "Is a blood bath. No one really survives, ya know?"

That hit me. What he said was really deep for my normally lighthearted BAFF. You could survive some things in body but not in mind or spirit. I had never forgotten about the night I was attacked, and if those asshole ash hadn't been scared off, I knew things would have been much worse – death of soul worse.

I raised my blood bottle to clink with his. "Here's to hoping they pay for therapy after we get through it."

He gave a deep genuine laugh and clinked my bottle before saying: "You should slurp that blood down, girl. Something tells me Ryder doesn't like tardiness."

Shit! He was so right. I downed my bottle and leapt for the shower.

I ENTERED the training gym slowly, part of me expecting Ryder to jump out of nowhere and whooping my ass without warning. It was empty. I peered up into the rafters and was pleased to see them empty as well. Now that I had a chance to have a proper look, I noticed rows of weapons lining the walls. At least four large walls' worth.

I was surprised to see that there looked to be something from a range of different cultures and martial art disciplines, including but not limited to samurai swords, whips with barbed ends, throwing knives, curved blades, crossbows, throwing axes – Jesus, my stomach rolled.

"Nervous?" a low voice said from behind me.

I jumped and grabbed my chest.

"Fucking A, Ryder!" I needed to get him a bell or something.

He smiled, showing those goddamn dimples, but then quickly replaced it with his signature clenched-jaw stare. "I didn't mean to scare you."

I took a shaky breath. "I wasn't scared," I lied. "I just don't like being snuck up on." That part was the truth at least.

His smile was back. "Right, well, in the culling there will be sneaking, so get used to it."

I eyed the weapons again. "Are there rules, or do I get to run over to the wall and grab an axe and try to cut some-one's heads off?"

He tilted his head slightly, as if trying to gauge whether I was serious or not. "There are a few rules – but not many. The weapons are out of your control. The oppo-nent's sponsor chooses your weapon, and Lucas will choose your opponent's weapon."

Great. I hadn't had weapon training in my defense class. And there were no guns up there.

"Let's start," he said, crossing over to the thickest of blue mats. I followed, taking note of the casual clothing Ryder was wearing. I didn't often see him out of black camo enforcer gear. He had on loose judo pants and a tight-back muscle shirt. He pulled a gun out from behind his back waist belt and laid it on a bench. The flash of that weapon reminded me of how he had saved my life, and Jayden's.

"Hey, about yesterday ... thanks."

Suddenly his eyes were locked on mine. "It's my job," he said.

I sighed. Okay.

"Get into your fighting stance." His voice was clipped now. He was in training mode.

I did, holding my fists in front of my face, right foot planted in front of me.

"Are you a southpaw?" He gazed at my stance, eyes roaming over me.

"Yes, I'm left handed."

He shook his head and then grabbed my hips and twisted me a little. I tried to stand firm, but he was strong. He clicked his tongue between his teeth. "You're weak."

"Screw you," I said, glaring at him.

"But you have some spunk, so I'm going to work with that. This scrappy fighting style of yours will only last as long as it takes for one of the ash to take you down to the ground."

"Guess you'd better have a magic wand then."

"I don't need magic." I could smell the faintest metallic scent on his lips. He'd recently fed.

I tried to focus as he took a step back. "Put your arms out, like you're flying."

I wanted to roll my eyes, but managed to simply sigh and do as he said.

"Resist," he commanded as he applied pressure to my arms, pushing them down with ease.

"Again."

I resisted him as hard as I could, but my arms still fell easily.

He nodded, his chestnut hair sweeping across his eyes. "Your left arm is stronger. On top of three times a day training, I'm recommending twice a day weight training. I'll have Jared train you. He loves his weights." I knew Jared was one of the sexy six. The blond Australian. I'd only ever seen him from across the way, but he definitely had impressive biceps. Still, that was a lot of training.

"When do I sleep?" I challenged Ryder.

"When you have survived the culling." His serious tone wiped the attitude off my face. Swallowing roughly, I nodded. The instinct to survive was strong in me and this guy was willing to help me. The least I could do was give it my all.

"I'm going to teach you a five step sequence. This sequence will be the only thing you do, three times a day for the next week. You will be so sick of it by the end of the week, you will be doing it in your sleep."

"Wow, you really know how to sell your services," I muttered.

He ignored me. "Left jab, right hook, left leg kick, drop and sweep." It sounded like a chant almost.

"Watch me," he commanded.

"Left jab." He lightly pushed his left hand out and brushed my chin.

"Right hook." His right hand swept around and lightly touched my right temple.

"Left leg kick." He took his left leg and slowly brought it up to touch my ribcage.

"Drop." He dropped to the ground. "And sweep."

From a crouched position, his leg snaked out and swept my legs out from under me. I fell back on the mat, my teeth clacking as I hit the ground. I had totally not expected that, since it was simply supposed to be a demonstration. He stood and looked down on me.

"You're a dick. You know that, right?" I waved away his hand.

He dropped his arm back to his side. "Would you rather have a dick teach you to stay alive or a nice guy babying you through training?"

Shit, the dick had a point. As soon as I was back on my feet, Ryder walked over to a wall and wheeled out this big-ass punching bag figure of a man. He put it right in front of me and stood like a sentinel next to it.

"Ready to sweat?" he rumbled. I forced myself to focus. It was really unfair that the unique rumbly quality of his voice totally threw my equilibrium off.

Taking my position, I began the sequence he showed me. I was unable to sweep the heavy mannequin, but I assumed we would work on that later. Maybe I'd be lucky enough to return the gesture from before and sweep Ryder on his ass.

Every time I punched, he intercepted and adjusted my hold, or twisted my arm. It made me feel like I didn't know shit about fighting. I grit my teeth and kept going. After twenty minutes of this my muscles were screaming at me to stop, but I wouldn't give Ryder the satisfaction of seeing me quit.

An hour later of non-stop "five step program," I heard the door creak open and glanced across to see Lucas. Vamp was still fully dressed in a suit and his white trench coat. He was hot, but I was starting to think he was a pimp in his spare time, or a Vegas card shark.

"How's our girl?" he asked, crossing toward us, smiling the entire time. I locked in on his beautiful face, appreciating the fallen angel look he was rocking. Hey, I was female and he was hot, and thankfully not my dad.

"Eyes forward." Ryder's voice was cold again. What was this guy's problem?

With a loud exhalation, just so he knew I was annoyed, I started up the sequence again. Ryder crossed the mat to meet Lucas off to the side. They started to chat, but in a tone too low for me to hear. Left jab, right hook, left leg kick, drop and sweep. It was irritating me already. I couldn't imagine three times a day for a week.

God, help me not die of boredom.

DINNER FOR JAYDEN and I consisted of a trip to the feeding room during our scheduled time. I had told Tessa only to meet me once a week, and we were still days away from that, so I didn't check with the receptionist for any scheduled feedings. I grabbed a couple bottles of O-negative and we left the feeding hall and made our way to the entertainment section. This was on a higher level of the Hive. Level forty-four. I followed Jayden to a plush lounge. Live music filled the space, low and jazzy. Soft green velvet couches circled the room; on a dais stood a baby grand piano. A sexy and voluptuous vampire with long golden brown hair was crooning out a sultry song as a man played on the piano.

No one came near us. The jumpsuits did their job of keeping the ash who had yet to survive the culling separate. We were nothing more than numbers.

We found a free lounge and sank into it. Jayden guzzled his blood, wincing as he banged his elbow on the side of the chair.

"You healing okay?" I asked him.

He'd been training separate from me, with the other male ash, and it was already starting to get brutal. Ryder had assured me that our training would continue to be different times from the rest. That way none of them could ferret out my weaknesses before the fights. It was under two weeks until the culling and everyone was freaking out. I'd trained twice already today, not to mention weights, and all I could think about was that stupid five-step program. One thing was for sure, those movements were going to be stuck in my head for a long time to come.

"Yeah, I'm sore but okay," Jayden answered, tilting his head back, the low lights shining across his perfect, dark skin. "Word got around that we were attacked and somehow survived. It's raised the odds on us, moved us toward the end of the culling schedule. So of course every ash and their dick have decided to take me out early."

I sat a little straighter. "I should be training with you. You need me in your corner." As little use as I might be, I could watch his back. "Fucking Ryder has me doing some stupid five step movement. I need weapons training. I need to know how to rip an ash's arm off and beat him to death with it. No five steps are going to help with that."

Jayden's dark eyes flashed as he opened his eyelids, and then he was laughing – throw-back-his-head-until-his-stomach-ached kind of laughing. "Girl, I could not have asked for a better roomie." It took him a few moments to compose himself. He even had me joining in his laughter; it was contagious. He finally pulled it together. "You should be grateful. Ryder is the shit. He is a scary mother and there is no one in here who would take him on. Whatever he is teaching you, you learn it until your brain bleeds. It will most probably save your life."

As if his words had conjured up the man himself, I sensed a dark gaze on me, and as I twisted to the side, my eyes clashed with a set which were looking quite silver at the moment. There was something between us, a spark. A moment happened then that was hard for me to describe, but all I knew was that I couldn't tear my gaze away from him. If he'd have beckoned me right then, I'd have gotten off my chair and hightailed it over to him. Which was not a feeling I had ever experienced before.

"Ever noticed that you and Ryder both have eyes which are a hell of a lot more vampire than ash?" Jayden was watching our exchange, and the boy was pretty much fanning himself as he grinned.

Ryder broke the spell, turning to one of the sexy six, and I was finally able to catch my breath. Wait! What had Jayden said?

"Vampire eyes?" I asked, letting my confusion release. "I have ash eyes. Only a little more intense."

Jayden nodded. "You do, even though your silver is a lot more defined than the others – and sometimes when your emotions are charged they get very silver, with this splash of green. It's almost ... alive."

I was guessing right now they were very silver, as he put it.

"I've seen the same thing with Ryder. It's almost as if the pair of you hold a little more of the virus in your DNA than the rest of us."

Was that possible? I wasn't sure what Jayden was talking about. They had tested my blood and I was an ash ... right? I couldn't actually remember if they had given me those results or if it was just assumed because, well, what the hell else could I be?

I took an extended sip of my blood, and almost against my will my eyes flicked back to where Ryder had been. He was gone. Some of the other enforcers lingered around the wide, wooden bar, but no tall, dark, and broody to be seen.

I noticed that a group of ash, all wearing jumpsuits, had just walked into the room. A few of them exchanged looks before strolling across to where Jayden and I sat.

"Something tells me there are a few alliances going on

before the culling," I murmured, sitting forward in my seat, the bottle of blood forgotten as I prepared myself. Surely they wouldn't start something here in a room filled with ash and vampires.

Jayden straightened also, and without saying a word both of us jumped to our feet. We would not be taken sitting down. The three male ash, two brunettes and a rather scrawny dirty-blond, paused about eight feet from us. A sense of hesitation came across them, and they exchanged another glance before turning and fading off into the crowd.

"Hell yeah," I said, "seems our reputation has gotten around."

A hand landed on my shoulder, and I suddenly knew that it wasn't our reputations which had sent those ash fleeing. I swung my head around, only to be visually assaulted by a very sharp-set of fangs. Lucas towered over me, his white trench glowing softly under the lights in this dim atmosphere.

"I need you to come with me, Charlie. Something has happened."

My immediate panicked thought was of my mom, but I was pretty sure that no one in the Hive cared or monitored the loved ones left out in the human world. It had to be something else. I'd just seen Ryder ... so who else was there?

I took a step toward Lucas, before stopping and flicking my head back to Jayden. "Hey, are you going to be okay? I don't want anyone to jump you while I'm gone."

He just gave me that cheeky grin and waved me on. "I'll be fine, you go and do your thing. I'll see you back in our room." The smile faltered a little as his eyes shifted across to the vampire at my side. Jayden was pretty up on the politics in the Hive and he knew Lucas was a big deal. All of the Quorum members were. This was not a request I could refuse, but he was worried for me all the same.

I wondered if I should be a little more worried myself. For someone who did not trust easily, who used to genuinely have a hate for anything to do with the Hive, I had come around awfully quick. But something about Ryder and Lucas gave me a sense of security. Like I knew they would not deliberately screw with me. Jayden was the same, and I was going to go with my gut on these three.

LUCAS WAS silent as he led me through the corridors and into the lower levels again. As we stepped off the elevator, I recognized the zone. I was back in the white-washed hospital wing, which was apparently on level two. I hadn't paid attention to the level the last time I was here. *Shit* ... what was I doing here? My heart rate increased again.

"Mom?" I gasped. Even if it was not a logical worry, I still had to ask. Lucas didn't answer immediately. I breathed deeply, trying to slow the rapid pulse of my blood, before grabbing at his trench coat. I was prepared to make him tell me what the hell was going on.

The vampire halted, surprise lighting up his eyes as I

pulled him closer to me. We locked gazes for an extended moment, and just as I was about to shake him for information, he leaned closer to me.

"Your friend is right, your eyes are very silver when you feel strong emotions."

Clearly he had been stalking me even before those ash had approached us.

"And your mother is perfectly fine. We just need to run a few more tests. The first ones were inconclusive, and without the results I cannot ascertain your lineage. It is needed for the culling. I would like to do this quietly before the rest of the Quorum get wind of it."

My lineage? As in who my father was? I knew his name, but for some reason instinct kept me silent on that. I realized then how close we were, my hands still tangled in his coat. I could see every facet in his silver eyes, which seemed to be swirling and pulsing in the fluorescent light. My grip loosened on his trench coat, and as I stepped back he smoothed down the creases I'd created. He seemed a little shaken, almost mesmerized in a manner, but before I noticed anything further he was back to normal.

"Come," he said, continuing along the path.

I tried not to breathe too deeply as I followed. Something about the disinfectant smell in the air of hospitals turned my stomach. And with developed ash senses, it was a hundred times worse. I hadn't noticed it as much the last time I was here – probably because I was too freaked out with the whole "your-mom-banged-a-vampire" revelation. This time though I was seeing everything. Why the hell were there so many rooms on this level? Was it really necessary? Surely, with our advanced healing, hospitals were only needed for those occasional ash who popped up out of the woodwork.

"Hey, what happens when a human receives the virus?" If my question startled Lucas, he didn't show it. "How come some take a really long time to turn, and isn't it illegal? How are new vampires still being made?" The longer I spent in the Hive, the more I wished I'd taken the classes on vamps in school.

Lucas paused outside of a door, one of the few that didn't have a massive viewing window. "It is illegal to make new vampires without Quorum permission. If you want to turn someone, you must apply. We grant very few of these. We must monitor our populations growth, and keep from starting another war with the humans."

Right, they didn't want to outgrow their food source or the Hive. I shuddered. I also knew there was a special branch of the human military devoted strictly to keeping vampire and ash at bay. We lived only because the humans allowed it. Nothing could stop them if they wanted to drop a nuke on the Hive in the middle of the night. On every Hive in the world. The vampire rights groups were the only thing keeping the fragile peace between our two races right now.

Lucas continued to answer my questions, and I had a brief thought of why he was so forthcoming with information. Probably this was all common knowledge for anybody who had actually attended the Virus 101 classes.

"The virus is generally fast acting, but we have known of some cases where it was dormant for years."

"And ash..." I prompted.

"Strictly forbidden, but we understand that sometimes things are outside of the humans' control." Ugh, was he talking about rape? "So we allow a small number of ash to survive each year."

Yeah, they were regular saints. The culling was their way of taking care of the problem without actually getting their hands dirty. It really didn't seem fair that the majority of vampires were allowed to live, but ash were culled like freaking animals.

I tried to dial down some of the simmering anger which was always close to the surface. "Why are there no female ash?" Lucas' eyes lingered on me for a few long moments. "I mean besides me."

"The virus destroys much of our reproductive system. Female vampires are unable to have children. No eggs remain intact. For the males, only the sperm which carry the Y chromosome survive. Which makes your existence all the more unusual."

He was telling me that even science dictated that my existence was impossible. So how the hell was I an ash?

Apparently question and answer time was over. He opened the door and gestured for me to step through first. There were two vampires dressed in lab coats waiting for me on the other side. They stood on either side of a chair, each holding a stack of charts.

"Please have a seat, Charlene," said the very blond

female. She was all sharp angles and pointy nose, interesting to look at, but not beautiful. There was more variation in vampires than in ash. Vampires were turned from humans, so they still retained much of their human looks, just all smoothed out. Ash were actually grown from mutated sperm, so it was ingrained into their DNA. Therefore, they were sexier.

I didn't like being surrounded or towered over, but in a room of three vampires I was not going to be able to fight myself out. Might as well do what they wanted. Lucas gave me a small smile, as if he'd heard my inner thoughts. I realized that the second vampire, the male with rows of black braids tightly woven to his head, was talking to me.

"...initial DNA test was inconclusive. Something must have tainted the sample, so we will need another one."

"What do you have to do?" I asked, suspicious. Mom always said my college major should have been investigating, not marketing.

"Cheek swab, hair sample, and we will also need some blood. We need a detailed DNA sequence to find your ancestry and place you in the proper house of ten."

I swallowed, but forced myself not to react. "Sure, poke away," I finally said.

I wasn't sure I quite believed their story, but I did not have a choice here. At no point had any of them asked my permission, so I knew this was part of the Hive protocol. Or maybe just for me because I was a special girl-ash.

The doctors were fast – benefits of the vampire virus. After swabbing my cheek and taking some hair, they pricked my finger. The moment my red blood beaded at the tip, the blond vampire inhaled deeply and hissed, her fangs extending.

An unusual scent slammed into me, and I realized it was my blood. What the hell was up with its potency? Shit, I almost wanted to bite myself. Lucas frowned and grabbed the woman's arm. I scanned each one of them as their eyes pulsed silver, green, silver, green.

I quickly wiped my bleeding finger on the test strip and placed it in my mouth. An odd taste washed across my tongue, but my finger healed before I could really sense why it was strange. Lucas led the female out of the room, and returned alone. He was staring at me like I was a complicated chess game. What Jayden had said about the allure of my blood was true, even for vamps.

Mental note: Don't. Bleed. Ever.

The male vampire with braids cleared his throat and bagged the specimen. "We will send across the results. Lucas, you'll be able to plan your culling schedule and make sure she's training in her specialty areas."

Since my finger had already healed and the unique scent of my blood was gone, the vampire's eyes were back to normal.

"I don't have any specialties. You don't need a DNA test to know that. Just watch me get my ass handed to me every day in training."

Lucas smiled in one of those full, breathtaking, rows of pearly whites. My breathing stuttered a little. He was potent when he wanted to be. "If we know who your sire is, then we know what your specialty is. Each of the ten houses has a specialty. More specifically, each vampire Original had a specialty which they passed on in diluted versions to their descendants. There is much we can discover from your ancestry."

Whoa. Interesting. The doctor left the room then, samples tucked into a lab bag. Lucas reached out and I took his hand, but still got to my feet without help. A part of me just wanted to hold his hand and see if he gave me the same tingles that Ryder could induce with just one of his famous stoic looks.

It was nice, no denying it, but not exactly the same. Staring into his silver eyes, I suddenly felt very brave. "Tell me what happened to the Originals," I blurted out.

He sort of froze, his human façade, which vampires tried to maintain, disappearing altogether as some sort of feral predator rose in his eyes.

"Even though they escaped the early cullings, they were eventually wiped out by humans," he said. "The blood of an Original is where the virus is strongest. It has been diluted down through the years, and now all that remains are the ten houses. We are very distant descendants."

His tone was clipped, as if he were reciting the standard brochure on the Originals or something.

"I thought after those initial years things got better between vampires and humans, so why were they wiped out?" I had to ask.

Lucas pulled his hand from mine and started to walk

toward the door. I didn't think he was going to answer. He pressed down on the handle and clicked open the door.

But then he swiveled his head back around and gave me a pointed stare. "For a long time there was a lot of misinformation and fear. Even though the original vectors, the bats, were gone, the humans still feared getting the virus from a cough, a touch, anything. On top of that, newly changed vampires didn't appreciate being weaker than the Originals. We believe a group of vampires coordinated an attack with an extremist group of humans. They came in the middle of the night and wiped out the entire Original lines.

My mouth fell open. Okay, yeah, I didn't exactly love the bloodsuckers, but killing off the bunch of them in the night was akin to genocide. They had all been humans before the virus, and I knew that they still had many human traits even now.

"After this loss of leadership the Quorum was formed, and some semblance of order has remained ever since. Ryder is the closest ash or vampire in the Hive with a direct link to an Original."

Whoa. My training instructor had just got that much more interesting.

"AGAIN!" Ryder yelled as I pounded on the boxing mannequin.

I groaned. I was sweating bullets, my pinky was broken, and I was bored out of my mind. It had been three days of this shit and I was considering killing myself so I didn't have to continue this insane regimen. Of course, soon I wouldn't have to worry too much about killing myself. Someone else was sure to do it in the culling.

"I can't," I confessed. "It's maddening. I need a change." My muscles ached from the weightlifting session I'd had before training, but I couldn't deny the definition forming in my arms and legs. Ash built muscle easily, and I was halfway home to a six-pack.

Ryder seemed to consider my words. He walked over and grabbed the mannequin, wheeling him to the far wall.

"Thank you, sweet baby Jesus!" I practically shouted. Finally this guy was listening to me.

Ryder planted himself opposite me, arms in front of his face. "Again."

I stared into his gorgeous face and cracked a smile. "You want me to kick your ass?" Oh man I had been dreaming of this day. This good-looking, smug bastard had electrocuted me – I was totes never letting that go – had kicked my legs out from under me, and made me work my ass off all week. He deserved some payback.

He tilted his head to the side in that observe-me-like-a-lab-rat way of his. "You're a little too happy about trying to hurt me."

I rolled my eyes. He waved me closer. "You think you've done the five steps enough? Let's see how you do with the real thing. I'm going to do basic blocks, but I will let you hit me. It's important you get used to the feel and sound of skin hitting skin, and bones crunching under impact."

My stomach rolled. Jesus this guy was a mercenary.

All of a sudden I didn't want to hit him, or break any bones in that gorgeous face. If I didn't have something pretty to look at every day, the Hive would be a real buzzkill. Sure, there were lots of pretty males here, but Ryder ... well, he was Ryder.

He saw me falter, and the beginnings of a grin lifting one side of his lips. "You were such a pain in my ass your first few days here. It felt kinda good to zap you after you broke my ankle."

Hah. I totally knew what he was doing. Bastard. It was working too.

Without warning, I threw the left jab. He blocked. I countered quickly with the right hook, which he let through to smash into his unprotected head. Shit. I was about to pull back, but I saw the glint in his eyes. He was daring me to continue, and he had barely flinched when I'd just hit him, so ... I finished the sequence with a knee to the ribs and then crouched and swept my leg out to flip him onto his back. He jumped up just in time.

I stumbled back before shaking out my throbbing hand. His face was made of stone or something.

He appraised me. "Your frame is stronger, your blows harder – you still don't quite have the feral push needed to kill, but that will come in the moment when you do literally fight for your life."

I really didn't want to think about that. I would probably throw up all over him or something.

"Again." He put his hands out in front of him.

Dammit, why was he being so pushy with this shit? My frustrations regarding the direction my life had taken flooded through me. This was not the life I wanted. This was not the life I'd expected. I wasn't even sure I would survive the next two weeks. I wanted to be stronger than I felt inside, I wanted to see Ryder in a position of weakness.

Instead of starting the sequence off correct, I pretended I was going to throw a left jab but instead went right for the leg sweep. Caught completely unaware, Ryder began to fall backward, then his hand snaked out and he grabbed my arm, pulling me with him. I landed on top of him as the breath whooshed out of both of us. Okay, dude was quick and I had totally not expected that to happen.

Conscious thought disappeared, and time stopped as I realized I was completely pressed against every inch of him. His hard muscles pushed into my softness and our eyes locked in a stare. So much silver flared to life in that one gaze. His eyes fell to my lips and I licked to wet them.

Before I could move though, the silver of his gaze darkened and his face turned cold. He rolled me off, jumping up to stand. "Pulling your old scrappy tricks," he said. "Give me five laps."

I blinked a few times, my daze wearing off in a blast of disbelief. What the hell was that? Was I crazy or had he been about to kiss me? For a split second I had wanted him to, so badly, but he clearly wasn't interested and I clearly needed to expand my circle of friends. Hanging out only with a gay guy and this insanely sexy badass was messing with my head. Stockholm syndrome was in full effect. I jumped up and hit the ground running, burning off the sexual tension that had crept in between Ryder and I. How long had it been since I got laid? That had to be the problem. Sexual deprivation was driving me crazy. There was no other explanation.

LATER THAT DAY I was on my way to the cafeteria to grab some human food when I found Lucas waiting off to the side of the double doors. As soon as he met my eyes, he flicked his head and motioned for me to follow him. He was all in white again. Did he have a problem with color or something? He was like a monochromatic painting. Perfect, but eerily white and shiny.

My muscles protested against any more running as I struggled to keep up with him. He quickly darted into an open door off of the hallway, and I followed him inside. On the other side was Ryder, Lucas, and an unfamiliar female vampire in a lab coat. She had a very short pixie haircut, her thick tresses an unusual silver color. Seriously, how many doctors and scientists did they have in the Hive?

"What the hell?" I said. Was this an ambush or something? Lucas shut the door behind me and motioned to the female.

"Everything is okay, Charlie, we just needed some privacy," Lucas said to me. "Tell them what you told me," he commanded, turning to the doctor.

She clutched at the few papers in her hands. "Well, sir, it's really difficult to explain – the virus has so many variants."

"Madeline," Lucas said, bestowing one of his rarely seen glares on her. I noticed that Ryder's expression was shuttered, hard to read. But still, I was sensing something in his black and silver eyes. Curiosity?

The doctor turned to me, her eyes fluttering and her expression sympathetic. "We ran the tests four times. The results keep coming back the same. Charlie appears to have been fathered by an Original. Her sire was the Original of the fourth house."

My mouth dropped open. For the first time there was an emotional response from Ryder – his eyes flashed and the silver took over his black iris. He moved beside me as if to protect me from impending attack. "She's twenty years old. The Originals died over two hundred years ago. It's not possible! I am two generations removed from the Original line, and that's the closest we know of." Ryder growled.

The female's expression hardened. "The science speaks differently. Her DNA is a direct branch of Carter Atwater of the fourth house."

Why were Ryder's brows drawn together like that? Not to mention his fists clenching? Was he scared? Ryder wasn't scared of anything.

"And the other thing you told me?" Lucas pushed.

She nervously fiddled with the paper. "It's just a theory, sir..."

Lucas' current stare could have cut glass.

She hurried out the next part. "I'm not one hundred percent sure that Charlie is an ash."

Okay, now I was even more confused. First she tells me I'm from a dead Original – sure, okay. I might buy that there was something weird going on there – Carter was the name my mom gave me for her rescuer after all. But now I also wasn't an ash? What other option was there? I knew I wasn't a vampire. I had been out in the sun and there was definitely black in my eyes. Was there a third option they hadn't told me about?

Ryder shook his head. "What is she then?"

Okay, if Ryder didn't know of a third option, then this woman was clearly a few blood bags short of a full load.

"She's not human or vampire, I know that. To tell more I need more time and more blood."

Lucas nodded. "I will provide you with whatever is needed, and you will testify to the Quorum tomorrow that she is a diluted descendant ash of the fourth house."

The woman clenched her jaw. "And if I do this, you will let my family go?" For the first time, some of her timidity fled and her fangs flashed as she glared at Lucas.

He smiled. "We'll see. Be a good girl." He opened the door and she stormed out.

Wait, what the hell just happened? Ryder was looking at me like I was going to sprout a second head. Lucas had kidnapped her family to keep this information private? I wasn't sure I wanted to know what was going to happen next. I really wanted to demand he release the captives, but I didn't have any pull with the powerful Quorum member. Poor Madeline ... I would have to try and figure out something later.

I realized that Ryder had started talking again, his words short and clipped. "This changes everything," he said to Lucas. "If she isn't ash and if she's a direct descendant, we can pull her from the culling. The Quorum will spare someone so special."

Did Ryder just call me special? I raised an eyebrow.

"Don't delude yourself! The Quorum would never let her live, for fear that she could overthrow them. You're not old enough to remember the dark days. We keep her in the culling and tell no one of this revelation."

Hey, I'm right here.

"Excuse me? What's the fourth house all about?"

The white-clad vampire wasted no time turning to me. "When Carter Atwater was bitten by the bat infected with Anima Mortem virus, and transformed to a vampire, he manifested the power of levitation. As a direct descendant, you too should be able to utilize this power to some extent."

Whoa. This was ... what the actual fuck was going on here? Carter Atwater was my father and an Original. Was that why he'd been in hiding and told my mom that things were rough for him. How had he not died with the other Originals? And if my mother was right about our Christmastime money deposits, he was still alive now. Something told me I shouldn't trust this knowledge to anyone. If they tried to kill him once, they would do it again.

Lucas met my eyes as if reading my train of thought. "Your mother didn't say anything about still being in contact with Carter, did she?"

Lie, Charlie, lie your ass off. I huffed. "Yeah, right. She was shocked as hell about what I turned out to be. Said the guy screwed her and ran off."

Lucas seemed like he wanted more of an answer. "You know there was a fire and Carter's body was never actually recovered. You can tell me if he has contacted you. Some say he might still be alive."

My eyes flicked to Ryder, who shook his head the tiniest bit.

I smiled at Lucas. "Trust me, if this dude was alive, I would have you drag his ass to the Hive so I could kick him in the nuts for ruining my life."

Lucas smiled, but it didn't quite reach those silver eyes. "Alright. Let's keep this all under wraps. Keep training. Charlie, I'd like to have you over to my place for dinner tomorrow night."

My eyebrows shot up as Ryder cleared his throat.

"I'd love to," I said with a fake smile. I trusted Lucas, but only to a certain extent. Still, there was no reason to let him know that.

THE NEXT NIGHT I was summoned to the fiftieth floor.

Jayden informed me that this level held the penthouses. Lucas lived the cushy life. I wondered what he'd been like as a human, before becoming vampire and all powerful Quorum member. Maybe I'd find out tonight.

Lucas opened the door and gestured for me to step inside. I crossed the threshold into his massive apartment, and wondered for a moment why the Quorum members would want their places up high with all that sunlight around. Made more sense for them to be in one of the twenty sub levels. Of course, the moment I ventured a little further into the room, my feet sinking into soft carpet, I understood exactly what the draw was. Floor to ceiling windows spanned the entire side of his apartment, and just like when I ran on the roof, the view was spectacular. He'd never see the sun rise across the city, but maybe the moonlight was enough for him. I guess it had to be enough.

Lucas' place was very open-plan, each room seamlessly blending into the next. The furniture was expensive but simple, all creams and whites. Which was not a surprise considering his love for that trench coat. Which he wasn't actually wearing right then, but still his slacks and button dress shirt were in shades of white.

"What happens when the sun rises?" I asked, taking in the wide expanse of windows which covered everything from the river to the edge of the Portland.

"The same shutters close over our floors." He stood next to me, both of us at the window of his main living area. "I could have taken one of the basement suites, but I already mourn the loss of the sun. I don't want to lose anything else."

His words mirrored my own thoughts from before. That was the most personal revelation I'd heard from the reticent vampire. For the hundredth time I wondered why he had taken such an interest in me. It felt like more than the fact I was an ash-unicorn – something deeper.

"Come," he finally said. "Dinner is almost ready and I don't want it to get cold."

I followed him through a few more impressive rooms, catching a glimpse of the massive stainless steel and marble-benched kitchen, before we ended up in a simply adorned medium sized room. It held not much more than an eight-seater dining table, which had two place settings made up on it. There was also an antique-looking hutch, which was oddly out of place in his very modern penthouse.

"That was my wife's." He must have noticed my interest – his words were so low I almost missed them, even with ash hearing. "She loved it, took her months to restore it, and I just couldn't part with it ... even after."

My breathing went a little ragged, matching with his. The usually cool, calm, and collected male was leaking emotions all over the place. It was hard hearing that tone of loss, and I wondered what had happened to his wife. What had happened to him? How did he become a vampire?

As we took our seats across from each other, I hoped that I might have some answers tonight. The silence between us grew, but it didn't really feel uncomfortable. I figured he must have someone cooking, because there was no way for him to be here and in the kitchen. Unless that was his superpower.

Nope. An ash male entered the room then, carrying a long tray which he placed gently into the center of the table. He proceeded to lift the very heavy looking silver-inlaid cover, and beneath was a veritable feast.

I sucked in deeply, the scents of seafood and pasta wafting toward me. My stomach roared to life and I had to restrain myself from actually launching across to fill my mouth with that goodness.

Lucas chuckled. "I do so miss that love for food. I pretty much just have blood now."

I knew vampires could still eat food, but they didn't need to, and they didn't particularly enjoy it. Another ash entered then, and in his hands was a bottle of red wine. He showed the label to Lucas and the vampire nodded. The ash popped the cork with a whoosh of release, and the wine was allowed to breathe. Lucas filled both of our glasses; the scent hit me immediately. It was all red grapes, sweet apples, oak barrels and ... blood. I straightened. Holy shit. They had alcohol with blood in it? Why the hell hadn't I known this before now?

He talked as he poured. "This is a special blend that my company is manufacturing. It's new to the market. I was hoping we could be the testers tonight." The silver in his eyes flashed at me as he lifted his head and lowered the bottle to the table again.

I was intrigued. Lucas not only was a Quorum member, which was a fulltime job on its own, he also had a company that made cool things. Like blood alcohol. I reached for my glass, the wine swishing against the sides a little as I brought it closer to my face. My eyelids fluttered closed as the deeper tones of the scent hit me. I allowed myself moments to breathe it in. Blood had such a tantalizing smell for me now, that copper filled with spice and heat and life. Team that with rich grapes, the juicy sweetness of red apples, and aged wine and, well, shit, I was pretty sure Lucas had a winner here.

The first sip was a blast of flavor. Every single one of my taste buds jumped to attention and started screaming for more.

"What do you think?" My eyelids flew open to find Lucas watching me closely.

"Un-freaking-believable." I almost moaned as I took another small sip. "I'll take ten bottles."

He laughed, flashing all those white teeth, the slightest tip of fang visible. "You survive the culling and you can have ten crates."

Incentive enough for me.

THE REST of dinner was relaxed. Lucas chatted to me about the general life and rules of the Hive while I devoured basically everything that wasn't tied down. We finished the first bottle of blood merlot before opening a second. This one was less fruity, and spicier, but equally delicious. It was even giving me a little buzz and I wondered if maybe the blood worked with the alcohol to give more impact to vampires and ash.

"So tell me about your life before you were a vampire. How did you get infected?"

As my artlessly worded questions left my mouth, the animation fell from Lucas' face and I realized that I might have pressed on a sore spot for him. The conversation before had been light and impersonal, and I'd just gone straight for personal. I opened my mouth to apologize and change the subject, but then he started to talk.

"I was infected in the late 1800s – I'm not even sure of the exact date any longer. Back then the bats had been culled, but the Originals had started to mass a decent number in their clans. But they weren't always successful at keeping control. Newly turned vampires were driven to attack, like a bad case of rabies that can never be cured." He swirled the liquid in his glass; my eyes remained locked on him. "I was a farmer, just a simple farmer. We grew wheat. My wife, Regina, she would stay at home and raise our two sons while I worked from daylight to dusk. It was a hard life, but it was perfect."

God, this was harder to hear than I expected, especially considering it had been a very long time ago. But I could tell that for Lucas it was not long at all.

"One night I was out with the plow. There had been storms that season and it was imperative I finished the field that night. Generally, we did not stay out after dark. Everyone was aware of the problem sweeping the human race, and caution after dark was always advised." He broke off then, ghosts of the past swirling in those captivating eyes.

"You were bitten?" I prompted.

He nodded a few times, his motions jagged. "Yes, a female, she came out of nowhere, attacking me. I managed to fight her off and in the struggle my horse took off dragging the plow over her, removing the head and covering my bite marks with her blood, infecting me. That was the only reason I survived. Well, sort of. I knew that everything I loved and worked so hard to provide for was gone. I could never go home to my family, I would kill them when the change happened and the bloodlust hit. So I ran. I ran for the city, to the humans who locked me and others like me away like science experiments. Luckily, technology was pretty sparse back then, so after I grew strong enough to control myself, I escaped and finally ended up in the Hive of those days, which was secreted away from humans."

"You never saw your family again?" I asked breathlessly.

He dropped the wine glass onto the table. A few drops spilled, marring the brilliant white of his tablecloth. "I did visit them one time, just to make sure they were doing okay. The farmhouse was empty, deserted, and it had clearly been looted." The depth of his anguish and anger filled his low tones. "I should have known that they'd be targeted, a single woman with two small children. I basically signed their death warrants when I deserted them."

Either way, his family had been doomed.

"I salvaged her hutch and a few other pieces before burning the house to the ground. I never found my wife or sons. I still do not know what happened to them, and it haunts my every single waking moment."

Gods, and I thought my story was horrible. I at least still had seen my mom and Tessa.

"That's why you allowed Mom to come and see me."

Lucas swallowed, his movements exaggerated as he worked to control his emotions. "You actually remind me a little of my wife. She was as tough and beautiful as you are. I ... I knew you wanted to have a final goodbye with your mother, and it was within my power to grant that."

I reminded him of his wife – it was all starting to make sense now. Lucas was a good guy, a good guy who'd had plenty of horrible things happen. Even now, with the cold ache of the vampire virus filling his veins, he was still being a good guy.

I reached across the table and took his free hand. "Thank you. I will never forget everything you've done for me."

He returned my squeeze once before letting go. "Do not die in the culling, Charlie. I will be very unhappy, and I'd hate to have to start hurting the ash who hurt you."

He would do it too. I could see it in his eyes. He was not happy about me going into this battle. But tradition was tradition, and not even a Quorum member could save me now. I was going to have to save myself.

SIX

The next ten days passed in a blur of training, blood hunger, and ass-kickings. And straight up, Ryder was doing ninety percent of said kicking. I was getting a little bit better at fighting, but if my fellow ash fought anything like Ryder, I was a dead woman. I was starting to wonder if Ryder was punishing me for the revelations that day with that doctor, where she'd spoken of the anomalies in my blood. He'd been riding the shit out of me since then – pun intended – determined to turn me into a ninja freak show, and he was dragging my aching butt out of bed all hours of the day and night to do it.

A week ago we'd started weapons training, though Ryder only trained me on one weapon, the samurai sword. He thought it gave me the reach I needed on these big tall ash males. I told him it was stupid to teach me to use one weapon, especially if we had no guarantee that I would get the sword in my fight. He had said to shut up and do what he said because he had a plan.

The culling was tomorrow. One final day of training. And I was flat on my ass again.

"I can't freaking levitate, Ryder. If you throw another fucking knife at me, I swear to the vampire gods I will find out where you sleep and I will sneak in and fill your bed with spiders – the kind that bite and kill."

The enforcer halted himself mid-throw. Apparently he thought I lacked proper motivation to tap into my supposed power of the fourth house of the Originals. I thought he lacked a freaking soul, and was determined to kill me before I even made it into the culling.

"Charlie, you have more than a little untapped potential. I see it rarely, but it's there. I'm struggling with a way to break down this wall of clumsy incompetence you hide behind. The culling starts tomorrow, and if you don't deal with your shit you're going to die." His broad chest heaved in and out as if he was struggling not to completely lose his shit on me.

Wait, had he called me clumsy and incompetent? What a bastard. I was trying my best. A surge of emotion knocked into my chest, tightening it before it rose up in a burning wave of righteous anger. I was so going to rip his arm off and beat him to death with it. That would show him who was clumsy. I flipped to my feet and leapt forward, ready to strike. The movements came easier, and I was finally starting to understand why he'd drilled them into me day after day.

In sparring I could hold my own now, even with Ryder, but I still lacked deeper technical training, which would be impossible for anyone to gain in such a short period.

I generally came at him front on and quite aggressive, but this time I did something different. I swung into his face, and right before I would have hit him, and he would have blocked me, I dropped down to my knees and drove both of my closed fists into his gut.

The shock reverberated up my arms and my hands ached instantly. There was not one ounce of fat on Ryder. Hitting his abs had been like smashing my fists into a wall. But I had hit him, and hard enough to stumble him back a little. I then swung one of my legs out, and ignoring the current pain in my knuckles, kicked out and smashed into his knee, hitting from the side and collapsing it in on itself.

The entire attack had taken no more than three seconds. I was fast. Ryder had been trying to get me to take advantage of my speed, and I was finally hearing his words. As he hit the ground, I dived across the long length of his body and straddled him, before slamming my fist down into his nose. He shifted his head at the last moment, and I knew he could have halted my movement – I saw that in his black and silver gaze – but he let me hit him, and it was this knowledge which stopped me from slamming into his face again.

We stared at each other, my breath heaving in and out as I fought for control. I knew I needed blood. I'd been trying to stretch myself out longer between feedings. But I was at the end. I wanted to bite Ryder so badly my teeth and gums were actually aching.

His expression was almost gentle as he stared up at me. "There is a wild strength in you, Charlie. You have beauty and brains. You need to figure out how to bring that all together. If you do that, there is no one who could stand against you."

Those soft words brushed against me, and for a fraction of a second his eyes flashed pure silver. I realized then I was still straddled across his muscled form, and needed to move now. I blinked a few times, but my body didn't seem to be responding.

Crap, Charlie, get your ass off him. He's already tried to kill you five times today. My pep talk wasn't doing its job either. I had to touch him, I needed to taste the skin on his neck. God he smelled so good. The way he stared up at me, before he raised his hands to my hips. His grip tightened and I almost moaned at the strength in his hold.

He leaned up, and as our faces moved closer together, he shifted his shoulders and ... lifted me to the side. Disappointment flashed through me as I lowered my head and fought for composure.

"I'm going to the feeding room," I blurted, stumbling to my feet and basically racing from the room. I glanced back just before I crossed out of the gym, and noticed that Ryder had moved across to one of the large bags hanging from the beams. He was already smashing the crap out of it, in a series of attacks that were controlled and smooth, leaving me breathless with jealously. I would never fight like him.

He snarled then, and in a show of unprecedented power drove his fist all the way through, completely destroying the bag and letting the seeds inside run out onto the floor.

That was all I got to see before I was out of sight. I'd never seen Ryder lose control like that before. He was always contained, but the pure fury as he ripped through that bag just then had my pulse racing and my heart stuttering.

I knew I frustrated him. But for some reason that had seemed more like he was fighting himself and his own control. I didn't understand Ryder very well. He was this strong, powerful enigma, and I guess I had never stopped to think about his story. How long had he been an ash? I knew we aged very slowly, not quite immortal like vampires, but there was a long life in front of us. I had never seen Ryder much in social situations. From the little I knew of him, he mostly hung around the other enforcers in the sexy six, trained me, and went out on missions – though they dialed that back during the culling period. They only contacted Ryder now when it was something the rest couldn't handle.

He was strong, he was their leader, and I was starting to find it hard to tear my gaze from him when we were in the same room together. I needed to get back to working on that getting laid thing. I wasn't easy or anything. I could count the number of guys I had slept with on one hand, but lately I was having a hard time dialing down my hormones. Tonight, right after I got me some blood and Tessa time – my bestie was scheduled on the feed tonight – I was heading out to the underground club, Base Level. It was embedded deep into the Hive on level three. Tomorrow might be my last day on Earth – if I was called to the early culling fights – and I was not going to spend it alone or crying in my bed.

Screw Ryder and his hot and cold bullshit. I was a strong, independent, bloodsucking ash. I did not need his sexy butt in my new life. It was confusing enough already.

I slowed my run as I finally made it to the elevator, taking it to floor eleven. I only visited the feeder room to see Tessa and stock up on blood. I still wasn't cool with sucking on a living person's neck. When I entered the double doors, I went straight to the fridge and grabbed three bottles, before ducking into my usual feeding room. Tessa was sprawled back in the chair, her skin clammy and pale – though she jumped up straight away and threw herself at me.

"Friggin' hell, Charlie, I've missed you so much."

She stumbled a little in my arms, and I grabbed at her to keep her on her feet, pulling back to see her better. "What's wrong, Tess? Are you sick?"

She waved me off. "No, nothing like that, just..." She held a hand over her neck to cover the right side.

I must have been slow or something tonight, because it was more than a few moments before I clicked in to what the hell had happened.

"Who?" I demanded, my hands gripping her biceps a little hard. "Who fed from you, Tess?"

No vampire or ash was allowed to just randomly feed, which meant she had signed up for this shit – additional feedings. Her round eyes widened a little and she dropped her gaze. I knew my own eyes would be a blaze of silvery green, so I closed them to try and regain control.

Placing my friend, with her overly pallid skin, back in the chair, I ripped into the top of my blood bottle. I was not going to be able to deal with this on an empty stomach.

She watched me warily as I prowled across the floor. "Why would you sign up to be a second feeder? You're going to get hurt, Tess!"

Her lips crinkled into a smile. "Babe, you worry too much. It's not like you actually feed from me, and maybe … well, you know, I might actually have a shot at being turned into a vamp."

The bottle fell from my fangs and smashed onto the floor, spattering out the remains of blood. My jaw hung open. "What … why … I don't… " I was spluttering away, trying to figure out what to say to her. "Why would you want to be a vamp?"

Yes, she had always been fascinated, but this was taking it a step too far. Tessa was officially a vamp groupie.

Some of her usual fire sprang back into her body, and she pulled herself up to meet me in a clash of female pissed-off-ness. Her finger jabbed at me while she spoke. "I have been here eight times in the past few weeks but have only seen you twice. You are busy or injured, or basi-

cally living a fucking life without me. I can't lose you."
Her breath huffed in time to her finger jabs. "I know it's
next to impossible to be turned, but I'm going to do my
best. Besides, Blake and I have been talking while I wait
for you to show up or not, and he's hot and sweet. Plus, the
feeding itself feels ... amazing."

Blake? I didn't know what to say. I loved this chick so
much; she was my person. If I ever killed someone, I'd call
her to help me dispose of the body. I could not blame her
for trying to keep us together, but I needed her to stop.

"Tess, I love you, but you can't do this. The Hive is not
a place you want to live. It's rough, and dangerous, and
there's a decent chance that you'll get killed by some
overzealous vampire long before they will turn you. I need
to know you are okay, that you and Mom are out there
living normal lives. It's what gets me through each shitty
day here."

"What about Ryder?" she said, ignoring all the nega-
tive I was saying. "Seems to be something going on with
you two."

I shook my head before reaching across to grab another
bottle of blood. "Ryder is my trainer, end of story. He's
helping out Lucas, making sure I don't die on my first day.
He doesn't have any interest in me."

He'd made that perfectly clear.

"But you are interested in him?"

I had told her a little about my weird attraction to him.

"You should just go for it, Charlie. Dive on that delicious piece of ash. Don't wait for him to figure shit out, you

take what you want and don't look back. There's no way he doesn't love you a little. You're hot as hell and funny and awesome. He's secretly crushing on you, I have no doubt."

And that was the second reason she was my person. Girl had my back no matter what. I ignored her Ryder pep talk. I knew there was something between me and him, but he clearly had some issues below the surface, something that held him back.

"So besides *Blake,* how's your love life going?" It felt like a million years since I'd lived with her in our college room. It was really hard missing all the things in the human world. I forgot about my old life when I was busy in my training bubble, but times like this it hit me hard that everything outside of the Hive continued to go on without me.

TESS and I talked for the next hour, which was the total allotted time we had together. She mainly talked about her new boy-toy Blake. I tried my best to dissuade her, but she said she'd be back no matter what. I knew that meant for more than me. She was still going to be a feeder. Dammit.

We also discussed my weird blood results. There was still no more word on the cryptic "not an ash" diagnosis and I had almost convinced myself that the vampire doctor was crazy. During my dinner with Lucas he had assured me that her family would be safe and free as soon as he knew she was keeping her end of the deal. He needed to make sure she kept her mouth shut about my Original father status. Not that it mattered. I apparently was the lamest descendent of an Original ever. No levitation here.

"Take care of yourself, Tess." I was trying to hold back tears as we hugged again. The vampire escort was waiting not very patiently to take her out of the feeding room. "I'll see you next week."

Her voice was rough. "You better. If you die during the culling, I am going to burn the Hive to the ground – I swear on Grandma Joan's grave."

She'd loved her cow-wrestling, gun-toting gran. Joan had been a hoot for sure.

I chuckled. "I'll be okay, I will survive." I let some of my confidence seep out in those words, hoping like hell the last thing I said to my best friend wasn't going to be a lie.

LATER THAT NIGHT I sat on the bathroom counter putting on mascara as Jayden coached me on how to pencil my eyebrows.

"It's the year of the brows," Jayden was saying when a knock came on the door. Tonight was party time, when all of the culling participants forgot about their shitty lives and had fun. My bestie cracked a smile. "My surprise is here."

I raised an eyebrow. *Please be a gorgeous straight boy here to take advantage of me.* Jayden returned with a bottle of homemade-looking liquor.

"Strong-ass vampire moonshine." He held up the bottle and I grinned. Second best thing.

"Will it get the job done for a change?" Beside the blood-wine, almost nothing else even gave me a buzz.

"My guy says if we split the whole bottle we'll be drunk for a few hours and it'll wear off long before the culling. Everyone is drinking it tonight."

"Your guy?" I raised an eyebrow.

He smiled, flashing his perfectly straight teeth. "One of Ryder's enforcers. It's only fun right now, but it looks like I landed me a sexy six." He winked.

Well damn, even Jayden was getting some. Which was the best thing I could hear about my best friend.

I leapt off the counter, pulling my short black dress down to cover my ass. Tessa had snuck me some sexy clothes. I really wished she was here with us now.

Jayden poured two glasses and clinked it with mine. "To surviving the next week."

I chugged the contents and erupted in a coughing fit. "Holy shit! I feel like I can breathe fire."

Jayden laughed and we poured more.

AN HOUR later I was feeling damn good. The buzz had hit me hard and the walls of Base Level were spinning a little. I was drunk for the first time in a year. Hip hop blasted out of the DJ booth and I danced, rubbing my butt all over Jayden. He laughed and spun me around. Then some hottie ash came up and put his hands around my waist, pressing me into him and grinning.

"Hey, beautiful," he whispered. His hair was shaved close to his head. I think he was blond, and like all ash he was hot as hell. Of course I was looking at him with moon-shine eyes, so he had extra hottie points. Was he in Ryder's crew? He wasn't a sexy six, but he might be in the extended group of enforcers. He did look familiar.

"Hey there," I said as I danced up on him. Maybe he would be my special friend tonight. Might as well have some fun before dying tomorrow.

"Johnson, back off," Ryder's growly voice echoed behind me.

The ash, who had just placed his hands on my waist, went rigid and backed away, before turning tail and scur-rying off.

I spun around, almost falling on my face, but managed to right myself at the last moment. Ryder was standing a few feet away, his expression unreadable.

"Uh-oh, you're no fun," I slurred.

Ryder narrowed his eyes as I continued to dance by myself, swiveling my hips and feeling the beat.

"You're drunk," he stated. "The males in here are like any other men. They will take advantage."

I gave him what I hoped were bedroom eyes and danced closer. "Maybe I want to get taken advantage of," I purred, and pressed myself into him.

He placed his hands on my hips and looked down on me. Was that a groan?

"Charlie... " I could see something stirring in those silver and black eyes. "You have no idea how beautiful you are, do you?" His voice went so low I almost wasn't sure I'd heard him right. Did Ryder just say I was beautiful? My Ryder? Try to kill me and push me away constantly Ryder? I swallowed hard, but before I could answer, he deposited me back a few feet. Okay, this was the Ryder I recognized, and I was sobering up quickly with him pulling out his usual bullshit.

"You've got issues," I stated. The flirtation left me, and I was hit with this weird ache in my chest.

His face took on a haunted expression. "I just came to tell you that you were a top pick, and slated for the last round of the individual fights."

Shit, he was here to give me some positive news, and I'd danced all up on him and practically thrown myself at him. Apparently moonshine made me drunk, slutty, and bitchy.

"Ryder..." I reached for his hand, but he turned and walked away. I remained where I was, half frozen on the dance floor, half wishing I was brave enough to run after him. My attention snagged on Jayden then. He was dancing with – holy shit, Oliver, the hot Latino sexy six. He really had scored one of the core group of enforcer hotties. The pair of them were watching me now, and that better not be pity I was seeing in their gazes.

I drifted closer. Ryder was gone from sight, but I still felt his presence out there. "What's his problem?" I said too loudly. Oliver's very dark eyes turned to the direction which Ryder had disappeared.

"Don't stress on it, Charlie. But you might want to give that one up as a lost cause. He's notoriously single, which is not a huge surprise after everything that happened."

My stomach dropped. I knew from his hot and cold behavior that he had demons littering his past, and I wasn't sure I was ready to know about them. Still, I had to ask. "What happened?" I was getting soberer by the second.

Oliver sighed and lowered his voice. I had to strain to hear it over the music. "I shouldn't be telling you this, but you're Jayden's best friend, and I promised I'd look out for you. When the boss man first found out he was an ash, the night he turned he was strong. Too strong."

My eyes widened as Jayden and I leaned in closer, so as not to miss a word. "He attacked and killed his fiancée before they could bring him in."

Oh shit. That was not what I'd expected him to say. Each word hit me like a slap to the face. My emotions were a complete tangle, but my heart truly ached for the pain I knew Ryder would have experienced that day and probably every day since. He was clearly still beating himself up. He must have loved his fiancée more than anything.

I rubbed at my eyes a few times. Jayden was hovering close by as if ready to hug me if I needed it. I gave him a half smile. It was my best attempt.

"I might call it a night, guys. Big day tomorrow." I was

no longer in the mood to party, and the alcohol seemed to have dissipated inside of me.

I waved goodbye and left, hoping like hell a good night's sleep would rid some of the terrible ache inside of me. Still, I preferred to know, no matter how painful. So much of Ryder's behavior made sense now – his aloofness, the rigid way he controlled himself. I understood it too. If I had hurt or killed Tessa or my mom, I would never have forgiven myself either. Of course, with the culling tomorrow, the timing of finding out this secret was not the best. There would be no true rest for me tonight.

Sure enough, that night I tossed and turned, dreaming of the culling, of blood and Ryder. By the time morning came, my head was heavy with the need for more sleep. As I pulled myself up, Jayden was sitting at the edge of his bed, staring at a blank wall.

What's wrong?" I dragged myself off the bed, surprised that I didn't feel hung over. Last night was intense.

"I'm slated to fight first." His voice sounded hollow. Shit. Ryder had told me I was last. Good for me, bad for Jayden.

Pep talk time. I crossed our small room, standing before him. "You're gay and black," I announced.

He forced a grin. "How very observant of you, darling."

I grasped both of his shoulders and made him look at me. "You're the underdog. No one expects you to whip ass, which is why you will. I've seen you fight. I'm jealous of how strong and controlled your movements are. Show everyone just how deadly an ash you can be!"

Jayden grinned and stood, raising one fist above his head. "For black gay ash everywhere!" he declared, and we both laughed. But a lump had formed in my throat. I loved this guy, for reals. He was my family now too. And family don't quit each other.

After getting ready and putting on my jumpsuit, I made my way with Jayden to the gym. As we neared I heard the rumbling of a crowd. Jayden looked nervously at me. Some of that blank stare was back on his face. I was pretty sure I was going to throw up. We took the side entrance and walked in through the locker room where Jayden's coach was.

His coach greeted him. I was pretty sure his name was Bryan. "Hey, big guy, you ready to make me proud?"

On the bench next to him I saw a long-handled axe. The weapon was a mid-sized one, and would have been too heavy for me to use effectively.

Jayden gave a weak smile. "Is that my weapon?"

His trainer nodded. "You got picked for the bottom because it's a popularity contest full of bribes and favoritism. Trust me, they have overlooked how strong you are. You will be fine."

I cringed at the mention of bribes. I had no doubt Lucas probably paid a shitload of money to get me at the top of the fighting roster, but still, Jayden's trainer's confidence in him made me happy.

I forced down the burning in my chest as Jayden turned to face me, eyes full of emotion.

"If I die, you can have my Coach wallet and my fancy tweezers. Don't let those eyebrows get too crazy."

I chuckled, tears springing to my eyes as I pulled him in for an extended hug. "Don't leave me," I whispered. Seriously, I needed him.

He squeezed me back, then his trainer asked me to go so he could get him prepared. I left the gym and suddenly I knew that I couldn't watch. There was no way in hell I could watch this fight. Not Jayden. I turned the corner to go to the cafeteria and slammed into Ryder. My breath whooshed out of me.

As he pulled back, his eyes ran over my face. He was doing that thing where he attempted to ferret out my secrets. Probably he was seeing quite clearly the anguish I was not hiding very well.

"You should watch the fights. It will help you learn the other ashes' moves, and it will desensitize you a small amount to the killing."

"Jayden's fighting. I can't ... I will watch the others," I mumbled, and my answer seemed to satisfy him. He nodded and turned to walk away towards the gym. I felt a need to say something more.

"Ryder, about last night ... I'm sor—"

He cut me off. "It's fine. You're right, I have issues." Without another word he stalked off.

I groaned and went in search of food. Blood hunger was not a good thing and I needed a major distraction from the fact that Jayden would be very shortly fighting for his life. I had every faith in my bestie, but that didn't make the next few hours any easier.

THEN NEXT FIVE days were the worst of my life. Ryder sat by my side and made me watch every fight. He was an expert at noting weaknesses, and he drilled it into me over and over. Of course, it was up to me to read the fighter once I was in the ring, to utilize any and all weaknesses. Twenty-five ash were dead. Each battle was a bloodbath of mammoth proportions, and sometimes as I sat there I wondered how the hell it could even be real. Though Ryder had been right about one thing: I was growing desensitized to the killing.

I mean, in the last fight, the middle-eastern-looking ash had torn out the spinal cord of his opponent – his mutha-freakin' spinal cord – and I'd barely even flinched. I didn't like the coldness which was starting to spread out from my chest, but I knew it was essential to me having the smallest chance of surviving. I just hoped when it was all over, if I survived, there would still be some of the old Charlie left inside.

Jayden, who had survived all his fights so far, was in the recovery wing, regrowing part of his calf muscle, and my first fight was in an hour. I forced myself to focus. I could do this. I was strong and smart and had boobs – surely boobs were a distraction I could use to my advantage in an all-male lineup.

After the spinal cord fight, I'd been escorted back into the locker room. I sat on the bench, my foot bouncing in a weird, agitated manner. I hadn't told my mom or Tessa I was fighting today, skirting around it every time they asked. I couldn't hear their goodbyes or any sappy shit. Even if that was unfair to them, I needed a clear head.

The door opened and I looked up to meet the eyes of my trainer. Ryder looked all kinds of badass and sexy today. His black-ribbed cotton shirt, tight across the biceps, did more than hint at the heavy muscle beneath. I stood and he crossed over to stand right beside me, dwarfing me as usual with his bulk and height. We clashed gazes. His eyes were a storm cloud of silver gray. I felt it then. The emotions from him were stronger than usual, and I somehow knew that If I died, Ryder would care.

I reached for my focus, starting to jump on the balls of my feet to keep my muscles warm, like he'd taught me.

He met my eyes and nodded. "Charlie."

I paused mid-jump; a smile spread across my face. "You called me Charlie. What happened to number forty-six?"

He shrugged. "I figured I should probably be nice to you in case you die."

I chuckled and smacked his tight bicep. He returned my smile but then his face became serious. "Your opponent is strong, but he fought yesterday, so he's tired and still healing."

My heart jackknifed in my chest at this news. Opponent. Right. I was going to have to kill a person today.

Well, an ash really, but it was the same damn thing to me now.

I felt the blood drain from my face when he reached down and produced the weapon my opponent's sponsor had chosen for me. It was a black case, which was open to reveal a set of five small throwing stars. I lifted my gaze to Ryder.

"Are you fucking kidding me? I couldn't kill a cat with those."

He grinned. "I know. That's why I told Lucas to assign the sword to your opponent. I want you to steal it from him."

My mouth dropped as the air wheezed out of me in a huff. That was either a brilliant plan or the stupidest thing I'd heard all week. So much of that relied on skills I probably didn't possess yet. I just really hoped Ryder knew what he was doing, and that I didn't let either of us down.

THE NEXT FORTY-FIVE minutes passed in a blur as Ryder made me practice stealing a weapon from him. We ran through about ten different scenarios, depending on how my opponent reacted to our plan. I felt about twelve percent more confident than before, so I was still pretty much up shit creek sans paddle again.

I had about ten minutes of rest time before the buzzer sounded, then it was my turn in the arena. Ryder, gleaming with sweat, turned to face me. "Charlie..."

Charlie. The way he said my name this time ... like

there were true emotions there, a sense of reverence. He never usually spoke to me like that. I played with the hem of my shirt, unsure of what to do or say. I mean, I had a lot of things to say to him and I could be dead in the next few minutes, but I couldn't find the right way to express all of my thoughts. Emotion overcame me and tears welled in my eyes. They weren't tears of fear or pain though, they were angry tears. This wasn't fair! We were just normal human kids who had free-lovin' mothers and now we had to kill each other over it.

"This is bullshit!" I pretty much shouted.

Ryder's hands snaked out and grabbed the sides of my face, cradling it as he brought me close to him, resting his forehead on mine. "Life isn't fair, Charlie." His breath tickled my nose; the delicious scents coming from him had me wanting to lean even closer, to touch my lips to his. Of course that was when he pulled away a little.

"I've seen a small fire smoldering inside of you since the day I brought you in. When those doors open, I need you to unleash that fire. Your opponent already has death on his hands. He won't hesitate to do it again. You need to be ready, you need to fight to survive."

His words roared through me like the fire he spoke of. Ryder had reminded me of the most important thing. It was simple math – the other ash or me. I nodded, relishing his warm hands on me. He left them there for one short moment and then pulled back quickly, his stoic façade falling back over his face. He tucked the throwing stars in my waist belt and opened the double doors.

"You can do this," was all he said, before nudging me out and shutting the doors behind me.

And just like that, I was in the culling arena.

I forced down the burn of fear and bile as my eyes alighted on the spectators, their feet pounding on the bleachers above. A vampire crossed the floor toward me. He was wearing the official uniform of the judges, a flamboyant royal purple full-length silk robe, with checkering of black and white.

He checked me over to make sure I wasn't holding any illegal weapons. I glanced across the room at my opponent, who was in the middle of the same checks, and was a little surprised to see it was one of the black-haired guys who had attacked Jayden and I outside that day. Some of my fear left, replaced by anger again. Bastard. Maybe this wouldn't be as hard as I feared. After all, karma was a bitch. And so was Charlie when she was cornered.

Black-haired ash was holding a samurai sword in an expert grip. I noted that his neck was bandaged, as was his ankle. These were the weak spots. The judge vamps left the field then and the fighter buzzer rang. I wasted no time sprinting toward him, prepared to meet him head on. We were separated by fifty feet of open gym, a scattering of low walls, hay bales and other shit to hide around was strewn about. It reminded me of a paintball course and it changed between every fight. Some of the floor was still lined with blue mats, other parts stone or cement.

I grabbed one of the throwing stars from where Ryder had stashed them, palming it. I would hold on to them until he was closer, especially since I had no clue how to throw them accurately.

I hesitated, even as the distance closed between us, and it wasn't until we were about fifteen feet apart, the black of his eyes reflecting the large spotlights above us, then I chucked one. He dodged in a rapid movement and it sailed past his left shoulder. Okay, I officially sucked at throwing shit. Why had we spent so much time training with a sword? The other guy's sponsor must have noted this, and chosen something I had barely touched.

I focused. I couldn't let him get near me with that sword. I loaded two stars into my hands this time. When he was ten feet from me – aggressively charging – I figured I couldn't miss him, and let them both go at the same time. One sailed right past but the other sank into the side of his injured neck. Hell yeah, luck was on my side.

He faltered, his muffled groan pain-filled as he stopped to rip the star free. Then, in the next moment, he did as Ryder and I had hoped. As he pulled the star free – my stomach churned at the chunk of flesh that went with it – he lowered his sword against his side. I ignored the blood and flesh. I didn't have time to deal with squeamish-ness right now, this was my best chance to relieve him of his weapon. I took the chance that he wouldn't expect me to come at him so violently.

I booked it, closing the gap between us, and before he could bring up the sword, I did my five step combo. It was like breathing for me now, no thought, just pure remem-bered instinct. My left hand flew out and sank into his jaw. I ignored the pain in my knuckles as my right fist connected with his temple. I heard the sword drop, but I didn't allow it to break my concentration. Knee to his ribs and he keeled over. Changing my routine, I improvised and pushed his shoulders, which were at my stomach level, shoving him backwards.

Thank you, Ryder, for drilling that boring-ass combo into my head. Who knew it would be so effective.

Dropping to the ground I retrieved the sword and the crowd went wild. My opponent recovered quickly, his dark eyes narrowing and fangs flashing as he spun himself on the ground. He was faster than I expected, and used his position to kick out and trip me. I kept my grip on the sword, knowing that if I lost it now I was as good as dead. I stumbled forward, somehow managing to keep my balance. I then righted myself. He flung his legs out, doing a kick up, and was suddenly standing before me.

He dodged my first attack with the blade. He was well trained, and definitely had spent time around weapons. But something told me the sword wasn't his first choice, just by the wary glare he gave it.

Adrenalin was flooding me, which was helpful in keeping the pure fear at bay. Fight to the death, fight to the death. I kept repeating it over and over, trying to make myself attack him again.

"You're weak," he spat, "and I'm going to enjoy tearing you limb from limb." He was confident as he started circling me. But I had been sparring with Ryder for weeks now, and there was no one scarier than him. This little punk was nothing.

I centered myself, drawing on whatever ounce of badass was inside of me. The sword fit my hand like it was made for it. Sword was definitely my weapon. I struck out at him, fast and without any indication I was going to move. His eyes shuttered. Before he recovered, I had already cut three long gashes into him, two on his right arm and one on his left.

I slashed in a three-step motion again, going for the softer kill zones. Throat, chest, gut.

He threw out an arm to protect his throat and my weapon sunk into his bicep with a sickening sound and I faltered. That was so much worse than the little cuts from before.

He took advantage of my hesitation and threw a knee into my stomach. The wind rushed out of me as I keeled forward. I kept my grip on the sword, but wasn't able to move before his foot clipped my forehead, throwing me backward. I hit the ground hard, and as his large form lunged over the top of me, I knew death was stalking me. Everything moved in slow motion then – the snarl, the fangs, the blood of his wounds raining across me. His hands were around my throat as he went in for the old fashioned kill. I knew he was strong enough to snap my neck and possibly take my head from my body. I felt the strength in his hands and limbs. But I was not prepared to die here today.

My eyes flashed across to the section where I knew

Jayden and Ryder were sitting. Lucas was close by. All three of them had believed in me; there was something special in my blood. I was the first freakin' female ash. I had to do this today. I had to be strong enough.

A surge of strength shot through me, despite the fact that I couldn't breathe and dick ash was about five seconds from killing me. I smashed up with my sword and at the same time bucked violently managing to dislodge him a little. I shouldn't have had so much reach from my position, but somehow I rolled to the side, tucking the sword against my body. Heat infused in my center, and I wondered if this was the fire that Ryder was talking about. I continued to roll, avoiding his heavy boot he had aiming for my face.

Time to die, asshole!

I jumped to my feet, my movements smooth and controlled for once. Must have been channeling my trainer. My opponent seemed to expect I would go for his head again, but the moment he was within arm's reach, I dropped again. His eyes widened, and I had more than enough time to slash out at his ankles. As the hilt of my sword whacked into his injured ankle, he came tumbling down flat on the ground. I got to my feet again, wasting no time, trying to think about what I was about to do next. I was a robot. All humanity had left me. My heart pumped with adrenaline as the sword came down and bit into his exposed neck.

The blade was sharp, and cut through the initial skin like paper, but there was resistance as I fought to finish the job. I was struggling to not stop. I wanted to scream, or vomit, or throw the fucking sword far away where I couldn't see it again. But this was kill or be killed. I had no choice, although sometimes it felt like that was just an excuse. I simply wanted to live, and today luck had fallen on my side.

My arms shook as I finally finished. The ash was still, his head connected by just by a sliver of muscle.

The crowd roared as I dropped the sword. There was a whining in my ears and I could no longer hear the shouts as my chest began to heave in shock. Suddenly Ryder was there, whisking me up into his arms. I fought him at first, but then let him take me back into the locker room. He set me down and was holding on to my biceps, his grip firm but not painful.

"Charlie!" His voice pushed past my shock.

Oh God. I killed someone. I cut his head off ... I cut his ... I tried to move my face away but I couldn't. I threw up all over Ryder's shirt.

He didn't seem fazed, those silver and green eyes flashing at me. "Your first kill is always the hardest."

As if I could ever get used to this. I wasn't sure I could do that again, but if I didn't I'd be the one missing my head.

SINCE THE FIGHTING was over for the day, Ryder took me to my room. I felt cold, chilled to my bones. I just walked behind him, mindlessly following and doing what he said. He sat me at the edge of my bed and handed me a bottle of blood and I drank it without pleasure. Then I lay back as Ryder unlaced my boots and I curled into a ball. He placed a blanket over me and told me to rest up until the next fight, in which I would be fighting doubles. A sliver of me was sad that I was too out of it to really enjoy this more caring side of Ryder, but I was already too far gone. I closed my eyes and the deep kiss of sleep engulfed my mind.

A soft hand stroked my neck. "Mmm ... Ryder," I mumbled, opening my eyes.

Jayden sat before me, black eyes twinkling and shit-eater grin in place. "Oh my God, if we weren't about to go into a battle for our lives, I would tease the shit out of you for that one."

I sat up quickly. "Wait, we?"

Jayden grinned. "Yep, your homeboy Lucas must have some pull with all of his high-up friends, because we happen to be paired together, and we happen to be fighting the two weakest and injured guys."

I squealed and jumped into his arms. He winced and pushed me back a little.

"Oh, damn. Sorry, Jay. Are you still hurt?"

He nodded and lifted his shirt to show stitches on his ribcage, and I noticed then that his calf was still bandaged.

"You don't mind having a gay gimp for a partner?"

My mouth dropped open. "You're gay?"

He rolled his eyes. "I love you, bitch."

I smiled. "Right back at ya, bitch."

And that was it. In our own special way we had just said goodbye.

JAYDEN and I stood in the training room with Bryan, Jayden's trainer, and Ryder. On the bench sat a short dagger and a short wooden stick with a spiked ball hanging from the end. Our two chosen-by-the-other-side weapons. Freak me. I shivered.

Ryder lifted one foot and rested it on the bench seat, which from my angle only emphasized his muscular thigh and ass cheek. Damn, Ryder's ass ... *not the time, Charlie.*

I focused on my trainer's words. "You two have a serious advantage here. No one in the culling becomes friends, it's every man for himself. Even these two will be against each other, trying to get the last spots. The buzzer rings as soon as two ash die. It doesn't even matter which two or which team."

Jayden and I shared a look and nodded. No way in hell was I letting anyone take out my new best friend.

Bryan shifted his focus to me. "I saw your fight. Well done. Jayden is pretty badly injured, so I think he should have the spike ball. The dagger will mean you will have to get closer to your opponent..."

The rest of his sentence was left unsaid, but we all knew what the words would have been. Jayden might not survive being close enough to use a dagger.

Ryder interjected. "But Jayden is stronger. If he gets pulled to the ground he can handle himself. She can't."

"No, I agree. I'll take the dagger." I shut them all up. Ryder's expression did that stoic, cold thing again. He seemed upset with my choice, but the buzzer sounded, eliminating any more time for arguing.

I grabbed the dagger, letting it roll in my hands, trying to ignore the dried blood at the tip. They couldn't even wipe the blade down? Sometimes the members of the Hive were true animals.

Ryder approached me and leaned in so close I thought he meant to kiss me. Instead, he whispered in my ear: "Charlene Bennett, you are a direct descendant of the fourth house. Don't forget that." His words were strangely smooth and echoey, and something unfurled inside my chest, seeking, strong. Before I could say or do anything, we were thrust out into the fight.

As per the previous rounds, we were checked for unauthorized weapons, then the fight buzzer rang out. The stomping and hollering from the crowd was sickening. It rang in my ears and had the blood pounding through my veins. Crazy mofos, how could anyone enjoy this? This was not sport or entertainment, this was real live ash getting slaughtered. It was sickening. I wanted this entire goddamn Hive to burn down! I might be an ash, and I might have had ash friends now and a possible ash crush, but my hatred of the system still remained.

I forced myself to focus on the fight. I couldn't change anything if I was dead. The two ash across from us definitely looked a little worse for wear. The shaved head ash, with his stupid pimp goatee, had his right arm in a hard cast; his other hand held the throwing stars. Great weapons choice from our sponsor. It was going to be near impossible for him to throw that with one arm all banged up. The other ash, who had long, light brown hair tied back at his neck, had a bandage over one eye and held a bow and arrow, which would totally screw with his depth perception. Still, they both had long range weapons. We needed to get in there fast.

"Stay by my side!" I roared, as Jayden and I took off. Bow and arrow guy dropped to one knee and expertly let loose an arrow. Shit! Even with sucky depth perception, he knew what he was doing. I hadn't expected him to move so quickly and I was too close to dodge his arrow. The razor sharp end slammed into my thigh, lodging itself quite deep. I screamed, turning to find Jayden right beside me. In a flash, before I could protest, my friend broke the end off, leaving the head embedded. *Holy mutha effing fuck*, that hurt so badly. Luckily the adrenalin kept me moving. I followed Jayden as he dropped and rolled behind an obstacle barrier. We crouched side by side as I panted in pain.

"Plan?" I huffed. Even injured, these guys were lethal. They had not made it this far without winning fights. And they wanted this desperately.

I realized Jayden wasn't even listening to me. His eyes were pulsing and his fangs distended. "Your blood."

Oh shit. I looked down at my bleeding thigh. Right, of course, the weird attractiveness of my unicorn blood. *Wait a freakin' minute.* The obvious answer had been staring me in the face the entire time. I knew my blood attracted these a-holes. I knew that it was some sort of special, weird, not-really-ash blood. Might be time to use this to our advantage. I wiped the blade of my dagger in my blood, letting it thickly coat the tip.

"Don't bite me, bitch," I said to Jayden. "This blood is going to be useful to us."

His eyes were crazed. "Trying not to," he said through clenched teeth.

I popped my head up and saw the two guys advancing slowly. They were close and I was confident enough to pull my arm back and let the dagger fly, giving up my only weapon. It sailed through the air and sank into bow and arrow guy's shoulder. Try shooting me with an arrow now, asshole.

He cried out at the thud, but then, almost in the same instance, his nostrils flared and his eyes widened. *Holy crap ... it worked.* Both guys were standing there stupidly, fighting the lure of my unicorn blood. I reached down and grabbed Jayden's weapon.

"Stay here!" I jumped out from behind the barrier and sprinted the ten feet between us in record time. The hot burn in my thigh faded a little as my mind focused on what I had to do. Both ash twisted to face me, fangs extended, and I felt my own descend in response. Their eyes were as black as night and pulsing. I expected them to snap out of their blood haze any moment and come at me double-team style, but despite the fact they were facing me head on, they still seemed stunned, especially the one with my bloody knife in his arm. Focusing on him first, I raised my arm up and whipped the flail in the air to gain momentum, bringing the spike down across his head. He didn't dodge it; the spike sank in with a sickening thud. Something awoke in him then and he grabbed my shoulder with a death grip, holding me in place.

I was focused on spike-head and hadn't expected the other guy to move so quickly. But as I felt fangs sink into my neck, shock ran through me. That fucker. Hell to the no! No one got to suck my blood, no freakin' ... *oh my gods.* It was like a sudden rush of euphoria flooded through me and spilled forbidden pleasure into my body. I didn't even feel his fangs any longer. All I felt was the weightless pleasure of the sucking motion on my neck.

"Charlie!" Ryder's deep bellowing voice carried through the cheering, those low tones hanging in the air, and a semblance of sanity started to filter into my hazy brain. What ... no! I kneed the guy with the spike hanging out of his head in the balls before dropping to the ground to get this neck sucker off of me. I could hear him growling and fighting like I was stealing away his favorite chew toy. What the fuck was up with my blood?! Was it Nutella flavored?

I pushed those thoughts from me as I heard Jayden come up from behind and engage neck biter. Although I was feeling a little woozy still from loss of blood and the last tingles of that feeding euphoria, I tracked the scene. I would admit to some surprise that the guy with the spike in his head was still very much alive. I'd hit him hard. Dammit, he was not just alive but fighting.

I attempted to dodge as he kicked out at my legs. Of course I managed to trip over my own feet, and landed hard on the mat anyways. The sharp jag of pain in my thigh increased as the head of the arrow went deeper. My eyes drifted across the floor and my heart started pounding as I realized the dagger lay five feet away. I lunged for it just as spike head caught my ankle, my fingers grazing the hilt. It was just out of my reach. Turning back, I flexed my knee and, as hard as I could, kicked at the spike which was still in his head. Was he not removing that because the injury would be worse?

As my foot connected for a second time, I gained enough distance to close my hand fully around the knife handle, and raising to my knees I leapt onto him before he could stand, slashing at the tender meat of his neck.

He was already covered in blood from the massive spike in his head, but the neck wound finished the job. I left his prone body, standing quickly, dagger still in hand as I sought desperately to find Jayden. I realized he was all the way across the gym and my heart literally stopped beating when I saw neck biter on top of him slicing at his neck with the throwing star. There was blood everywhere, doing that little spurting thing which meant something serious had been hit. I wouldn't make it in time.

"No!" I screamed. Desperation flooded through me – I would not lose Jayden here today. I would never give up on my friend like that, and I knew he would never have given up on me. I had to make it there in time.

The heat that had begun before, after hearing Ryder's words, started to burn in my center, like a forest fire which had just been doused with an ass-ton of fuel. I sensed that this was what everyone kept harping on about – my special blood, the unusual test, my genetic linage from the fourth house. This was what burned inside of me. Everything about my life started to make sense then, the reasons I was different. I took off to give myself a proper speed for launching, and without a second thought bent down and sprang up with all of the strength I had. I had planned on trying to jump in large leaps, closing the distance fast, but apparently the fire had a different plan.

I freakin' flew, like some sort of strange bird, across the arena. The crowd gasped, and a weird sort of dead-air silence fell over the fight. That's right, bitches. Levitation. I worked hard to land close as possible to the ash who was hurting my friend. Dude hadn't even looked up; he didn't know death stalked him from the air. But he was about to find out. I came down hard, knocking into him, throwing the asshole off of Jayden, the pain in my leg roaring back to life with an intensity that had my vision flashing with black dots.

I wobbled for a second, breathing deeply. Not the time to pass out, no matter how much I wanted to. Neck biter jumped up, and I was relieved to see Jayden was alive – clutching his bleeding throat but alive.

Neck biter circled me like a lion about to strike. Anger

was coming off him in waves. I forced myself to envision how I would kill him. Then of course, the moment I did that I started raging at myself. This entire situation was screwed up. Why the hell was I having to become a murdering monster? Because the vampires needed to conserve space for their huge luxury Hive apartments?

Neck biter lunged, but I was ready – I was so ready. I might not want to kill him, but I wanted to end this. I dodged and threw out a high kick to the side of his temple. He wobbled and I dropped to my knees, stabbing him in the stomach. Not a kill shot, but a debilitating one.

He folded over and I took the chance to tackle him to the ground, straddling him, his hands pinned under my legs as he clutched his bleeding stomach. I couldn't meet his eyes as I brought the dagger up and slid it straight under his chin and into his neck. Ryder had shown me many times the best ways to kill and debilitate quickly, information that had been very useful during the culling, but which no twenty-one-year-old should ever have to know.

I had no choice. I told myself that over and over. I had no mother-effing choice. But I still hated myself for it.

He started bleeding out, and I clenched my thighs to keep him from lifting his hands and stanching any of the blood. It was only that he was weak and injured already that I'd even had a chance. If Lucas hadn't used his money and influence to ensure I was one of the last fighters ... fuck this! This was so wrong. Tears lined my eyes as the last of my innocence died. I wasn't Charlie anymore, that girl who liked to check out boys at Starbucks and get mani-pedis with Tessa...

It was inevitable of course. I had to harden all of my soft edges if I was going to survive my new life as a tasty Nutella unicorn, but it still pissed me off.

The ash beneath me ceased to breathe, and stopped moving, and I stood up to the roaring crowd as the buzzer sounded. I threw my dagger on the ground and met the eyes of my new society. Then I raised both hands and gave them all the middle finger, turning in a slow circle to make sure they all saw. Fuck you crazy assholes and your sadistic game. My gesture was met with mostly glares and a few sparse chuckles. Yeah, glare on, freaks, I didn't give a shit.

I turned to Jayden, relieved to see he had wound a shirt around his neck and was sitting up. Together we left the arena, never looking back. Ryder came out of a side entrance and approached me with a solemn face.

"You did it."

I could only nod. I had just fought for the right to live in a society that I wanted nothing to do with. Yay. Life was great.

SEVEN

It had been a week since the culling and life in the Hive had completely changed. We were given ID badges with our actual names. Jayden and I received a nice two-bedroom apartment that happened to be down the hall from Ryder and the enforcers. Level thirty-three. We got to wear normal clothes and were assigned shitty jobs. Jayden worked the front desk at the feeding center and I helped in the communications room. I got to dispatch Ryder and his enforcer team to different situations that got called in. It was hella boring and I would much rather be going to the actual calls and enforcing, but I guess it was fine for now. The nightmares from the culling were also starting to ease. The fact that I'd ended lives and had to fight to the death still weighed heavily on me, but last night I'd actually slept five hours in a row. First time since that day.

I would never forget what the vampires had forced me

to do, but for now I was going to bide my time. I couldn't change anything yet, but one day I wanted to give it my best shot to end the culling. I was relieved to know that even as a full-fledged member of the Hive, vampires were still not around much. I wasn't sure what those suckers did in their spare time – stuck to their own levels of the compound probably – but either way I was much more comfortable with ash now. Which was good, since that's all I ever saw.

Thank God for emails from my mom and Tessa, some much needed female interactions. They'd been more than relieved to learn I had survived the culling, and both were happy to know that I was applying for permission to go back to my college classes. As an ash of course. I would have to sit in a special section and not with Tessa, but it would be nice to get back to some semblance of normalcy. Of course, I wasn't allowed back for a year. That was how long new ash were monitored. Which left me bored and edgy in the Hive. Cell phones didn't work in lower levels of the Hive, so for daily communications Tessa and I had to email each other. I smiled as I saw an email pop up.

'CLUBBIN', read the title.

Hey bitch,

I miss your blood drinking ass and now that you're not on ash probation, I thought we could meet up at Club Shade. Blake invited me, I will stay out after curfew. Please come, I miss your ability to down an entire bottle of tequila. Don't dress like a boy, show the goods.

P.S invite Ryder, I gotta see this guy in person.

Love,

Tessa

MY SMILE GREW LARGER. I glanced over my shoulder. The communications room was pretty empty right now. Just Markus, the Scottish enforcer, and my current communications job trainer.

"Hey, Markus, what's the protocol for new ash going out during curfew hours?"

He gave me a look that said I might not like the answer. "For the first year, all requests go through Ryder."

Ugh. This monitored for a year thing was going to get old real fast. I drummed my nails on the table top and then stood to go find the elusive ash. He had just gotten back from a call where one of the eleven new ash that survived the culling had tried to run away. He hadn't made it far, of course. Ryder was very good at his job.

I knocked on the enforcer locker room door.

"Come in," Ryder said.

I opened the door and had to keep my jaw from dropping as Ryder was standing before me wearing only a white towel. His skin still had droplets of water beading and rolling down. Good God, this man was trying to kill me.

"What's up?" he said as he pulled on a black t-shirt. I

followed the movement as it rolled over his tan delicious body.

In the short time since we'd stopped training together, I had almost forgotten how perfect Ryder was. Shit, okay, I hadn't exactly forgotten, more like I made myself to think of him as only my friend and an enforcer. No one wanted to lust after someone who was not interested, no matter how many blazing looks he threw my way. I needed to meet up with Tessa ... or meet a nice ash ready to settle down. Ugh, no, not an ash. A human maybe ... screw the rules. It had definitely been way too long since I had had a boyfriend.

I stared at his mesmerizing eyes, the silver so prominent tonight. I wondered what emotion he was feeling strongly. "Just wanted to see if I could meet Tessa – my best friend who is human – at a night club tonight. During ash curfew hours of course."

He took a moment before answering. "I don't know ... you're new, and the Quorum brought a shit storm of questions down on Lucas after your levitation incident at the culling."

Apparently it was rare for a new ash to tap into their houses special skill like that. Thankfully, the questioning had been brief, but the Quorum were now "keeping an eye on me".

I forced myself not to lower my gaze. I wouldn't beg, but I had to make him understand. "I need this."

It was either he let me out or I really would start

begging him to take that shirt off again so I could gawk at his perfection.

His chiseled jaw actually softened. "Okay, I'm off duty tonight. I'll go with you. I don't want any trouble."

I gave a little excited jump and wiggle. "Thank you! Can Jayden come?"

He threw his hands up. "Sure, invite all the newbies. I love to babysit."

I threw him a grin. "You're not such a bad guy after all."

He returned my grin with a withering glare. "You can go now so I can finish getting dressed."

I sighed and left, trying not to imagine Ryder replacing the towel with pants. Stupid pants. What use were they anyway?

I pretty much bounced the entire way back to my room. This was what I had been waiting for since the moment I collapsed at my mom's place – time to feel normal, to pretend for just one night that I wasn't some weird, mythical creature that needed bottled blood to live. Now that I had survived the culling, I was hoping for a lot more normal moments in my life. I wasted no time smashing into Jayden's room in our apartment.

As expected, he pretty much squealed when I told him of our upcoming field trip from the Hive. "Seriously? Yummy Ryder is escorting us to a club in town?"

I rolled my eyes at "yummy Ryder." Jayden had his own sexy six. He had to stop with all the man greed.

"Yes, get ready," I told him. It was midnight and Ryder would be here soon.

Jayden lurched to his feet. "Me get ready? What about you?" He eyed my skinny jeans and tank-top like they were dirt-covered canvas bags. I flipped him off but he persisted.

"Honey, a body like that needs to be showed off. Please, please, please, let me dress you."

Well shit, Tessa had been replaced by her clone. Knowing my new bestie pretty darn well already, I knew he would not give up. And I was too excited to care tonight.

"Whatever," I declared, and just like that he attacked me with all of his gayness.

My hair was pulled down and curled in loose waves, my makeup applied with expert precision – darker than I usually wore, but still perfect. He finished with a red stain brushed upon my lips. Then Jayden ducked out of the room, he was gone for a bit so I guessed had headed to the Hive's clothes stores, before he returned holding what looked like nipple pasties triumphantly in the air.

I put my hands up. "Hell no, I'm not a stripper." Jayden was even worse than Tessa.

He rolled his eyes. "Duh, strippers don't wear pasties."

He dropped the packet on the bed and whipped out this small black scarf.

"What's that scarf for?" It was cold outside now. We were well into October, but ash were naturally warmer than humans. I wouldn't need a scarf.

He smiled. "It's not a scarf, it's a top." He motioned for me to lift my arms.

With a sigh I complied, somehow knowing I was totally going to regret allowing him free rein here.

Ten minutes later, I was looking in the mirror – *Good lord* – wearing a black backless shirt that scooped so low in the front you almost saw my belly button. It fastened at my neck, and if I leaned forward the pasties were the only thing keeping my modesty. Jayden let me keep the skinny jeans and ass-kicking boots. My upper half was stripper central and my lower half was Lara Croft Tomb Raider. Which was actually kind of perfect.

A knock on the door startled me. Shit, my eyes flashed back to my outfit.

I had forgotten for a second that Ryder, and who knows how many other ash, might be at the club tonight. With my freaky blood, maybe it wasn't the best idea to have so much exposed skin.

Before I could voice my protest, Jayden opened the door and I turned to meet two silver eyes.

The head enforcer took one of his large strides into the room. He wasn't alone. His five guys were with him, the core group of his enforcers, AKA the sexy six.

I took a second to stop and stare, at all of them, but mostly Ryder. This was the first time I had seen him in civilian clothes. First time I had seen any of the enforcers in civilian clothes.

I already sort of knew Oliver and Markus, and had been briefly introduced to the other three. One was Kyle, with his mess of dirty-blond hair and NFL player's physique. He was Ryder's second and best bro. Those two were always together. They had epic bromance written all over them. Kyle had been off on a long mission during my culling, so this was the first time for us to really hang out.

One of the other two was Jared. With his hot-ass Australian accent and blond curls, he was the epitome of surfer dude. I sort of guessed his eyes had been sky blue before the ash transformation, but now were the same black, with slight rings of silver. He was a funny, laidback guy, seeming to bring lightness to the other more serious ash. He had been the one Ryder wanted to train me in weights, and as I had admired his biceps on more than one occasion, I'd been looking forward to it. Unfortunately, he'd had to leave with Kyle, so some other random enforcer had helped.

The final of the six was Sam. Sam was a bit of a dark horse. I wasn't sure I'd ever heard him speak. He just stood there with his black hair cut militarily short and his features hard. He wasn't the tallest of the enforcers – that went to the mammoth of Markus, who was at least six and a half feet – and he wasn't the scariest – that was definitely Ryder – but there was something about him, a contained energy. He was one to watch.

I found my eyes drawn again to Ryder. I was like a fucking bee with a flower, needing to suck out whatever sweetness I knew was inside. He wore clothes like no one's business. He had on a dark blue polo shirt and dark-wash jeans. As my eyes dragged across his broad shoulders and slim hips, I realized he was checking me out almost as closely. His silver eyes were hooded now, his expression hard to read. I wasn't sure if he appreciated all my skin or was hoping I had a large coat to throw over it.

He didn't say anything about my outfit though, he just flicked his head to the hallway. "Let's go."

Oliver gave me a grin, his teeth very white against the dark tones of his skin. He crossed the space, and show-casing not an ounce of shame, interlocked fingers with my bestie. *Go Jayden!* I had quite the happy feels. Nothing like knowing your bestie was all hooked up with some hottie.

Ryder gave me a side glance, distracting me. "The boys have been bugging me to go out." He flicked his head to the group. Kyle fell in on my other side. I tilted my head back to meet his lazy smile. Strangely enough, I was immediately comfortable with this guy. He induced no confusing and often x-rated feelings like Ryder, and even though he had the same tough, badass vibe going on, he seemed a little more relaxed.

"Fuck yes," Kyle said. "It's been boring as shit here for a while. Even my request in the UK proved to be nothing. The action has dried up since we got that call all those weeks ago about our mythical ash girl."

Those black eyes twinkled at me and I found myself smiling in return.

"I'll bet you thought that was some sort of system malfunction."

He gave me a wink. "I was more focused on keeping

Ryder from smashing the shit out of every single one of the ash who were at your mom's house when we got there."

My eyes shifted across to the silent enforcer again. "What did they do?" I asked, as some worry seeped into my voice.

He shrugged. "Nothing much, but they were too caught up in what you were. They abandoned protocol."

"And the fact that one of them was cradling her in his lap while she convulsed had nothing to do with it?"

Ryder turned that dark stare on Kyle, who just laughed. You could tell they'd been friends for a long time. He was one of the few males not afraid of him. We walked in silence for a bit. I was still pondering Kyle's words, even though I really didn't want to be. Ryder shifted a little closer, and as my eyes rose to meet his, he said, "Your hair looks good down."

Whoa. That was completely unexpected and I didn't know what to say. I wasn't used to Ryder dishing out compliments. I didn't want to read too closely into it. He was an honest guy. Probably there was nothing more than simple approval.

"Thanks," I finally murmured.

You look good in a towel.

We traveled the rest of the way through the Hive in silence, before ending up in the courtyard. Everyone piled into a big black unmarked van and then we headed to the club. Hell yes. Finally, some normalcy in my life.

· · ·

THE DOORMAN WAS A VAMPIRE. They must completely change shifts when the curfew ended. I had no idea, I wasn't one to break curfew much. Ryder nodded at the bouncer and we all strode in without paying or ID checks. Ryder posse perk.

The club was pumping, the music louder and more bass driven than the last time I was here. I felt my body loosen up as we strode further in. This was my world, not the fucking Hive.

"Charlie!" my bestie shrieked, bounding over to me with blond curls bouncing. Girl looked all kinds of gorgeous in her short, tight blue dress, eyes extra blue against the dark liner. She slammed into me with the force of a truck and I laughed as I hugged her. We stayed like that for an extended moment, flashes of our past flittering through my head, and I knew she'd be thinking the same thing. The last time we were in a club everything had been normal. Then that very same night, everything changed. You really couldn't take anything in life for granted, it could be gone before you even had a chance to really know you had it. Eventually we had to untangle ourselves and I handed her over to my other bestie. Tessa and Jayden had been chatting over email but hadn't met in person.

"Girl, your hair is Marilyn Monroe gorgeous," he told her. She grinned and hugged him. My heart overflowed at my two BFFs finally meeting.

"It's nice to finally meet you. Thanks for dressing Charlie tonight."

I scowled. "What! How do you know he dressed me?"

Tessa rolled her eyes. "Please…"

Her next words were cut off as she finally focused on the enforcers, her eyes running across the six tall, buff, and badass guys. She lingered the longest on Ryder. Somehow she knew which one he was. She had never really met him; the last time she'd been passed out. I was a little nervous about the glint in her eye.

Please don't say anything stupid, Tessa.

"So, you're Ryder," Tessa said. Her words made it sound like he was some important person in my life. Shit. My cheeks reddened.

Ryder extended his hand and shook hers. As he pulled away, a vampire strode in beside her and put an arm around her shoulders. I bristled at the sight of a blood-sucker so close to her.

Tessa smiled up at the guy with his strawberry blond curls. Damn, he was sort of a cute, sexy version of a grown-up Cabbage Patch Doll.

"Guys, this is Blake."

I really did not like the idea of Tessa having a regular vampire feeder, especially not one that acted possessive of her.

Blake nodded to all of us, then his eyes settled on the tall enforcer at my side.

"Ryder," he said.

Ryder nodded back. "Blake."

It was clear Ryder had the respect of all the vampires, which was an achievement since they thought of ash as mongrel dogs.

The song changed then and Tessa squealed, ducking out from under Blake's arm and grabbing Jayden and my hands, dragging us to the dance floor. Typical Tessa, she was a sucker for Britney Spears. It felt good to let loose, and I got lost in the music for some time. After dancing inside of a Jayden and Tessa sandwich for almost a half an hour, I broke away to get some water. I was laying off the liquor for a bit. Human alcohol was pretty much a waste now anyways.

As the crowd parted, I noticed Ryder leaning against the bar, his eyes locked on me as I approached. He lowered his glass from where he'd just taken a drink, his eyes traveling across me. I approached him slowly, taken aback by the intensity of his gaze.

"Having fun?" I queried.

His reached around and pulled me close to him, speaking in my ear. It was the only way to be heard in here. "What did you say? I can't hear you over the music?" he shouted.

His muscular thigh was partly lodged between my legs, and to steady myself I reached out and let my hand rest on his bicep. The only thing ruining this moment was the reek of alcohol on his breath.

"Got a hold of some vamp moonshine I see," I shouted back.

He gave me a slow but insanely sexy smile. "I'm told I need to lighten up."

I grinned. Well, well, well ... if I didn't know any better, I'd think Ryder was more than a little drunk. My straight-laced, overly rigid, tough as shit Ryder. And I was starting to get the feeling that in his drunken state he wanted a piece of Charlie.

I knew I could lean into him now ... I could kiss him. But something held me back. This wasn't how I wanted it. Tomorrow the steel door to his emotions would close again and I knew on instinct that one night with Ryder would never be enough, and I didn't want a taste only to lose it forever.

Before I could respond, he leaned in so close that my hair covered his face and his cheek touched mine. "I should have told you this long ago, but watching you fight in that culling was among the worst moments of my life. I was half a second from jumping in the fight and killing them all."

My heart beat wildly in my chest at his proclamation. Who was this ash? He seemed relaxed, his words flowing more freely than usual. He pulled back then, slipping his leg out from under me, leaning farther back onto the bar. He was then casually watching people dance like he hadn't just said the most romantic thing in the world. I sank in next to him and ordered my water.

After taking a few sips, I decided to be bold. "You wanna dance?" I gave him my bedroom eyes. This look had never failed me. I was wearing nipple pasties, for Christ's sake. No way would he say no.

He swallowed before shaking his head. "I shouldn't."

Well, there's a first time for everything. Awesome. *I'm a complete loser.* I noticed Kyle heading our way, and not wanting to break down like a full-on girl, I swiveled around.

"Right, see you later." I booked it for the bathroom, trying to remember where it was.

Stupid, Charlie! He didn't like me, he was just drunk and my boobs looked amazing in this shirt – he got distracted.

I took a wrong turn down the hallway before remembering that this led to an outside patio and smoking area. Frustrated, I turned around and ran smack into a vampire.

He caught me by the shoulders to keep me from falling. His grip was firm.

"Oh sorry," I said as I tried to pull out of his grasp. He didn't let go, and my eyes shot up to his face. His hair was slicked back and jet black; he had a pointy nose, and his eyes were doing the pulsing thing.

"I've been waiting all week to meet you. Your performance in the culling was superb," he purred, tightening his hold on my shoulders.

"Thanks, I really need to use the bathroom." I reached up to brush his hands off. He tightened them again, his grip an iron vice. *What the actual fu–*

"Ow!" I shrieked as his breathing hitched and he began to pant. Fangs slid from his upper lip. Shit. I had never fought a full-fledged vampire before. I knew they were stronger than ash, but not sure how much. I had a feeling I was about to find out.

I put both hands on his chest and shoved him, hard. He stumbled backward a little, but my push only served to enrage him more. He smelled of vamp alcohol and had clearly lost control.

He slammed into me before I could even track his movement. The back of my head cracked into the wall and I yelped. He had me pinned against the brickwork; we were alone in this dark hallway. His eyes pulsed from solid silver to some weird gray color.

"Help!" I screamed again, hoping like hell someone would hear me this time. I felt the graze of razor sharp points on my neck, and I knew he was just about to pierce my skin. Pleasure chased along my spine, my body remembering how it felt to be fed on, but it was quickly doused with how awful this situation was. Vamp asshole then decided to take his time with me, slowly pushing his chompers into me. His wet mouth sucked at my neck with greed. Gross. Vampire hickey. Just what I needed. I kneed him firmly in the groin, but he just bit down on me harder.

"Got off, asshole!" I screamed, but it was no use. He was like a two-hundred-pound mosquito.

Suddenly Ryder's and Kyle's faces zoomed into focus, and before the relief even had time to hit, the enforcers had grabbed the vamp by the neck, ripping him off of me. The vamp went airborne and was slammed onto the ground. Kyle reached over and yanked me up, holding me against his hard frame as one of his hands lifted to rest against the side of my neck. Both of us froze as we watched Ryder go completely into warrior mode, throwing a series of powerful blows to the vamp's head, his arms moving so fast I couldn't track them. Holy shit, he was a monster.

The force at which the punches connected with the vamp's face made sounds that I was pretty sure would haunt my dreams. It was in this moment I truly realized how easy Ryder had been going on me in training. I had not even the slightest clue of his true abilities.

Kyle held me close until my shaking stopped. "You okay, Charlie?" His dark eyes lifted from Ryder to lock on me. "Shit, sorry girl, we got here as soon as we heard you scream."

I tried to swallow, some of the pain in my neck easing. Kyle lifted his hand away and his eyes swirled as he stared. "The wound has closed over. You're going to need some blood."

He pulled himself away from me and I realized that my blood was tempting him. I propped myself against the wall as Kyle strode across to help Ryder. Markus, Jared, and Sam ran down the hall then, and together the enforcers helped Kyle pull Ryder off the unconscious vamp. I remained against the wall, too shaken to move yet, my focus locked in on the one man who always had my back. Ryder's eyes were wild, his knuckles already bruised, cuts littering them. He left the vampire to his men, crossing the space to crowd into me.

"Are you hurt?" His words were barely audible, so much feral in his gaze.

Hurt? Oh right, I was attacked.

My hand went up to my neck, even though Kyle had told me it was healed. "He bit me."

Ryder breathed deeply, his serious eyes never leaving

me. He didn't seem drunk anymore, the fight having washed away whatever buzz he'd had.

Finally, he turned back to his guys, even though he did not shift out of my personal space. He spoke in a low voice to the enforcers, and I used the time to move off the wall. My limbs were shaking a little, the adrenalin starting to wear off. Why were these bastards always trying to bite me? It didn't seem normal.

Ryder turned back around, and finding me moved, stepped back into my personal space. "If he were an ash, I would kill him right here." His hazy silver and black eyes flickered to the lump on the floor.

Kyle nodded. He'd moved close to Ryder's back. "I think we should kill him anyways. Who cares what the Quorum says."

Ryder seemed to consider this, then he grinned, catching me totally off guard. "No, I have a better idea. Throw him in the pit for a month."

Jared let out a low whistle. "A month in the pit. Dude is going to be fried." Damn that accent was good. I needed to visit Australia one day. Also, note to self: Don't get on Ryder's bad side and find out what the hell the pit was.

Ryder placed a hand on my lower back. "Fun's over. Let's go."

I got the distinct feeling he would not be letting me out again soon. "I wouldn't consider being attacked by a vampire fun," I retorted.

He frowned. "Yeah, bad joke. Sorry." He stopped and faced me. "Seriously, are you okay?" His hair was tousled from the fight, and the protective way his hand rested against my spine had my stomach all aflutter.

No.

"I'm fine," I said.

This was not Ryder's problem. I was the delicious, chocolate-covered unicorn donut, and while I'd love it if Ryder were my own delicious chocolate-covered donut, the feeling clearly wasn't mutual.

I turned and left the hallway with Ryder hot on my heels. The night of fun was over, and we were heading back to the Hive. Back to the world of blood and vamps. If I didn't figure this out soon, how to stop all of this blood-lusting after me, I wasn't going to survive long past the culling anyways.

THE NEXT DAY I awoke to a loud banging on my door. This wasn't a friendly, just-stopping-by knock. It was a police-raid I'm-going-to-Taser-your-ass, bang-bang-bang sort of knock. I leapt off the bed, heart hammering and crossed the hallway as Jayden flew out of his room, eyes wide.

"What the hell?" Jayden looked half dead. Ryder and Kyle might have brought me home early from the club, but Jayden and Tessa had stayed out with their men.

"Open the damn door!"

It was Ryder.

I flung the door open and he stepped inside and slammed it behind him.

"The Quorum is on their way." His words were short and sharp. "They want another blood test after the culling and what happened at the club. They don't trust Lucas."

My eyes went wide and Jayden looked confused. I hadn't told him about the direct descendent thing. Not because I didn't trust him, but because there wasn't really anything to say. No one knew what I was, they just knew I wasn't normal.

"What do I do?"

Would it be so bad for the Quorum to find out I was directly linked to an Original? No one had really explained the end results for me if everyone found out. But since Ryder looked worried and usually nothing fazed that man, there was definitely room for me to start stressing.

Ryder tilted his head to the side, exposing his neck. "Bite me," he declared.

Heck yes! I mean ... what?

I raised one eyebrow as Jayden looked at me, grinning. Okay, I'm not gonna lie, I had fantasized about Ryder saying those exact words, but not in front of Jayden. And not in response to the stupid Quorum. I hadn't fed directly off anyone before and now really didn't seem like the right time to start – the freakin' Quorum was on its way. I closed my mouth abruptly, trying to figure out what he was on about. "You want me to ... bite you? Why?"

Ryder grabbed my hand and pulled me closer to him. "Feed from me and then from Jayden, and when they take your blood it will be a diluted mix. It's the only chance we have."

Holy. Shit. Was it man-candy Monday?

Realizing there wasn't time to ponder this, I slipped one hand behind Ryder's neck and stood on my tiptoes as instinct kicked in and my fangs slid from my upper gums. I had about a thousand-percent more control over my fangs now than when I first turned, but right at this moment they wanted Ryder. As I leaned in, I barely even noticed that Jayden turned and left the room, giving me privacy. My nose grazed against Ryder – Mmm, he smelled so good. I lightly scraped my fangs against his neck, but paused. I had never fed from a living person. Would I hurt him? Would warm blood be gross?

His hands clamped down on my hips. "Do it, I want you to."

That was all I needed to hear. I sank my teeth into his deliciously plump vein and his warm blood trickled into my mouth. We both moaned at the same time. He tasted like cinnamon and copper. Holy shit – bottled blood was like old ass compared to this. Ryder's blood was potent and warm, filled with power and energy. It was like hitting an electrical socket and frying a thousand volts through me, but instead of pain all I got was the huge boost of power.

I gulped greedily as his hands tightened on my hips. I lost sense of time completely, but still sort of knew that he let me feed from him for an extended period.

Finally he halted me. "Stop, Charlie."

I pulled away gasping, feeling his warmth in my body,

182 JAYMIN EVE & LEIA STONE

and the burning of my cheeks. I knew they would be bright red. When I met Ryder's eyes I could see desire flashing there.

A bang on the door ripped me from my trance.

Ryder silently grabbed my arm and pulled me into Jayden's room. My best friend was ready.

"Bite me, bitch – but you better tell me everything later," he whispered softly. I nodded and sank into his neck without any of the sensuality that I'd reserved for Ryder. It was more uncomfortable without the intimacy. Let's just say I was much more aware that I was feeding on another person. After a few big gulps, I pulled off.

Ryder nodded and handed me a type-O blood bottle.

"Answer the door," he murmured as he slipped inside of Jayden's closet. For some reason he did not want the Quorum to know he was here.

I chugged the bottle, throwing it in the trash as I crossed the space to answer the door. As I opened the door, strong vampire energy flooded through the entrance and I almost took a step back. A group of very pissed, very powerful looking vampires stood before me. My eyes catalogued them, wondering if I was about to find out how strong the Quorum really was.

"Hello, Charlene, we require your presence in the medical wing," one of them told me with a gritty voice. It took me a second, but I realized that I knew his distinct voice. This was the vampire who had spoken with Ryder outside of the medical wing when I was first brought in, who told him I would be treated like every other ash and join in the culling. He was tall, with slicked black hair and a bent hooked nose. He must have been an ugly mofo before the virus, because even with all the smoothing out he was still fugly as hell.

I acted dumb. "Okay. What's this about?"

"Just a routine blood test."

Damn liar.

Where was Lucas? There were – I quickly counted in my head – nine of the members here, but no Lucas. "Wow, the entire Quorum accompanying me to a routine blood test. I must be pretty important," I mused out loud. I couldn't act too dumb.

I stepped out and they closed rank behind me, boxing me in.

Ugly sneered at me as we walked together. "We just want to see with our own eyes that the test is done properly. Your... *talents* ... don't seem to line up with your lineage."

I tried to slow my heart rate, knowing they could sense it. "Whatever." I shrugged. I was getting good at feigning disinterest. But in my head I was all *fuck-fuck-fuck*. My damn unicorn blood better not shoot rainbows when they looked at it, or I had a feeling I was a dead woman.

I was led to a medical room, where a male doctor I had never seen was waiting in a lab coat with a needle kit before him.

"How many doctors does the Hive need? You guys heal," I said in the sweetest voice I could muster.

One of the Quorum members smiled, a woman with reddish hair. "She's bright."

Another Quorum member scowled at me. "They aren't just doctors, they're also scientists. The humans allow a small number of vampires to be privately educated. We have a highly contagious virus that the humans aren't keen to catch. Now sit down."

I sat down in the red leather padded chair and hoped that my resting bitch face was on. These people were really starting to annoy me. No more words were spoken at the *scientist* pinned my arm down and jabbed it with a needle. I had forgotten the affect my blood had on them until the aroma hit the air and they all stiffened.

"Why do you think her blood is so tempting?" one of them asked as his fangs extended onto his lower lip.

The scientist holding the tube of my blood shook his head as if to clear his own lusting thoughts. "I don't know, but I'm about to find out."

"Maybe because she is the first female ash," another Quorum member offered.

The ugly one shook his head, that crooked nose looking even more bent in the fluorescent lighting down here. "No, I think there is more to it. When will the results be ready?"

The scientist placed the tube into a glass cylinder compartment inside a machine.

"About eight hours."

Ugly turned his dark, silver eyes on me. "You may go. Don't leave your apartment today. All right?"

House arrest. Awesome.

I nodded. Would it kill them to get cable in the Hive? At least then I could at least spend the hours until my doom with some good TV viewing. I'd choose those badass brothers from *Supernatural*. The door opened and an ash was there to collect me.

What? No Quorum escort back to my room?

As I followed the ash wordlessly down the hall, the severity of the situation began to press down on me. What if it didn't work? What would happen when my blood showed that my father was an Original? Would they kill me? I needed to talk to Ryder, he would know what to expect from this.

The ash dumped me at my door and left without a word. I'll bet that he thought the Quorum warning was more than enough to keep me from wandering during the next eight hours. Little did he know, I was most probably going to be running for my life, and a little rule breaking would be the least of my worries.

I crashed into my apartment, closing the door tightly behind me. I scented that Jayden was here, but Ryder's spiciness was missing.

Jayden strode out of his bedroom, bottle of blood in hand. "Girl! What the actual fuck is going on? They had your shit searched while you were gone. You need to tell me everything and you need to do it now."

He drained his bottle before throwing it in the trash and basically kicking my ass across to our couch. I interrupted his next little hissy fit.

"Where's Ryder? I'm pretty sure I'm in a crap-ton of trouble and I have no idea what the hell I'm supposed to do now."

I was not sitting around waiting for them to kill me. No freakin' way. Still, there weren't many options for me. I might never have wanted to be an ash and live in the Hive, but there was no life left for me in the human world. They feared my kind, and I would be hunted by the government. If these tests went badly, I was going to end up with nowhere to escape.

"He did that growly, sexy-as-sin thing, then took off just after you were escorted out by the *Night of the Living Dead* crew. He hasn't come back yet."

I could tell by the way Jayden had me pinned with his dark eyes, and the hand on my shoulder, that he was not letting me leave until I told him everything. I just had to hope this knowledge wouldn't come back to bite him.

"They did some tests when I first turned, trying to figure out how the hell there was a female ash. Apparently they had some odd results. They believe my father was an Original."

I had just thrown it out there, and Jayden was surprisingly calm about it. So either he didn't know the stories or he wasn't worried. Maybe it wasn't a big deal. His perfectly shaped brows drew together as he seemed to contemplate my words further. "Closely descended from an Original is not a huge deal, but sired directly is ... I thought all the Originals were dead."

He was starting to understand now, understand the trouble I was in.

"What else was wrong with your blood, Charlie?"

I swallowed loudly, working hard to try and clear the lump in my throat so I could talk. "I wasn't showing the standard blood work of an ash, and yet it wasn't vampire blood either. The lab technician was confused, said she was going to run more tests, but I haven't heard from her or Lucas since then."

Lucas or Ryder, I needed one of those big bastards. Someone needed to tell me what level of freak-the-fuck-out I needed to be having.

Jayden rubbed a hand over his eyes, looking confused. "So if you're not an ash or vamp, what the hell are you?"

I pulled myself from his grip and began to pace the room. "I have no idea. What is there beside ash or vampire? I'm definitely not human."

Jayden fluttered those crazy long lashes. "I wouldn't worry about that right now. Let's deal with problem number one – you being a direct descendant of an Original. The Originals were all murdered for fear of them being too powerful."

I stopped and looked up at him. "So ... if they find out?"

Anger began rise up in me. I did not just fight my way through the culling to be killed by some old-ass Quorum bitches. Jayden got to his feet, crossed the room and grabbed my hand.

"Then we run. I don't have a family anymore. Never

really did. You're my family now. I will go with you and we will figure it out."

Emotion tightened my throat. It was a sweet offer. It wasn't logical or practical, of course. We wouldn't be able to get jobs because of what we were. And no jobs meant no food, no blood, and no place to call home. Still, I really appreciated his loyalty. A light tap came at the door. I moved instantly, hoping like hell it was Lucas or Ryder. As I flung open the door I was shocked to see Blake, Tessa's feeder boyfriend.

"Umm, it's not a good time," I told him.

Ignoring this, he pushed past me and shut the door behind him. Umm, excuse me? "Come right on in," I muttered.

"Lucas sent me," he said quietly. Okay, in that case I would tolerate his presence.

"Does he have a message for me?" I urged in my most hurried voice, whispers of bitchy leaking through – this vamp asshole was chomping on my best friend. I wasn't a fan of him.

Blake glared at me, which looked odd on his pretty, cherub face. "I love Tessa, you don't have to worry about me hurting her."

A sound left my voice, somewhere between a snarl and a gag. "You love her? Please, you barely know her."

He stepped closer to me, eyes fierce, jaw set. "You're her best friend, so I know it's your job to worry about her, and I will take whatever you dish out. But I want her and I will fight for her."

Well shit. Maybe I was letting some of my frustration over the whole Ryder thing bleed across to Tessa and Blake. Sure, I was annoyed that she was with a vampire, but that declaration was pretty damn perfect. Even Jayden had tears in his eyes.

I sighed. "You better look after her, Blake, or I am going to cut your dick off and feed it to you." He blanched at my threat. I meant every word of it too. "I must be the only one in this hive that's single. Can a girl get some action?" I told the room.

Blake, already recovered, was back to wearing his cocky grin. "I'm sure you would be getting action if Ryder hadn't told every guy in the Hive to stay away from you."

My heart jackhammered in my chest. "Wha ... wait, what? He said that? To who? Why? When?"

I will kill that asshole. He couldn't just reject me and still make a declaration like that. Who did he think he was? Jayden had walked closer and was hanging on Blake's every word.

Blake shrugged. "I'm not sure if it came from Ryder or the Quorum. Apparently they don't know if you're fertile."

And just like that my dreams went up in flames. I was seriously pathetic, thinking Ryder told every guy to stay away from me so he could have me. Jesus. Jayden squeezed my hand in BFF solidarity.

I changed the subject. "So ... what's the word from Lucas?"

Blake ran a hand through his perfect curls. "Lucas said

to stay put for now, and that if stuff heats up any more there will be an exit plan in place. He said you would know what that meant."

Shit. So if the Quorum wanted to kill me, Lucas would be helping me run away from the Hive. I sighed.

"Yep. I understand. Thanks."

Blake gave me a long glance. "Tessa misses you and she has asked me to get permission from the Quorum to change her into a vampire. I'm considering it." Then he turned on his heels and left.

As the door slammed, I was knocked out of my shock. Okay, now I was back to hating him again. Tessa would be turned over my dead body. Seriously, what else could go wrong today?

Jayden's comforting arm around my shoulders did very little to ease my pain. He gave me a tight squeeze, and I realized silent laughter was shaking him.

"Oh my God, when he said Ryder told all the guys to leave you alone, you should have seen your face. You were like an orphaned puppy that finally found a family."

What? I totally had not – okay, I must have looked a bit pathetic. I tried my best to glare at him, but his amused expression was ridiculous. Asshole. Finally I busted out laughing too, until tears ran down my face and my stomach ached. It was a nice stress reliever, that was for sure.

. . .

SEVEN HOURS, three games of Scrabble, thirteen magazines, a thousand YouTube videos, and fifty-seven emails to Tessa later, there was a knock at the door. I bolted upright from my position sprawled on the couch, my head darting to the side to meet Jayden's gaze. Was this the results? Early?

I pulled myself up, brushing off the crumbs from my many snacks, before crossing the room confidently. When I was a foot from the door, I smelled the familiar spicy scent. Ryder.

Opening the door, he was alone. My eyes ran over his tan smooth neck and the memory of biting him floated into my mind. I pushed that aside.

"Hey, come in." I stepped aside and Ryder entered the apartment. I turned to see Jayden had gone into his room. Sigh. If only there was a reason for him to leave us in private.

"The Quorum sent me." He was less relaxed than usual, his posture stiff and his features cold.

I planted my feet, hands on hips. "If you're going to give me news from the Quorum, I would rather hear it from a friend, not the military enforcer ash you're pulling right now."

The words slipped out before I could censor them and I regretted them immediately. Why was I all of sudden taking my sexual frustrations out on him?

Still, something I said worked. His face softened just a little, and concern lined his eyes. His hand shifted at his side, as if he were reaching out for me, but then thought differently, stuffing it back in his pocket. "You're right, I'm sorry. Are you okay?"

Guys were so dense sometimes. I really wanted to smack him upside the head, or kiss him. Maybe both.

"Just tell me." I was the cold one now, pushing off his concern. Ryder and I were never going to sort our shit out. The timing just never seemed right.

He must have sensed my mood, and decided to just get to the point. "Your blood work showed that you do not have the DNA of an ash or a vampire. That has them in a total scientific mind-freak. But the blood was diluted and mixed, so you look to be about as close as I am to an Original. Nothing to kill over." He smiled.

I returned the smile. "Did you just say 'scientific mind-freak.' Oh my God, have I ever heard you cuss?"

Ryder stared at me. "Believe it or not, I'm a gentleman. I don't like cussing."

My mouth dropped open; laughter bubbled up inside of me and I grabbed his arm. "Oh my God, delicious Ryder, token ash, killer and enforcer, doesn't say 'fuck?'"

He looked at my lips briefly before resting on my eyes. "Delicious?"

I decided hard-to-get was a good play right about now. "Jayden's words, not mine."

Ryder nodded. "I figured. You're free to leave your apartment and go anywhere within the Hive grounds."

He turned to leave. What, just within the grounds? Damn, that meant no more human field trips, no more Tessa.

"Ryder..." I reached out and grabbed his hand, pulling him back around to face me. His body was inches from mine.

I was going to take a risk. If one of us didn't, we would always exist in this in-between place. I felt something between us, and sometimes I thought he did too.

"Why are you helping me?"

He was quiet so long I was afraid he wouldn't answer. His jaw clenched as he seemed to be battling something I couldn't see. Just when I was going to speak again, he muttered, "Many reasons, Charlie, so many. But for now, let's just say that it's my job."

Then he turned and strode away from me. Okay, that was it. I had given this guy too many opportunities to stake a claim. Time to move on. I slammed the door harder than I should have for someone at my maturity level. Whatever. I turned to go sulk in my bedroom when he knocked again. Oh yeah, asshole, come say sorry after that? I don't think so.

I opened the door. "Screw off!"

Shit! Lucas was standing there, dressed in his whites. Luckily my verbal attack didn't faze him.

"Having a rough day, Charlene?"

I chuckled. "You could say that." I waved him inside.

He entered the apartment, exuding that air of sophistication he always wore. I couldn't hook up with a vampire, could I? I scanned Lucas and decided no, he gave off too many dad-vibes. But I wouldn't tell him that, because I was pretty sure the only reason he was helping me was that I reminded him of his late wife.

"I'm in the clear. Ryder just told me."

Lucas nodded. "Yes, I would have been here much earlier if that had not been the case. I have some other news from my own private blood results."

Oh. I sat down. Something told me this wouldn't be good and I wanted my butt firmly planted for any more news today.

Lucas sat across from me. "I'm not very good with this type of information."

"Just tell me." I was in full freak-out mode now. Was I a new race? Holy gods ... was I dying?

"You can't have children," he stated in a sympathetic tone. His eyes were a swirl of emotions and I wondered if he was thinking about his own long lost children right then.

I blinked a few times. At no point had I expected him to say that. "Okay, well ... shit. Is that the big news? I thought I had vampire cancer."

A smile replaced his sympathetic frown. "No, I just wanted to tell you that you're infertile like the male ash and the female vampires, in case that is something you would like to know for future relationships."

I was still confused about why they were even checking my fertility? I supposed it was just because I was an unknown ash, and reproducing for our kind was against the law. Lucas gracefully changed the subject. "There's more. My lab technician also thought she saw some sort of immune response to the virus in your blood. This is not her expertise of course, but still, worth us looking into for the future."

I recoiled, confused. "An immune response? What does that even mean?"

Lucas's expression was all serious. "Like you were fighting it."

My mouth dropped open. "Okay." I put both hands up. "Enough crazy for today. I have reached my limit. Maybe tomorrow." I stood and Lucas followed my action. The serious look never left his face. "Charlie, if this gets out..."

"Lucas." My voice was clipped. "I literally can't take one more damned thing. I'm done."

I had the strongest urge to hurt him, to unleash this pent up anger I had at the Hive. I was being pushed backed into a corner and I had an instinct that said *Fight your way out.*

Lucas nodded understandingly. "You know where to find me," he said, and left.

I shut the door and let my head rest against it. Hot tears rolled down my cheeks. I wanted my mom. I had been doing way too much adulting in the past month. I didn't ask for this life. I would give it back in a heartbeat. But it appeared I was stuck with these freaks.

EIGHT

Sometimes, when life gets really shitty, your best bet is to live in denial. That's exactly what I had been doing for the past week. I didn't even think about my special unicorn blood, I ignored the glances Ryder sent my way, and pushed off Jayden's comments asking if I was okay. Denial. It was better than reality.

Sitting at my computer desk in the comms room, I was ready to fall asleep if something didn't happen soon.

When the phone rang, I was actually excited to talk to someone, even if it was usually a panicking human thinking their dog had somehow gotten the vamp virus and was about to slaughter their entire family.

"Hive hotline, this is Charlie."

At first all I heard was screaming in the background. Then: "My son – he's not well. I think ... he's an ash."

I sat bolt upright. I hadn't had one of these calls yet – a newly turned ash. I looked around and saw that I was alone. Shit! Usually one of the enforcers was lingering around, but today they seemed to be MIA.

What was I supposed to do? We weren't taking in any more ash. We were referring them to the Seattle Hive? No, they'd pulled Seattle too, they were full. Was it the one in Denver? Shit.

There were screams in the background, although they sounded a little closer. "Okay, ma'am, give me your address and I will send someone over."

The woman rattled off an address and I scribbled it down.

"I'm thirsty!" a male voice screamed, and then the phone went dead. Shit!

I bolted out of the room holding my piece of paper and burst into the enforcer dressing room. Generally one of them was in here.

Kyle was standing there half naked, looking at me like a deer in headlights. I took a second to admire his ripped chest and arms, not to mention his tousled dirty-blond mane. What? Don't judge me, I was only human ... well, sort of.

"Where's Ryder?" I burst out. "I got a call. A newly turned ash just attacked his mom, I think."

Kyle swore and pulled on his clothes, lightning quick. He grabbed some weapons from a locker and shoved a gun in my hand.

"Ryder is gone for the day. The rest of the boys are on the roof track running. The human will be drained dry be the time I get them. Let's go! You're coming with me."

I didn't have time to register this breach in protocol. Leave the Hive? Carry a gun? Hells to the yeah. This was what I needed right now, some action and time out of this place. Kyle was on his walkie-talkie as we left the locker room, letting the other sexy six know what was up. They'd be right behind us. Following him, I ran faster than I ever had before and practically flew into the black van's passenger seat. Kyle moved at ash speed, peeling out of the garage and down the gated side street.

"The address is only a few miles away, over by the airport!" I yelled, holding on as he took a corner at a super speed. It felt like we went up on two wheels.

He must have called ahead, because the Hive gate was open, and we flew through no problem. Kyle's grip was tight on the wheel, but he remained in complete control as I started to give him directions to the house.

"What happens if she's dead?" I blurted out.

Kyle swallowed. "The humans can press charges against the ash. They will fine the Hive a shit-ton of money, and the ash that killed her will never forgive himself."

Shit. Suddenly I thought of Ryder. He hadn't forgiven himself yet, had he? Now wasn't the time to ask and I was sure best friend code kept Kyle from telling me.

The van screeched around another corner and turned onto Monroe Street. We were at the right street now. This was where the woman lived.

As we ground to a halt in front of a sprawling, ranch-style house, Kyle swung around to face me. "You haven't been trained, so let me take the lead. Newly turned ash are jacked up from the change and are super strong. They also have an unquenchable thirst. If he bites me, kill him. He will not hesitate to kill me, and then he will move on to you."

Holy shit balls. I felt my palms sweating, and was suddenly a tiny bit grateful for the culling. At least I had some experience fighting.

"Was I that strong?" I asked.

"You were the strongest call Ryder and I have ever taken."

Well, damn. Kyle opened his door and hit the ground running. I did the same, following him right up to the door. Two hard kicks and it was down. One day I was totes going to learn how to kick down a door.

"Ash enforcers! Lay down with your hands behind your head," Kyle yelled, and I finally noticed that he had two bottles of blood in his hand, and what looked like a couple more in his pockets. When the hell had he grabbed those?

I stepped out from behind Kyle's broad shoulders and saw a young man with dark hair leaning over a limp, pale woman. The male stopped feeding on her; his face shot up and he started to growl. Kyle pulled his weapon and I followed suit, figuring he had a much better chance of knowing what the hell to do.

Kyle flicked open one of the bottle lids. "Want some nice blood?" He slowly bent and set the bottle on the ground, about three feet from the ash.

The young man's chest was heaving, eyes black as night, with the slightest silver ring. He ignored Kyle's offer and leaned back down to bite his mother. The second he clamped down, I saw her fingers twitch. No! She was still alive. I acted on instinct, firing a shot into the guy's back. He snapped his head up and looked at me.

"Shit, Charlie," Kyle said calmly. "Don't poke the lion while he's feeding."

My eyes widened as I got what he was saying. Too late. The guy stood, dropping his limp mother and lurching up, smashing aside furniture to get to me.

"Don't kill him!" I shouted at Kyle. Something inside of me felt bad for him. It wasn't his fault. This was me a few months ago. He came at me like a zombie, arms out, fangs distended.

I jumped up and did a roundhouse kick to his temple, but he caught my leg midair, and an instant later I heard a loud snap.

Son of a bitch...

I let out a strangled scream and shot him again, this time in the gut, mostly to stop him from ripping my leg off. The guy folded over on himself, clutching his stomach, and I used this opportunity to bring the butt of the gun down on the back of his head. Kyle was right there to pin him down and wrestle reinforced steel zip ties onto his hands. Which was great because I was in a world of pain, and about to be completely useless. I favored my good leg while waiting for Kyle to finish securing the ash. All the while I was trying not to cry.

Kyle stood then, and I could see the new ash was out cold. The enforcer appraised me. "I'm kind of impressed, although Ryder is going to kill my ass for letting you get injured."

I tried to smile. It felt more like a grimace. "What do we do now?" I asked, hoping like hell we were heading back to the Hive. I needed blood, and rest, and more blood. And possibly a good hour with Jayden to cry about how people kept breaking me.

"The others are almost here."

When he said others I knew it was members of the sexy six. This core group of enforcers were the badasses of the ash and vampire world. They stepped in when no one else would take the job. And since Ryder trusted all of them, I was also starting to think of them as part of my people.

Kyle left me then to attend to the boy's mother. She was very still and pale, and I wondered if we were too late. Kyle's dirty blond hair shone in the half light as he leaned over her, feeling for a pulse and shifting her into a better position. "She's still alive, her pulse is steady," he said, lifting his head so I could see the very dark of his eyes. "The human doctors will take care of her. She's going to be fine – just a little blood loss."

I sank against the wall, which was currently holding me up. "That's great!" From the first moment I heard those screams on the phone, I'd feared we were going to be too late. Seems we'd made it just on time.

Noise drew my attention then, starting low and

increasing as more than one set of heavy boots clomped outside the single-story house. The front door Kyle had slammed into when we'd first entered had been leaning into the doorframe, and now slid to the side to reveal Markus, Jared, Sam, and Oliver. As usual when they were all together, the room shrank in from all the tall, beautiful, and deadly they were throwing around. Oliver noticed me first and broke ranks to come and assess my leg.

I winced as he tried flex my ankle. "Ow!"

He shook his head. "What happened? Ryder will want a full report when he gets back from paying his respects."

I frowned. Paying his respects? What was he talking about?

Kyle glared at Oliver. "She took a call. It was an emergency and I needed backup. I didn't think she would roundhouse kick a newly-turned ash in the face."

The other four guys whistled low and appraised me with pride. Markus' deep brogue drifted across the room. "No shit? Our unicorn is kind of a badass."

Great, unicorn had officially stuck as a nickname. Sirens could be heard coming down the street.

Kyle looked me in the eyes, both respect and a glint of something extra there. Like acceptance. "What do you expect from someone trained by Ryder?"

Since the humans were on their way, we needed to bail. Oliver scooped me up into his arms, which I didn't love, but walking was out of the question. Kyle and silent Sam lifted the newly-turned ash by the armpits. He was groaning and just beginning to wake.

"Come on, you know the drill. We need to leave so the human medics can help the mom." Kyle ushered us all outside and we loaded into the two Hive vans just as the paramedics pulled up. There was an awkward moment as our two groups crossed paths, the human medics glaring us down. Really? We just saved her life. Well ... we wouldn't have had to if one of our monsters hadn't bitten her. Okay, point taken. Humans hated us, and rightfully so.

The new ash was taken with some of the enforcers back to the Hive to await a transfer to another city, whichever one was still taking ash, or had a culling coming up. Poor guy, he had no clue the shit storm that was about to be his life. *Good luck in the killing – I mean culling – buddy.*

Oliver and Kyle let me stretch out on the back seat, resting my leg for the trip home. Truth be told, my leg hurt like hell, but that was the most fun I'd had all week. Screw answering phones, I wanted to be an enforcer.

LATER THAT DAY, as I was hobbling around the enforcer locker room, I heard the distinct clip of shit-kicker boots. I had a moment to wonder which of the males it was, then Ryder strode in. He did a double-take as our eyes met. The silver around his iris started to glow and swirl, and the air between us thickened. I watched his breathing grow deeper. He seemed to be working on controlling himself. Did he already know what had happened? Had he heard about the call out?

I managed to blink a few times when he wrenched his gaze from mine and strode back out of the room. Not one word had been spoken, but the air felt heavier now. The tension was palpable. Within minutes, I heard steps again, and Kyle, Oliver, Markus, Sam, and Jared followed the hard-as-stone lead enforcer into the locker room. As they stood there in a line like that, I realized how different each of them truly looked from one another, and yet the way they moved ... it was fluid, like a team that had been together for a long time. There was history there. True family style.

Still, that didn't stop Ryder from losing his shit.

"Someone better explain to me right the fuck now why Charlie is not only injured, but rumor has it she was out on a call today?"

Uh oh, the lead enforcer rarely raised his voice, and he never swore. He seemed to be able to command a room with no more than a few tersely spoken words, but today his cool was missing.

I did find it kind of hot to hear him say fuck.

Kyle, who was all casually leaning back against one of the gray metal cabinets, met his best friend's eyes. "I had no choice. This was an emergency call – a new ash attacked a human, his mother. We both know that a second's hesitation could mean the difference between life and death."

Ryder's jaw clenched. "You brought an untrained ash to a dangerous situation? It could have been life and death for her. And you thought it was an even better idea to give her a gun? What the hell, Kyle?"

A slight pink flooded across the tips of Kyle's cheeks, and his eyes darkened even further. "I was thinking I took an oath! I was thinking of my best friend visiting his fiancée's grave today and how I didn't want this new ash to live with killing his mother, like you live with killing Molly!"

Holy Shit. That was so not what I'd expected Kyle to say. The enforcer's dirty-blond hair hung forward as he dropped his head. I could tell he was already regretting using such harsh words with his friend. But still, that was freakin' deep. Ryder sort of looked like he'd been punched in the gut. More than one of us in the room were staring at our feet now – except for Sam, who was staring at the far wall like he wanted to put his fist through it. I struggled to hold back my tears. That's where he had been, paying his respects to the fiancée he killed years ago?

The room remained in this bubble of uncomfortable silence for a few minutes, but then the strangest thing happened. Instead of another explosion of anger from Ryder, he simply stepped forward, clapped Kyle on his shoulder, nodded to the rest of us and walked away.

"Ryder..." Kyle's handsome face fell as he called out, but Ryder didn't stop. He exited the locker room, leaving us all to our silence.

"Dammit!" Kyle slammed his fist into a locker and I winced as I heard the crunch of bone. Tragedy affected so much more than just one person. Molly's death took something from every person who cared for Ryder. I wondered then if Kyle had known the couple before the ash thing. How far back did their ties go?

DECIDING it was time to give everyone a moment to cool off, I slowly hobbled back to the control room. Walking was not pleasant. God, these assholes could create super-human freaks with their sperm, why the hell couldn't they invent ash pain meds? I at least needed some vampire moonshine to take the edge off of my shattered ankle. Although, I was told by tomorrow it would only be slightly bruised and nearly fully healed. Another ash perk.

Opening my email, I saw Jayden had sent out an invite. It was addressed to Ryder, Kyle, Oliver, Sam, Jared, Markus, and a few other random ash.

DEAR BITCHES,

I have recently come across some fabulous information while gossiping in the feeder room. The Hive has just opened a brand new club and it features karaoke. Join me tonight for laughs, drinks and a damn good Diana Ross impression. Level 55.

Sincerely,

Jayden AKA Diana Ross

I SMILED. If God were real, then he'd created Jayden just

to keep me sane in this hellhole. I loved karaoke and needed to take my mind off everything. I replied with a big fat yes. I highly doubted Ryder would be attending, and couldn't believe Jayden referred to him as one of his bitches. That alone was enough to brighten my mood.

AFTER FINISHING MY BORING-ASS SHIFT, I hobbled home to get ready for karaoke. My leg was feeling better already and I was so pumped for tonight. Hells yeah. A little Celine, a few Whitneys – not to mention some Cindy Lauper – and I'd be in song heaven. Yeah, I had a penchant for 8os power women.

I chugged a bottle of O-negative and then put on some low-rise black skinny jeans, tucking one side into a knee-high flat boot, and the broken ankle side into the walking boot. I then threw on a vintage cut-off *Star Wars* shirt that exposed my stomach. Remembering Ryder's compliment last time, I decided to leave my hair down, shaking out the kink from my ponytail. The front door closed and I walked out of my room to find Jayden just getting home from work. He looked at my outfit and I braced myself for his comment about how shitty it was.

"Hmm, it works ... in a tomboy, grunge, gothic way."

I rolled my eyes, but then he eyed my walking boot and his face became serious. "Oliver told me what happened today."

I grinned. "It was actually fun."

He raised one perfectly-shaped eyebrow. "Say what? Getting your ankle shattered was fun?"

"No, obviously not that – the excitement of going out on an emergency call, helping save the woman, subduing the ash. It was a thrill. I want to be an enforcer!" I blurted the last part because I wasn't sure I could keep it in any longer. I hadn't stopped thinking about it since I went out with Kyle.

Jayden laughed. "Hah hah, like for Halloween?"

I smacked his big-ass arm. "No, asshat, like every day. Do I look like I'm destined to answer phones for the rest of my life?" I put a hand on my hip.

He smirked. "You have a point."

My eyes lit up. "Really? You think Ryder would let me?"

Jayden's smirk fell. "No, honey, I don't."

I growled. Dammit, weren't friends supposed to support your dreams?

THE BRAND new Hive karaoke club was on level fifty-five and had the most banging view of Portland. The club had a stage and high-tech karaoke setup, with an oxygen bar off to the side, and some hot-ass female vamp waitresses wearing cut-off jean shorts and tight white tank-tops with brown cowboy boots. It was interesting to see the vampires serving the ash. Rarely in Hive society did that happen. These girls looked like they took the job just to be able to bag a hot ash – judging by the sultry looks and lingering touches between the vamp females and male ash.

As a perky blond vamp with some seriously gorgeous full lips took our drink order, I plugged in a song for Jayden and I to sing next. I couldn't wait to let loose and feel the beat. My attention shifted then as a familiar group walked into the bar – the sexy six, only they were missing a member, so right now they were the fine ass five. My eyes remained glued on the door for a few extra beats, but there was no Ryder. Sigh. I really needed to get over that shit. I was getting pathetic.

Oliver spotted us first, and with eyes for his boy, reached our table and dropped a kiss on Jayden's cheek. He turned and gave me a hug, whispering in my ear, "Word has gotten around that you're no longer off limits. Fair warning."

He pulled away and I tried to mask my confusion. Was he talking about the blood test results? My eyes darted around, trying to figure out if everyone knew I was infertile now, and why that would make them all think I was open for lots of casual sex?

I seriously hated my private shit out there in the Hive world. This information was something I intended to sit on for like five or six years before thinking too much about it. I'd probably cry about it on that day in the future, and then move on because you can't change the past.

Unease trickled down my spine and I felt super aware of all the hot ash around us. Was I imagining things or were they all looking at me? I was distracted then by the speaker system. It called for Jayden and me, and at the same time the intro to our song started. My BFF grabbed my hand and together we ran to the stage. As the spotlight hit us, I was suddenly in my element. I was a Leo, and there were two things Leos love: attention and more attention. Thank God for karaoke.

We grabbed the mics and stood together on the stage as the lyrics rolled up. Jayden flashed his full range of pearly whites and opened wide to belt out the tune.

We were pretty tame, right up until the chorus hit, and then it was time to let loose.

"Girls just wanna have fu-un! Oh girls, just wanna have fun!"

I cracked up on the last line as I noticed Oliver, Kyle, and Jared had left their booth and were crowded around the stage. I wasn't sure if they were singing along or mocking the shit out of us. Either way, they were finally less badass and more relaxed-ass. Even the ash boogiemen needed a night off on occasion. Markus was laughing in the booth but hadn't joined them. Sam was still in the shadows, nursing his vamp booze. That man had some demons. Even more than...

As if I'd conjured him with thought, a figure stepped out of the shadowy entrance and strode across to the bar. I almost dropped the mic, my palms suddenly sweaty and mouth dry. It was Ryder. He'd actually showed up. Our eyes locked and the rest of the room fell away.

What power did this man have over me?

He hadn't looked away and I was barely singing

anymore, totally forgetting the lines to a song I had sung a thousand times before. Our moment was broken then as a jostling almost knocked me off the stage. I swung around to find an ash behind me. He was clearly wasted as he jumped around and sent a few pelvic thrusts my way.

I wasn't sure whether to be amused or horrified, but his dancing was borderline obscene, so I had to laugh. Oliver took control of the situation by throwing a lemon wedge at the interloper, which actually knocked him down. Glancing back up, my eyes zoomed back to the find Ryder leaning sexily up against the bar, eyes still on me, like he had not removed them for even one moment. *Oh my.* His expression was doing all sorts of hot things to my insides, and there was something different about him. Like he had less walls around him. Was he drunk again? Vampire moonshine seemed to be his warrior juice with the ladies.

A female waitress approached him but he waved her off, continuing to stare. Hot damn, was I sweating? This was intense. The song ended and Jayden flicked his eyes to Ryder and raised an eyebrow at me. I shrugged and left the stage with him. The typical thing to do would be to walk over to the hot guy that had been staring at you. But typical didn't work for me, so I followed everyone back to the table, squeezing in next to Jayden. Kyle left us then and my gaze followed him as he approached Ryder. The head enforcer removed his eyes from me to give Kyle a bro hug.

I finally had a breather from the intensity that was

Ryder, and a butt-load of air whooshed back into my lungs. It was like I couldn't breathe when Ryder locked me in his gaze. The force was scorching, and my belly heated at the naughty thoughts running through my head.

Jayden fanned himself. "Woo it's getting hot in here! What's up with Mr. Tasty?"

Oliver smacked his arm. "Hey, I thought I was Mr. Tasty."

I shrugged. "Maybe he's drunk."

A tall dark ash approached our table with a red drink and set it in front of me. "Hey, beautiful."

Not interested, buddy.

I stood quickly. "Oh, I was just going to find the bathroom." I walked away quickly, making a run for the girls' bathroom.

I walked down the dimly lit hallway and shouldered the door, then stood in front of the mirror. I took a moment to stare at my reflection. As always, the first thing to capture my attention were my eyes. They were just so weird and it never got normal to see silver instead of my original brown – not to mention the way they swirled and held such an intense light. Just another thing which was gone from the old Charlie Bennett's life.

I turned on the water and washed away some of the stickiness from my drink, all the time thinking of Ryder. What was up with him? Since the first day I met him, he'd been my knight in shining armor, stepping in and saving me. He'd saved me from hurting my mom, brought me into the Hive, trained me to survive. Why? Because it was his job? Or something more?

My body heated as I recalled drinking his blood. That had probably been the single most intense and confusing moment of my life. And I so wanted to do it again. I ran fingers through my hair, yanking at the tangles in frustration. I was so confused! I didn't get confused about guys, I went for the one I wanted and didn't have a problem.

Seriously, Charlie...

Was I really standing in the bathroom mooning over a guy? Okay, back to reality. Plan: get kissed senseless tonight by a really hot ash and forget Ryder. I'd give him no satisfaction in seeing the way he tied me up in knots. He was clearly still hung up on Molly, his fiancée, and I couldn't compete with her. She would forever and always be the woman he lost. I had enough pride to know that I deserved better than that. I wouldn't be second best, not even for Ryder.

Crossing the bathroom floor with quick even strides, I opened the door and ground to a halt, almost smashing into the very man who was dominating my thoughts. Ryder was leaning against the wall, one hand in his pocket, the other rubbing across his five o' clock shadow. Sweet baby Jesus. All of my previous reasoning flew out the door as I was assaulted by all of his hotness.

"Dance with me." He offered his hand.

Wait, what? Just as I had made the decision to give the chase a rest, he was stepping in. Not to mention that I had asked him to dance before and still hadn't washed off the sting of that rejection. I decided to give him a taste of his own medicine.

"I shouldn't." I shrugged, tossing his own words back at him and walking right past him.

I felt a strong hand on my waist. He stopped me with ease, then spun me around to look down at me. I wasn't a tiny female, just average height with a slim build, but Ryder made me feel downright delicate with all of his power surrounding me.

"I wasn't asking." And there it was again, that sexual tension between Ryder and I. It was tangible.

I was just about to shake my head, but before I could he slowly lifted his other hand and gripped me gently behind my neck. Our eyes were locked in a stare that held more passion than I'd felt in my entire lousy sex life.

Some sort of fire took over, starting low in my belly and spreading like a forest fire that just had its first taste of fuel. I stood on my tiptoes, wanting to be closer, needing to feel our bodies pressed together. He'd held me at arm's length for so long, keeping it just enforcer and ash, but those walls were down. Something had shifted between us. I could feel his breath on my face. We were no more than an inch apart now. Ryder had to lower his head to reach my level, even when I was standing on my toes.

I hadn't actually been sure he was going to kiss me, but my worries were finally unfounded. His soft lips descended to press on mine. The first touch was gentle, barely the brush of our mouths together, but as I fell further into him, his breath hitched and his hands came around my waist. This movement brought our hips together, and just like that my body was plastered to his. He took control then, opening his mouth and deepening the kiss, demanding more, his teeth nipping at me as he sought entry between my lips. I could deny him nothing; the taste was intoxicating and I wanted more.

I moaned softly as our tongues slowly explored each other. God damn the boy could kiss. The gentle play started to ease as hormones took over. My body was humming now and I had the strangest urge to climb up onto Ryder. I wanted more. I wanted to be closer to him. As if he'd read my thoughts, he grabbed my butt and hoisted me up with one hand. My body knew what to do then, and as I wrapped my legs around him, crossing my ankles behind, this position felt like home. He turned around and pressed me back up against the wall, our mouths still locked, kissing me like I was the only woman in the world. Like he needed me to survive. Like I was everything.

"Ryder!" Kyle broke through my bliss. Ryder didn't falter, although he did pull those lips away from me as he turned to his best friend. Through my hazy lust vision, I noticed that the other enforcer looked stressed. His hair was even messier than usual.

"There's been a mass illegal outbreak and hostage situation involving the Quorum in Seattle. Helicopter is waiting." Kyle had to shout to be heard over the music. I was still fuzzy from the most amazing kiss of my life, but what he said sounded pretty darn serious.

Ryder looked down at me, regret and so many more things in those flashing silver eyes. "Charlie ... damn, I have to go." He lowered me gently to the ground. My feet had barely hit the floor before he was gone, Kyle close behind.

I exhaled a shaky breath, leaning against the wall and giving my legs a chance to regain some feeling. Ryder had kissed me ... and then run off in the line of duty. Well, it wasn't exactly how I'd imagined ending that kiss – was kind of hoping we'd make it back to my bedroom for a heavy make-out session, but ... I guess I had to take it.

I had planned on being kissed by a hot ash tonight, and there was no denying that was exactly what had happened.

NINE

The next three days were among the worst of my life.

Dear Men everywhere, the absolute worst thing in the world you can do is kiss a woman like you haven't kissed in years and then run off like your ass is on fire and don't contact her. Go screw yourself. With love, Charlie.

Jayden was allowing me to mope around, but I knew he was sick of my shit. Frankly, I was sick of my own shit too. I had all but convinced myself early on that night at karaoke that I was okay without Ryder, that I deserved better ... and then he kissed me – with a skill that should be banned, as it was most definitely some sort of weapon. That kiss had blown my previous pep talk straight out the window and I had done nothing since he left than bitch and whine, take phone calls, whine some more, jog, more whining, and think about that damn sexy man. Jayden had all but slapped me up the side of the head today and told me that Oliver had emailed him and the ash were due back tonight.

Yep, freakin' Jayden got an email and I got nothing. I was seriously going to kick Ryder in the teeth when he finally got back here.

It was time for my feeding, and I headed there at the pace of an elderly cripple. I just couldn't find the joy in bottled blood any longer. It was bland and cold. I was really starting to hate that I'd fed off a living being. It was too hard to go back. Everything felt too hard. Still, at least I now had the answer to what happened when an ash bit another ash. The blood wasn't as sustaining in the long term as bottled blood, which was probably why we generally didn't feed from each other. But with Ryder, that hadn't seemed to matter. It was perfect.

I finally dragged myself to floor eleven, striding past the ash on the desk and grabbing my usual bottles of blood. Slipping into my cubicle, I almost shrieked as a familiar blond head of hair sprang into my vision.

"Tess!" I forced myself not to bowl her over in my enthusiasm. This was not a scheduled visit but she must have known how badly I needed her. We were totally due some girl talk.

In my distracted state, it took me longer than usual to notice how glammed-up my best friend was. She had always dressed nicely. Her mother's family had more than enough money to indulge her sense of fashion, but this was a whole other level. Her icy blue dress was skin-tight and clearly designer. Its thin straps barely held her boobs in, and there were these gold drapings of chain crisscrossing over the backless part. Gold, which looked real. You could always tell that cheesy yellow from the true golden color of the real stuff. Real freakin' gold on her dress! Her boots were thigh-highs, and looked to be made from the skin of a seal or something, soft and rich. What the hell? This was Tess Couture Barbie.

We stared for a few more moments. I was trying to wrap my head around this new Tess. Even her makeup was different, heavy but tasteful, and her hair was tightly pulled against her head. Which she usually hated.

"You look different," I finally said, hoping she would start bouncing around in her usual manner. It hadn't really been that long since I'd seen her. What had changed?

Some of my icy fear dissipated as a smile crossed her lips; the ghost of my best friend was still there. "I've missed you, bitch." A trickle of relief followed, and I took the opportunity to cross the room and throw my arms around her.

"I've missed you too," I said, before pulling back from her. "What's up with all the Hollywood bling-bling? You going out after this? Paris fashion week?"

We sat then. I chugged into the first bottle of blood, which slightly eased the ache in my stomach.

"No, Blake owns a design house. He'd been helping me out. Styling me so I fit in more."

My face fell. It hit me then what this was all about. Blake wanted to ask permission to turn Tessa. He'd said so the last time I talked to him, and he was trying to slowly work her into Hive society before that. Very few humans were allowed to become vampires. Firstly, the human government took any forced infection seriously, and no one wanted scrutiny from them. And secondly, Hives across the world were very limited in space.

I wanted to lean forward, grab her hands, and start begging her to not be so stupid, to not throw her life away on a dude that she had just met. Blake seemed like a pretty good guy, but he was still a vampire. Just like me and Ryder were still ash. None of us could be trusted. None of us were human any longer, and I wasn't sure about the other two, but I'd have given anything to have my old life back. I missed my mom. I missed school. I missed the normalcy.

But there was no going back for me. It was too late. Tessa, on the other hand, she was choosing this and I wasn't sure I could sit back and let that happen. I wrenched the bottle from my fangs, throwing it into the trash. "I am begging you not to do this, Tessa. Think about your family. Think about everything you will be giving up. This is not the glamorous life you believe. And you will never be able to have kids."

My eyelashes fluttered for a moment as a heavy weight descended in my chest. "I can never have kids," I said with barely a whisper. "This is not a gift, it's a fucking curse."

And with those last words I tore out of the room and left my wide-eyed, slack-jawed friend sitting there. I was so all over the place. In all honesty, despite my words to Tessa, I didn't actually hate my life here that much. But it wasn't a choice I'd have made either. I wanted to scare her, make her question this thing with Blake. I wasn't sure it was enough, I knew how stubborn she was. Maybe I needed to pay a visit to Blake, or even Lucas. My previous sponsor was the head of the sixth house, and that was Blake's house.

Maybe he could have a word with him. I wasn't sure how much control the heads of the houses had over their members. The heads were the Quorum leaders of course, and as a group they were scary, but they didn't seem to do much individual day to day monitoring of anything. I had never even officially met the head of the fourth house, even though I was in that branch. Which led me to believe that they were always off doing other things. The rules of the Hive were basically enforced by Ryder and his men. Despite the fact that vampires thought of themselves as superior, they seemed to do jack all in regards to the heavy lifting.

I often wondered why they gave so much power to the very race which might one day band together and rise up against them. It hadn't happened yet, but one day the ash would revolt. The culling was barbaric, and I wasn't sure I could be in the Hive for the next one. I still, on occasion, had nightmares thinking of the men I'd killed.

I didn't know where Lucas was, but I figured the best place to start would be his penthouse. I practically ran my ass through the Hive, up the elevator, and out onto level fifty. I didn't pause before I reached his suite and started slamming my fist repeatedly against the white door.

"Lucas!" Patience was not my strongest suit right now. I was panicking, and this made me do stupid shit.

There was no answer and I could hear nothing on the other side. He wasn't here. Dammit! I'd have to come back later. I couldn't hang around now, I was due for my shift in the call center. At least the enforcers should be back. Maybe I'd work off some of this frustration by kicking the shit out of kiss-me-and-not-call-for-three-days Ryder. Yes, I decided, as I turned away from Lucas' suite, that sounded like a perfect plan.

THERE WERE two ash in the room when I entered ten minutes later, neither of them enforcers, both lowly shit-kickers like me. I so badly wanted to be an enforcer. It was unfair they were out there doing things and I was stuck here taking calls. Ninety percent of which were false alarms. Their shift was over, so they left without a word. I was still getting plenty of extra looks, and more than a few had approached me about spending some *quality* time with them, but these two were professional. They did their job and barely talked to me. Which was how I liked it.

I settled back into my padded, high-backed chair. For some reason, even though it was generally a two person shift, I was always in here alone. Or with one of the sexy six or the extended group of enforcers.

Speaking of, they should have been back by now. I swiveled in the chair, one eye on the door at all times. I'd like to think I wasn't so much acting like a crazy girlfriend as much as I was acting like a concerned friend. But, in reality I was dying to see Ryder. For so many reasons. But mostly to stare into those silver and black eyes for the first time since "the kiss" and see if the same heavy emotions still laced them. I needed to see if he had missed me too.

In my musing, I didn't hear the scuff of boots, and by the time my head shot up, Kyle was in the doorway. I jumped to my feet, taking the two steps across the room to stand right before him.

"Hey..." I sounded a little breathless, and knew I needed to try and find some cool again. I was officially screwed right now, and my feels were leaking all over the place. "How was the call out?"

Details on their operation were limited and had seemed a little sketchy. Oliver had told Jayden that the Hive in Seattle had had some sort of internal problem which required specialist treatment. And Ryder and his men were the best enforcers in America, so they'd had to step in. It just seemed awfully strange that no one else had heard of any mass craziness in other Hives. To take away all of our top enforcers, it should have been huge enough to make the gossip-vine light up. They'd left us virtually unprotected. But clearly I was just a worrier, because they were back now and nothing terrible had happened while they were gone.

"Hey, Charlie bear," Kyle said with a massive grin. He leaned forward and swept me into a hug. "Good to see you holding this place together while we were gone." I hadn't expected the show of affection from him. I think I had officially been accepted into the enforcer inner circle.

Yes!

I couldn't hold back the grin. Ryder's best friend was such a relaxed dude. The only time I'd seen him lose his cool was in regards to Ryder. Their history clearly had some pain buried deep down.

"It's been quiet here. What was the big deal in Seattle?"

Kyle, who was dressed in the usual black on black, patted me on the head as he strode in and dropped heavily into the chair I hadn't been using before. "Seattle was a pain in my ass. Their culling ash rioted and joined forces to hold the Quorum hostage. They killed their lead enforcer. Bloody mess. We're called in for anything to do with Quorum members. By the time we got there, it had died down a bit. Only one member was in any danger, and that was mild at best. We had to stay for a few days of the culling to make sure no trouble stirred up again, but it was all calm. Ryder and I barely slept. Spent nearly the entire time throwing ash bitches in their version of the pit."

He lifted his long legs and dropped heavy boots onto the bench, stretching back in his chair.

"We were supposed to be there for another day. Their Quorum had some sort of fancy-ass dinner for us, but Ryder was at the end of his patience with politics. He sent us back behind their backs, and stuck around just long enough to ream them a new one for wasting our time. He should be back tonight."

I sort of knew I wasn't hiding my interest in Ryder, even though I hadn't said anything specific. Kyle wasn't stupid, and he'd seen our heavy make-out session. I worked hard to conceal my disappointment that he wasn't back yet, but clearly failed at that task.

"All good, little unicorn. Our big bad leader will be back before you know it. He told me to tell you he says hello."

I tried to conceal the middle-school squeal that wanted to rip from my throat. Instead, I nodded.

THE REST of the day passed agonizingly slow. Oliver and Jayden were shacked up in the room, so after my shift I took off to the roof and spent the better part of an hour jogging my ass off. It didn't help with the frustration at all, and the fact that Lucas still wasn't home the five other times I checked that day didn't help either. Tessa could be in the middle of any shitty situation and I would never know, because for the first time in ages I had no emails from her. My little outburst had pretty much ensured she wouldn't be telling me much about her vampire excursions.

I had to stop her before she did something stupid, but of course the moment I needed Lucas, the white-trenched-coat vampire was nowhere to be found.

I trudged back to my apartment, grateful to find Jayden there alone, looking a whole lot relaxed. "Hey, ready for dinner?" he said as I stormed through the door.

"Yeah, just give me five minutes." I was starving, but definitely needed to shower off my run sweat.

I was done in about eight minutes, taking an extra second to choose my clothing and add a little makeup. I might be a tad pissed at Ryder, but I sure as shit wanted to look my best when we first saw each other. Three days and no email? Jerk ... even if he was busy working.

"Hot damn, baby, you could turn this gay ash's head any day of the week." Jayden whistled as he took in my skinny jeans, flat ankle boots, and skintight tank. It was one of those which was ripped in places and held together by these little scraps of lace. Everything was black, and I'd gone a little heavier on my eyes than normal. Not to mention leaving my hair down to hang in straight layers to mid-back.

I blew Jayden a kiss, crossing to link arms with him. We rolled out and made our way into the ash dining room. It was packed; we were late as usual, and as always the entire room basically paused for a second when we entered.

Jayden didn't sweat shit like that, simply dragging me across the room toward the enforcers' table. We had the privilege of sitting there. Not many were accepted into their little group, but the thing with Ryder and me, not to mention Jayden and Oliver, assured that we made the cut. The sexy six might need a new name. Exciting eight. Exotic eight ... I'd work on a name for us.

I paused as I counted only five heads there. Before the disappointment could bowl me over, I was distracted by the way they were leaning into each other, conversing too low to hear. Their tense faces sent trills of fear through me.

Something was wrong.

Jayden left me and took off for the long rows of food. As usual he was more than starving, and would soon be back with his Mount Everest size plate of food. I didn't follow. My appetite was now nonexistent as I took the last few stumbling steps to fall down into the spare chair beside Kyle. Five sets of black eyes locked on me, and even though each of the enforcers' looks were unique, right then they were all wearing the same expression.

"Just give it to me straight," I said, wasting no time on bullshit. "You all look like you're about to kill the next fucking person who glances sideways at you, so I know something has happened."

Kyle and Markus – the red-headed enforcer, looking surprisingly clean cut and handsome, having trimmed his bushy beard and man bun – exchanged a glance and I forced myself not to scream and stamp my foot. Just as I was about to jump up and start beating the shit out of them, even though they could wipe the floor with me every day and twice on Sunday, Markus answered.

His voice was gruff, the thickness of his accent making the growl worse. "Ryder was supposed to check in when he left, and then again when he landed. He should have been back at the compound thirty minutes ago."

Kyle picked up the conversation. "He did text me when he got to the airport. The private plane was ready to take off. He never checked in upon landing, and when I called the flight control, they said Ryder never showed. He didn't make the flight."

While they were talking, there was this strange ringing in my head, like a buzz or something. It was my panic, and it was distracting enough that it took me more than a few moments to wrap my head around what they were saying. Ryder was missing. Ryder who was the most badass ash in America. What the hell could have happened to him?

I forced the nausea down, and clenching both fists in front of me landed hard eyes on each and every single one of the boys. "Well, what the fuck are we waiting for? Let's go find out what happened to him!" I get all cursey when I'm scared or worried.

Kyle's lips thinned, and I realized he was forcing back a smile. He wasn't the only one either. The rest of them looked both amused and impressed. "It's dangerous, Charlie." Oliver's voice was low and smooth. "Not much could take down Ryder. We have no idea what we're walking into."

I was already on my feet. "Only one way to find out." I turned then, and without looking back or locking eyes with the many curious faces around us, I strode through the hall and out the door.

I didn't have to check, I could feel the boy's energy behind me, and I felt more than safe having them at my back. I knew I should have told Jayden what was up, he'd be pissed at us ditching him, but he'd be safer here at the Hive.

Kyle strode faster to fall in line beside me. "What's the plan?"

I gave it two seconds' thought. "Say we got an emergency call, drive out of here in the van, sirens blazing. Start driving to Seattle, asking questions wherever we stop. Interview the pilot, rough up the Seattle Hive. Do whatever we have to."

Kyle shook his head a few times, his eyes drooping down as his entire body tensed. "I should have stayed back with him," he said as we turned the corner and opened the door leading to the garage.

I shrugged. "I shouldn't have given my virginity to Seth Peters. Can't live life in the past." I tended to lean on inappropriate humor and sarcasm to avoid serious emotions and get through stressful times.

Oliver, Markus, and Jared all chuckled. Not Sam though, he was immune to all of Charlie's charm. As we reached the Humvee, I grabbed the keys and moved to open the driver's side door. Kyle placed a hand on the glass, barring me from opening it.

"Nice try. Get in back and hide." He pulled the keys from my hand as all of the guys piled in.

Dammit. Bossy-ass ash. Still, Ryder was gone and we were the only ones looking for him. I would obey for now because I didn't want them to waste any more time. I lay in the back and piled some thermal blankets over myself. The engine roared to life and then we were hauling ass. It was much rougher back here with no seatbelt. I felt one of the guys drop a heavy hand on my side, which definitely helped to keep me in place. A few minutes later Kyle called back to me.

"Okay, Charlie, you can sit up."

Whew! I sat up gasping for fresh air and took in the rigid postures of the five massive ash enforcers. I wasn't sure right then, but I thought it was Sam who had held me in place. Which was unexpected but nice from the reticent ash.

All of the boys looked tense and ready for anything. I forced myself to focus, my mind going through all of the places Ryder could be. If he had been taken by humans, he could be anywhere, but if he had been taken by our kind, his locations were limited.

A cell phone rang somewhere in the car. Kyle fumbled to get it out and glanced down.

"It's Ryder!" He put it on speaker. "Where are you?" His voice was sharp and tense.

"Having pepperoni pizza," Ryder said coolly, but he sounded out of breath and his voice was raspy.

What the actual fuck? If he was out having pizza, I was going to kill him myself. But I saw the color drain from Kyle's face through the rearview mirror, and all of the guys shared a look.

"Where at?" Kyle said casually.

"That place we went for my sixteenth birthday."

How long had Kyle and Ryder known each other and why were they speaking in code?

"Kyle, bring my lucky jacket. *Don't* leave it behind," Ryder insisted.

Kyle met my eyes through the rearview and nodded. "It's with me now." Then he hung up and tossed the phone out the open window.

"Phones," he barked, and everyone pulled out their phones and tossed them out the window. Oh my God. Five smartphones. That was three grand gone, just like that. I climbed over the back seat, my ass hitting Markus's pretty man bun, and shoved myself in between Kyle's driver seat and Oliver's shotgun.

"What the hell is going on?" I quipped. I didn't have a phone to toss out the window and I didn't know what had just happened.

Kyle gave it to me straight. "Pepperoni pizza is our code word for if some shit goes down and phones are tapped. Never had to use it. Ryder hates pepperoni, he would never eat it."

I shouldn't have let myself get distracted, but seriously, who hates pepperoni pizza? I needed to get to know more about this man, because pepperoni was right up there with bacon in my book. It might be a deal breaker if he didn't like bacon.

"So, we're going to a pizza place and the phones were tapped?"

Kyle took a hard left. "No, we're going to a fishing lake, and the phones were tapped, and you're the lucky jacket."

I smiled at that part. Ryder had a code word for me.

"And if the phones are tapped, we most likely have an inside mole," Markus offered.

Well ... shit. At least Ryder was safe. Silver lining. Not

to mention he'd cared enough to make sure they brought me along. That had to mean something.

AFTER ABOUT THIRTY minutes of tense atmosphere in the car, we pulled up to a private Lake in a fancy suburb of Portland.

"This is where he had his sixteenth birthday?" I looked around and saw one thing: money. Big houses, fancy cars, and a beautiful lake with a huge clubhouse overlooking it.

Kyle crept the SUV up to the farthest parking spot, encasing it in the darkness.

"The clubhouse, yeah. We were rich kids. Get over it."

Ouch. Sensitive subject. They should have tried being a not rich kid. I had my sixteenth birthday in a Chucky Cheese.

"How is it that you and Ryder both grew up in the same neighborhood and were both ash?" Seriously, what were the odds of that.

Kyle lifted his full lips into a smile, kind of creepy that grin. "Our mothers were best friends, rich girls with overindulgent families. It was the '60s, free love and all that shit. They both got knocked up by vampires at the same party. This was right around the time that groups were lobbying for equal rights. They were supposed to stop all the testing on our kind, and it was sort of the in thing to try and have an ash baby."

I vaguely remember Tessa telling me that the '60s had

been the biggest time for ash in all of vampire history. So Ryder and Kyle were over fifty years old. Of course, they didn't look a day out of their early twenties. Ash aged so slowly, it was like twenty human years to one ash. We lived a very long time.

"Ryder and I have been buds since birth, and there is no better human or ash in the world. We are lucky to have him." Kyle finished his little speech, sinking back to wait out the rest of the time in silence. Which was okay by me, I had plenty of thoughts to keep me occupied. Especially about the enigmatic and quite mysterious head enforcer.

We sat in the van for what felt like forever. After a certain amount of time I was no longer able to be patient. I was seriously about five seconds from losing my shit when, finally, I saw a familiar shadow hobble out of some tall, thick reeds. My heart started to beat double-time and I had to stop myself from rushing out of the vehicle and throwing myself at him. Ryder was looking a little worse for wear, limping and holding his right shoulder.

Kyle burst out of the SUV, gun drawn, and I decided that I was definitely following him. Thank God it was dark out, 'cause Kyle and I looked shady as shit, especially with his gun waving around.

I forced myself to stop a few feet from Ryder. I wanted to hug him but wasn't sure if I should. It felt a little weird between us, so much unresolved after that kiss. Before I could mentally break apart our relationship any further, Kyle swooped in, his long arms loping across Ryder's shoulders, taking his weight.

"Charlie's not safe," he mumbled as we walked back to the van.

Kyle and I exchanged a glance. Ryder was barely audible. He was in worse shape than I'd thought. What had happened? What did this have to do with me and the fact that he knew something about me "not being safe?" When we reached the car, Markus and Oliver piled into the far back. I squeezed in between Jared and Sam, allowing Ryder to take shotgun. The injured ash took the white gauze which Sam had pulled from the med kit for him and wiped away some of the red on his forehead, the cuts looked to have already healed. In the close confines of the car, his copper blood hit me and I was instantly reminded of drinking from him.

Trying my best to ignore this, I leaned forward, peeking through the middle seat. "What happened? Pilot said you didn't make your flight? How are you here?" Seattle was a three-hour drive from Portland – he had gotten back somehow.

Ryder barked out a laugh. "Is that what he told you? I made the flight. Bastard set me up. I got jumped by some enforcers from another Hive when the pilot landed in this field just outside of Portland. Said we needed to pick up another person. I didn't trust him, so I was ready."

Holy shit. Ryder fought a group of enforcers and got away alive?

Ryder met my eyes. "Charlie, they had your original blood work. They know that you're not showing normal ash blood and that you're a direct descendant of the fourth house. They're after you. They were trying to recruit me to their cause. Offered me money and plenty of other incentives to turn against you."

Bastards. Guess I was lucky Ryder had an honor code. I had never doubted that he was a good guy deep down, even if he had electrocuted me.

"How much money did they offer?" Kyle flashed his pearly whites at me. "Always good to know the going rate for Charlie's life."

I flipped him off and his grin widened further.

"Three mil," Ryder said.

My mouth actually dropped open. "Like ... three million dollars? American dollars?"

Ryder gave a short nod of confirmation. Well, what do you know. For that ridiculous amount of money I should turn myself in.

The CB radio on the dash blared to life and all of the men stopped their joking and focused.

"This is command. Bring in all enforcers. The Hive has been infiltrated. I repeat, the Hive has been infiltrated. ETA on a secure channel." It was Jason's voice, a guy I knew and worked with. Sirens could be heard in the background.

My blood chilled. "Jayden!" Oh shit. I'd left my best friend behind. Oliver made a noise then and I spun around to lock him in my gaze. I knew I wasn't the only one panicking about this attack.

Ryder grabbed Kyle's hand mid-air as he was about to respond. "Five ash enforcers attacked me. Four of them were regular, run of the mill, but the fifth one, the one who offered me the money, had a fighting style I recognized. We were evenly matched, and before I could hurt him too bad he got away."

The two shared a look that sent chills up my spine. "Don't say it." Kyle was looking as pale as Markus right now. And the Scottish ash was definitely on the fair side.

Ryder didn't hesitate. "I think it's the Sanctum."

"The who?" I didn't like being out of the loop. The entire car clearly knew who they were. The collective curses had told me more than enough. If they were worried, then I had no doubt that the Sanctum was not to be effed with.

Ryder was silent for a moment. "The Sanctum are an elite group of ash mercenaries. They offer sanctuary to any ash who does not wish to live within the Hive. But there is a price to pay. They have no morals, no loyalties, and no end goal. They are highly trained killers who do what they do for money. Glorified hit men. I think a price has been put on your head."

The air whooshed out of me. "How do you know all this?"

The entire car was silent. Ryder looked out the car window as if reminiscing. His voice was hollow. "Because I was recruited by them. I was lost for a few years after I changed, and they offered me a way to focus through the pain. I trained and worked with them on a few jobs until I realized we were killing innocents. Then I left."

Holy shit. That's how Ryder had become so deadly.

Something told me that if these Sanctum had trained Ryder, they were not people I wanted to meet.

"You're sure it's them?" Kyle asked.

Ryder nodded. "I didn't recognize him, but his fighting style screamed Sanctum. He was there to see if I was susceptible to turning, to join them again. And if that failed, to put me out of commission before attacking the Hive. Should have sent two of them if they wanted to make sure of that."

I wanted to roll my eyes, but he was really just stating a fact. They probably should have sent three.

Ryder continued: "I'm going to say, judging on that call from the control room, they decided not to wait and went looking for Charlie. Of course she's not there, she's here with us, so they have made their presence known. They're drawing her back."

A searing flood of panic filled every part of my jittery brain. This was worse than I'd thought. Jayden wasn't just in the Hive while it was under attack, he was in there with highly trained mercenaries, who were after me and probably knew he was my best friend and roommate.

"Step on the gas, Kyle! Jayden is in there with those psychos!" I screamed. God, less talk and more driving to save my best friend.

Ryder turned and met my gaze. "Did you not listen to what I just said. The Sanctum won't be seen unless they want to, won't be heard unless they want to. They want us to know they're there. They're waiting for you to do something stupid like run straight into their trap. You're not going back. I won't risk you."

I had to keep myself from full on freaking out on everyone in this car. No way in hell was I leaving Jayden. "I don't care. My best friend is still stuck in there and I am going back."

All six of the big, scary-ass men groaned then. What? Surely they hadn't expected I would do this the easy way.

"We should just knock her out and stash her somewhere so we can deal with this."

I almost fell over as I realized that that had come from Sam. He had finally decided to talk, his voice low and gravely, with a faint accent. Russian or something.

"Seriously?" I threw my hands up as frustration rocked me. "You never speak, and the first time you do, it's to tell everyone to knock me out. If any of you boneheads lay a single finger on me I am going to make you pay. Every single one of you will have hair remover in your shampoo, and wax strips stuck to your ass." I jabbed a finger at Markus. "Even you, pretty boy man-bun. You will take me with you now, and together we will save Jayden and our Hive."

Some of the tension left the car then. Jared's eyes were flat-out laughing as he locked in on me, his blond curls messy as he ran a hand through them. "She's got us there, mates, I certainly don't want no hair grabber stuck on my arse."

Ryder got very close to me then, his eyes boring into mine, his scent enveloping me and pretty much knocking me over. "You will stay with me the entire time, Charlie. If you can't promise that, I won't take you back. We go in there knowing that they plan on taking or killing you. You have to understand this before you agree."

I swallowed, trying to remember how to speak. What was my name again? I had to blink a few times to clear my hazy thoughts. "I promise to stay close to one of the enforcers, but you also have to promise me that we will make Jayden a priority. He is my family."

Ryder and I remained eye-locked for some endless moments, his eyes dropping for a second to stare at my lips. I wondered if he was remembering our kiss too. Finally he gave me a head nod and I knew it was settled.

Kyle threw me a grin. "We're with you all the way. Your family is our family, Charlie. You should know that by now."

That gave me all the warm feels. It had always been just me, my mom, and Tessa. But now my family was so much larger. Maybe becoming an ash wasn't the curse I had always believed. Maybe it was so much more.

IT WAS pitch black by the time we reached the outer limits of Portland. The drive had been silent. Ryder had downed a few bottles of blood before crashing out and sleeping most of the way.

"How did he managed to fight off a group of ash enforcers?" I finally asked Kyle as the familiar outskirts came into view. "And one of these Sanctum mercenaries. Is he a normal ash?"

I heard more than one snort from the crew around me, and I guess that was a pretty stupid thing to say. We all knew Ryder was beyond a normal ash by a million, but why? Was it just because he was so close to an Original? I mean, why was he so kickass and awesome and I was just ... me? I was directly sired by an Original ... or something. It was so confusing, because my results said I wasn't really an ash. I probably sucked as an Original descendant because I was not one at all. The blood work was inconclusive, which basically meant they didn't have a fucking clue what I was.

Ryder answered my earlier question. "I had more than a little motivation." He shifted in his seat, stretching out a little, waking up. "They mentioned that you were the target, offered me the bribe, and I kind of lost it."

"What happened to the rest of them?" Oliver asked. His tanned skin was looking even darker than usual.

"Dead," Ryder said, his tone flat.

I actually shivered then, and it was in that moment I realized that Ryder was really scary. I mean, I'd always known he was scary, but I'd never felt the force of that emotion around him before.

The CB radio blared to life: "Core Enforcer team, come in! What's your status? We have been infiltrated by suspected rival Hive. Although no one is in sight. Quorum is going into lockdown."

The enforcers exchanged a glance, but none of them

picked up the radio. They believed that not only was there a mercenary group hired to find me, but a traitor in our Hive. They would not give any heads-up at this stage.

Kyle spoke this time. "The Sanctum are very good at making Hives think they are under attack from countless assailants. They are fast, deadly, and kill quickly."

My eyes darted around as I tried to take in both of the males in the front. "So we don't know if the attack is just the Sanctum, or if there is another Hive involved as well?" All this double-talk was confusing.

Ryder's lips curled up a little. "Doesn't matter. Either way, our goals remain the same – rescue Jayden, get him and Charlie to safety, and then go back for the Quorum. That's the order of business."

I saw more than one head nod, and I was okay with that. I wasn't going to be much use against elite mercenaries. The gates of the Hive came into view and we were all distracted. Driving in at night like this always gave me the creeps. It reminded me of that night a year ago – when everything changed.

Remembering was easier now, although it still churned my stomach and sat bile at the base of my throat. I'd been out partying with Tessa, and we'd been separated on the street. Before I knew what had happened, I was grabbed by two ash. One of them punched me in the face, and by the time I managed to pull myself together I was in behind the security fence.

They were like rabid dogs, pawing at me, trying to tear my clothes away, and I had been helpless, unable to fight, unable to even scream for help as one of them had his hand firmly clamped over my mouth.

I cut off the thoughts. I didn't dwell on that night. I'd been saved. The two ash had been yanked off me by some guy, who then ripped their heads right from their shoulders. I didn't know who had saved me, I only got brief glimpses of him, but he sort of reminded me of a blond Viking, with braids and feathers and shit in his hair. Probably I'd imagined that part or something, because I'd never seen a single member of the Hive who came close to his description.

My biggest regret was that I hadn't stuck around and thanked him. All I'd thought of was escape. I dragged myself out of the compound and called my mom to get me. I'd been beat up, scratched, bruised, and bloodied. But I had not been raped or fed on, and I counted myself lucky. Other human women were not usually so lucky when it came to the ash.

That was why I'd hated ash, right up until the moment I became one. Now I realized it was wrong to hate an entire race just because of a few bad souls. Just like with humans, there were good and bad in the Hive. I could see that now, and I was more than ready to protect my newfound home and family. I was prepared to embrace my ash side and kick some ass.

TEN

Ryder was grim-faced as he stared out of his window, seeming to be lost in thought. Kyle pulled the Humvee in behind some trees, on the outer perimeter of the Hive fence. Blue lights and sirens were flickering around, casting everyone's faces in a ghostly shadowing. Our Hive was in lockdown, standard operating procedure in these situations. Ryder leaned down and pulled a duffle bag out from under the seat. He rifled through for a moment, retrieving two pairs of hand suction cups. I recognized them from the training room.

"Sam, Markus, you scale the outside windows and hang outside of Charlie's apartment."

He tossed them the suction cups. Holy shit, like seriously? They were going to scale the thirty-three floors to my apartment with only a suction cup to keep them from falling? Before I could express both my worry and incredulity of this, the boys had already slipped from the

Humvee and taken off into the dark of night. I glimpsed them scaling the high razor wire wall like it was no big deal. Then they were gone.

Ryder looked at Kyle. "You and Jared create a big-ass distraction. Drive the Humvee into the lobby for all I care, just make sure all eyes and cameras are on you."

"No worries, mate." The surfer dude Aussie looked completely relaxed, like he'd just agreed to ride some gnarly waves, not crash his car into a building.

Ryder then turned to Oliver and I. "Oliver, you're with me and Charlie. We'll head to her apartment, where I'm almost certain the Sanctum will be waiting for us, with Jayden as a hostage."

Oliver clenched his teeth and nodded. My stomach dropped. No, no, no, no! Jayden better be okay, or mercenaries or not I was killing myself some ash tonight.

"I'm coming with you?" I hadn't expected him to allow that so easily.

Ryder's face was scary warrior right now. I got legit chills. "You, Charlie, are my shadow. Where I walk, you walk. If I tell you to get down, you get down. If I am not satisfied that you are listening to me, I will knock you out and stuff you in a closet. Do you understand?"

Damn. Ryder didn't fuck around. "Glue myself to your ass – got it!"

He cracked a hint of a smile then and handed me a sleek black pistol. "I'm told you know how to use one of these." He glared at Kyle, who tried to hide a smirk. No guns were used in the culling, but subduing the ash on that call last week hadn't been the first time I'd fired a gun. After my attack I took defense classes, and right now the cool weight of it in my hand was oddly comforting.

Ryder took a deep breath, rolling his head side to side, "Oliver, if after we get in the apartment I say to get Jayden and Charlie out of there..."

Oliver nodded. "I get them out."

Ryder seemed satisfied. "Let's do this." He picked up the CB radio. It was time to let them know we were coming in. Of course, they didn't know that most of us wouldn't be coming in the front door. "Core enforcer team inbound, ETA sixty seconds."

Jason's voice returned immediately: "Thank God. Three men breeched security, killed ten of ours, and now can't be found."

Shit. Three mercenaries crawling around my home? I would never sleep again.

"We'll take care of it," Ryder radioed back, and looked at all of us. "Happy hunting."

Kyle grinned. "You know that CB isn't secure from the Sanctum."

Ryder grinned back. "I know."

His boots slammed down on the asphalt, and Oliver and I followed. Thank God I decided to wear my flat boots tonight. Tires screeched as Kyle peeled out in the Humvee with Jared. They were our distraction. In seconds we were at the chain-link fence. Once we crossed it we'd be right outside the huge laundry room, and our best way in undetected.

I groaned as I looked at the tall fence with razor wire at the top. "Why don't we go in through the front door?"

Ryder gave me a look from the corner of his eye. "Because of Manuel." I raised an eyebrow, and lucky for him he continued his explanation. "The Sanctum's sniper. Come on. Enough talk."

He jumped up and began climbing the fence. Oliver and I followed. Shit, this was harder than it looked. My fingers were cutting into the wire and the holes weren't big enough for my feet. The cold wasn't helping at all, but at least there was no snow or rain to dampen the journey. The boys were smoother than me, but they had gloves on and I didn't. Halfway up, I winced. My fingers looked like they were turning purple.

Ryder looked down at me. "What's wrong?"

I shook my head, "Nothing." I went to reach that next section of fence when my fingers slipped. Thankfully, I caught myself at the last second. The plunge to the ground would not have been pleasant.

Near the top, Ryder grabbed a chunk of the barbed fence and pulled himself over. He reached down to help me over the last part. His strength easily hoisted me up, and I was just swinging my leg over, my butt close to his face, when I slipped again, and we both almost fell off the side. I was about to recover my position when a snapping sound drew my attention. Ryder knocked me down again, the barbs cutting into my body, and I realized what it had been. A bullet. Which had scraped right between us, only missing because I'd slipped at that last second.

Ryder wasted no time then. His huge hand basically lifted me up and hoisted me off the fence. "Soft landing and roll, Charlie!" he shouted.

I flailed for the entire fifteen-foot drop but was proud that I didn't scream. I braced for the jolt as my legs slammed on the ground and sharp pain shot up my shins. Apparently the soft landing part had completely passed me by.

Soft landing and roll? Was this man for reals?

I felt Ryder slam down behind me. Oliver was there too. The three of us took off running in a zigzag, more bullets raining around us, but we were moving too fast for them to track us. We made it into the side entrance, and using Ryder's ID badge were inside in seconds. We were on target too, right near the laundry chutes. I scanned Ryder quickly. He seemed to be unhurt, then I turned to Oliver. *Holy shit.* The enforcer was holding his right shoulder, which was bleeding freely. I wasn't sure if he'd hurt himself on the fence or if he'd been hit.

"Oliver," I said, reaching out for him.

He brushed me off. "I'm fine. Jayden is the priority."

I hesitated for a moment, before nodding. Neither of us would worry about injuries until Jayden was safe.

Ryder moved into my personal space then. "They aren't here to kill you, Charlie. Manuel never misses. He was aiming to hurt you, not kill. They intend to capture you alive."

And I'd thought the sniper had missed because of our

awesome dodging skills. Wait? Take me alive? I would much rather they wanted to kill me.

"This changes the plan slightly. But no matter what happens in there, you stay close to me. The boys can handle the Sanctum. They made a mistake when they brought only three. I know one will be down in the lobby investigating Jared and Kyle. So that leaves two for us, plus the sniper."

Ah, so even though the Hive thought there were three, Ryder knew there were at least four of them...

Ryder hunched over and crept silently down the hall to the stairwell. I followed his movements to a T. I had no doubt that if anyone could keep me alive in a dangerous situation, it would be Ryder. He drew his weapon and then quietly opened the stairwell door, he and Oliver taking a side each, heads craning around first before their bodies followed. They continued moving, looking left and right. Ryder put a finger to his lips to indicate complete quiet for the rest of the trip. We all padded like cats up the thirty-three floors to the apartment I shared with Jayden. It was a very long-ass trip, and I wanted to complain like a mofo, but kept quiet. No other ash or vampire crossed our path. The Hive was on lockdown, which was a good thing as I was jumpy and would probably shoot anybody who appeared.

We finally reached my floor. Ryder took point, and was just about to hit the handle when I felt a slight shift in the air. This was my only indication that something was above us, and then a black shadow pretty much fell from the sky. My finger sort of did a spasm, and sure enough I managed to shoot out the light above us. Great, not only could I have killed someone, but I also plunged everything into darkness.

This didn't seem to bother Ryder. He managed in one movement to spin, block the masked man's outstretched arm, and step in front of me in a protective stance. My ash sight was advanced enough to see a gun fly off and clatter against the wall, but I couldn't tell who it had come from. It didn't fire at least. I backed up to the wall and stood there silently, my own weapon still grasped in my sweaty hand. I couldn't use it. It was too dark and I wouldn't risk hitting one of my guys.

Oliver moved in to help Ryder, swift and silent even with his injury. He kicked out, cracking the guy in the back. The black-clad man – legit dressed like a ninja, face mask and all – had been busy keeping Ryder from breaking his limbs and hadn't seen Oliver. The ninja dropped to the ground now, and on the way managed to kick out his leg and push Oliver down the flight of stairs.

Before I could dive down the steps to see if my friend was okay, the ninja popped up and pivoted himself to the left. He practically flew across the stairwell in my direction. I started to lift my gun, which had fallen uselessly to my side, but instinctively knew I was going to be too slow. This guy moved like a shadow, so fast he almost looked blurry. Just as his hands landed on my throat, and I was tightening my finger on the trigger – I didn't even care if I only managed to shoot his nuts off, that would certainly slow him down – Ryder leapt out of the shadows, moving in the same blurry way, cracking the ninja straight in the temple. As the Sanctum guy stumbled, Ryder whipped up his weapon and pressed the barrel to the back of the ninja's head.

It was like time stopped. I could see Ryder's hesitation. He wasn't a cold-hearted killer. And for all he knew this Sanctum ninja was very possibly an old friend of his.

"Call off this job and I will let you walk," Ryder said, his voice clipped.

I could see the ninja breathing deeply. "She's worth more than any job we've had, and you were always too weak to be one of us." The ninja folded himself over, doing a front flip, his feet kicking Ryder in the stomach, knocking him back. The ninja didn't take time to fight again. He jumped up high and spun over the side of the railing, down the stairs and out of sight.

I didn't hesitate then to scramble down the steps to Oliver. My breath came a little easier when I saw the Latino enforcer gaining consciousness. He groaned. I almost tripped over the final few stairs – he'd fallen down a set of ten – and skidded to his side.

His eye fluttered a few times before focusing on me. "I'm fine. Get Jayden!" He was all business, and I knew he would never forgive me if I didn't leave him in this stairwell right now. Of course, if anything happened to Oliver, Jayden probably wouldn't forgive me either.

I leaned down and kissed him on the cheek. "Stay

hidden. Do not get yourself killed. We will rescue Jayden and come back for you."

He propped himself up. "I'm going to try and make it to the other guys. They'll drop me at the medical ward. I just need some blood and I'll be fine."

He didn't look fine. His arm was bleeding pretty badly again, and bones were definitely broken in his hand. I wondered why he wasn't going to the feeding area for blood. Probably it was in lockdown too.

I felt heat at my back. Ryder was standing protectively over both of us. "Get some extra blood. We will probably need it. Meet us back at the Humvee."

Oliver gave his leader a nod, and something passed between them. The sexy six were family, and none of this situation was easy on any of them. Especially the splitting up part.

Ryder reached down then, and before I could say anything he stashed a gun into the side of my boot. I recognized it as the one from the ninja. I didn't question him – he would have a reason and I would be okay with that reason.

He started to move then, his gun on display. I picked up my original weapon from where it had dropped. I needed to start training again. Guns started to feel scary and odd when you didn't have regular contact with them.

No one jumped us this time. The door silently opened, and my eyes remained glued on the broad shoulders in front of me. I didn't question, I just followed him down the hall. My apartment door was unlocked, but

Ryder kicked it open hard, like it was no more than a piece of paper, and it banged against the wall.

I couldn't see anything at first. Ryder went in front, gun drawn and his scary face in play. He blocked my sight for about eight seconds, but the moment I could see around him my blood did this strange thing where it boiled and froze all at the same time. Jayden was tied to a chair, an unmasked mercenary standing behind him. He was not particularly tall or broad, and had no real defining features. He was sort of bland in a mousy brown-haired way. But his eyes, they were scary – ash black, literally no silver – and they looked flat … dead. This was not a good dude.

As I focused in on my best friend, I could see that Jayden looked a little drowsy, like they'd either hit him hard enough to stun or tranqued him. Boring dude had a gun trained on the back of Jayden's head, his hand steady, not even the slightest shake, like he could stand there for hours in the same position. The window behind him was open and I wondered if Sam and Markus were there waiting. Why would the Sanctum have that window open? Was that how he'd gotten inside?

"Ryder…" His voice was as bland as his appearance. It was so odd, but I felt like I could forget everything about this guy the moment he was gone. Which was probably the appeal. Except his dead eyes, they were seared into my brain.

He continued: "So nice of you to bring the target."

Ryder was about two feet inside the apartment. I was

right up in his business, because I knew he would freak if I didn't attach myself to him. Of course that didn't stop me from looking up and around more than once. I was pretty sure there were no other Sanctum members in here, but you could never be too sure.

"Laz, I was kind of hoping I wouldn't see your ugly face again." Ryder sounded calm, but I could feel his tension.

Laz's expression finally morphed into something resembling an expression, sort of a sneer or a shrug. Hard to tell. "You know the drill, you've done this plenty of times before. Drop your weapons on the floor, and if you haven't handed over the target within ten seconds, I shoot the friend."

My stomach dropped as I saw fear flash in Jayden's eyes. Ryder was smooth as he dropped his weapon, then took mine from me and tossed it on the ground also. The heavy weight was still in my boot, and I was relieved to think we still had that backup.

"Kick them toward me," the Sanctum mercenary said.

"I'll pay you double to call off the job," Ryder said as he slid both guns across the tiles. They bumped near Jayden's bound feet.

Laz looked a little surprised. "It's not like golden-child Ryder to give a shit about a girl. Looks like this one is special to you in more ways than one. I might enjoy her before I hand her over."

Not happening, asshole.

Then Laz focused fully on Ryder. "We both know you

can't afford it. This target is worth almost my entire year, and I *will* be bringing her in. The people who want her, they are willing to pay anything. She's more important than you think."

There I went again, being the all-important freakin' unicorn. I would be okay with just being a regular horse right now. Unicorn was overrated.

Ryder grinned then, and it was sort of scary and sexy at the same time. "I know her exact worth. And they will never get their hands on her."

Laz pressed the gun harder against Jayden. My friend's head snapped forward from the impact. "Say goodbye to your friend," he said.

"No," I screamed, and right then I didn't care about Ryder's previous orders, I was handing myself over. If Jayden died because of me, I might as well be dead. I would never be able to live with myself. I shoved Ryder, who was not ready for it and stumbled. This gave me an opening, but before I could step out, Sam flew through the window. He held a gun in each hand and was shooting before he even landed. I felt a hot weight on my leg, and glanced down to find Ryder's hand capturing my ankle, yanking me down beside him.

"Jayden!" I screamed again as bullets flew. My best friend had better not get hurt or heads would fucking roll!

I heard grunting, and I was able to flip over and see that Jayden's chair had been knocked forward. *Thank God.* He seemed fine and was squirming to break free. The bullets stopped as Laz and Sam crashed into each other and started fighting. Laz seemed to favor grappling. He immediately brought the large enforcer down, but Sam recovered instantly. He was quick, and managed to flip Laz over and crack him twice with his elbow.

I was distracted as Ryder silently rose and crossed the room, moving in to help his teammate. Just before he reached them, though, another dark shadow flew in through the window. I expected it to be Markus, but the fully black-clad figure didn't look like the Scottish enforcer. It was one of the Sanctum. He landed on Ryder, the two of them trading blows. I started to drag myself across to Jayden. If I freed him, we could escape together. I'd come back for Ryder as soon as my friend was safe.

I gasped as Laz gained the upper hand on Sam. He pulled a knife from within his black fatigues and stabbed him a few times in the gut. Ryder's eyes practically glowed then, and with a snarl he locked his Sanctum under his arm and with the slightest twist snapped his neck. But he didn't stop there, continuing to twist until the head was completely removed from the body. Blood spurted everywhere, slowing to a drizzle in seconds. Ash bled a lot less than humans. But seriously, *what?* What sort of strength would anyone have to possess to be able to literally tear a head from a person? It was inconceivable.

Ryder launched himself at Laz, knocking him off Sam. Laz pushed Ryder and took off then, heading toward the open window, and then he ... *jumped.* I stumbled up and ran to the open window with Ryder hot on my heels. We got there in time to see Laz falling rapidly, right before he pulled a cord and a wingsuit flipped out from his black outfit, like a base jumper.

I gave a little shriek as Markus popped his head up from outside the window, hanging by the suction cups. He grinned. "Sorry, was a little tied up with the sniper. He jumped with his boss." I noticed then the second wingsuit zooming out across the Hive grounds. "But I can head after them if you want." His eyes flicked to Ryder.

Ryder shook his head. "No, you'll never catch them. They will be gone before you even hit the ground.

"Shit, so they all just get away?" I asked, frustrated. "Well, except for dead guy..." Who I guessed was the ninja-clad dude from the stairwell. Since he had thrown Oliver down the stairs, I couldn't dredge up much sadness for him.

Ryder's hands were clenched on the window sill, but he finally turned to face me. "They'll be back. This was just a test run. They hoped for an easy mark with me out of commission. Next time they'll come in force."

Great, awesome news to end this shit day.

"Not to interrupt your little powwow here, but can I get some goddamn help? Where's my man?" Jayden had loosened his gag, and was looking pissed from his position on the floor.

Whoops, I'd never gotten around to freeing him.

I scrambled to untie his bindings, and in that same moment Oliver and Kyle appeared in the doorway. Oliver was holding about eight bottles of blood and was looking a lot better.

"I thought I said meet at the vehicle." Ryder didn't sound that pissed.

Oliver ignored him; his sole focus was on Jayden. My fingers fumbled a few times with the thick ropes, and before I could loosen them Oliver stepped in and softly moved me so he could take over. His eyes were dancing with silver; he looked murderous, but his hands were gentle as he cut away the binds.

"Did he hurt you?" Oliver ground out when Jayden was finally free. The enforcer reached down and hauled his man to his feet.

Jayden's muscular arms trembled as he launched himself at Oliver. "Yes, he had god awful taste in music and his breath reeked. It was awful."

This was why we were best friends – we both had terrible comedic timing.

Still, it worked to break the tension. Even Oliver's expression lightened. Ahhh Jayden, the world would truly be a dark place without you. I couldn't stop myself then from stepping into them, joining Oliver and Jayden for a group hug. Strong arms surrounded me, and I was so relieved to know that no one had been hurt badly today. My family was safe for now. We had been lucky. But I hadn't forgotten what Ryder said. They'd be back, and soon. Would we be so lucky the next time?

Ryder stood apart from us, his jaw rigid enough that he was looking quite statue-like. He was making it very clear that he was in no mood to celebrate. His worries would not ease tonight. In the depths of his silver eyes swirled a windstorm of emotions. The worst, though, was the coldness there. This situation had done something to him ... to us. I wasn't sure what, but it didn't feel good. I felt him going distant again, putting up the walls.

Great. Looked like we were back to the old days, treating me like no more than number forty-six in the ash culling members.

ELEVEN

Ryder inserted the code into the alarm system, which halted the lights and blaring sirens. It took two of them – Markus and Kyle – to use fingerprint and retinal scanning before the Quorum suites security gates were lifted. The elevators had been halted, and the entire Hive sectioned off during the breach. I was not surprised, but the level of security in the building was impressive. Of course, now the mercenaries knew about all of that – they had a general layout, they knew procedure – they would not make the same mistakes next time.

I was sitting in the control room, Markus stretched out on one side of me and Sam on the other. The dark-haired enforcer had gone back to being silent and deadly, not speaking to me, but his presence was as comforting as Markus', who chatted away in his Scottish tones.

"I just about lost my grip when the car crashed into the building. It drew away the sniper immediately. He dashed in to make sure it wasn't his men. That gave Sam and I enough time to get into position by the window."

Turned out the sniper had been in the window next to our apartment. He would have taken out the boys if it wasn't for the few distractions we had set up. Jayden had thought it was awesome they had gotten to smash up the main level. Of course, that was before Ryder sent him and Kyle back there to start repairing it, along with the rest of the enforcer group. Even though there were only six in the core group, there were dozens in the main enforcer team. Ten of their men had lost their lives, and I knew the Quorum was preparing the burial now. Ash didn't get quite the same sendoff as the vamps, but they still had a ceremony.

I had not seen Ryder since those moments in my apartment. He was everywhere at once, dealing with everything, and—

"He's calling in favors, you know." Markus stopped randomly chatting, changing subjects to the one I was most interested in. "Ryder. Using his contacts to make sure the Sanctum don't come for you again, finding out who hired them for the job in the first place."

I shook my head, my arms automatically wrapping around myself as a comfort. "I don't understand. I know I'm unusual. I know I'm apparently descended directly from an Original, but besides a little levitation one time, I've done nothing else. Why would they go to all of this trouble? Three million dollars is a lot of money. It doesn't make sense. What do they want from me?"

Sam shifted. He was monitoring some security footage, going back through the mercenaries' initial entrance. His job was to try and figure out how the security was so easily breached, how ten men were killed before the lockdown was initiated. His eyes flicked across to me once or twice, but he didn't speculate with Markus and me.

The Scottish enforcer rested his massive feet on the desk, leaning back in his favorite position. "I don't know, lass, but whatever happens, we have your back. Ain't no one stealing our unicorn on our watch."

I wanted to punch and hug him at the same time. Our unicorn. They were so arrogant. But they were my family now, and I kind of like that they claimed me as theirs.

"I should check on Jayden," I mused, unwrapping my arms and placing them on the cool metal desk. "He was still shaken up, and I don't want him to be alone stressing about how close he came to dying."

Sam stopped me as I got to my feet; a single hand on my forearm did the trick. "Oliver is with him."

That was all he said, before releasing me and going back to his footage. I had to shake my head a few times. His intensity was a little disconcerting, but I was starting to see the many layers to the mostly silent enforcer.

A noise in the doorway had all three of us swinging about to find Lucas perched in the entrance, his white trench coat billowing out around him. He looked tired. The last twelve hours had been stressful for everyone in the Hive.

"Can I talk with you, Charlene?" His voice was low, and sort of raspy.

I jumped up, and with a last wink for Markus, took off toward Lucas. I needed to talk with him too. I still hadn't asked him to step in with Tessa and Blake. I hoped nothing had gone too far with those two yet. I had to save her.

Lucas and I walked side by side through the hall, ending up on the cafeteria level, which was deserted at the moment, hundreds of bench seats spread out, letting us see the true size of the space. It kind of blew my mind to think that every mealtime these tables were all full. The Hive really was too small for the growing number of ash. Each culling, fewer and fewer were going to be allowed to survive. In the next few years, being an ash would pretty much be a death sentence. Not for the vampires though – every single one of those assholes were welcome.

I pushed down my bitterness and focused on Lucas across from me. We were seated near the entrance, the space around us cool and quiet.

"I'm so glad you're okay." He reached out and took my hand, his grip comforting. "I was very angry about being locked in with the Quorum, especially when my people and you were out there unprotected. But when a head of a house dies, the entire line is weakened. It happens time to time but not a lot. It is to be avoided at all costs, so they always lock us in the secure chambers during conflict."

I returned his squeeze. "All good, Lucas. We weren't even here when the initial infiltration happened." I told him bits and pieces about our theories – why the Sanctum had been hired, how they'd tried to take out Ryder first. I kept a lot of information secret though. There was a mole somewhere in this Hive. I trusted Lucas mostly, but it never hurt to be a little cautious, even if he had done nothing but keep me alive.

"I will organize a security detail for you also," he bit out at the end of my story. "I know Ryder will be on top of it, but I have to do whatever I can to keep you safe."

I started to shake my head. I didn't want a security detail, I didn't want to be followed and watched every second of the day. It was bad enough being stuck in here, and I wanted to be able to go back to college soon. I couldn't let them stop me.

I quickly changed the subject to Tessa, hoping Lucas would forget about his plans to sic his guards on me. "You have to do something to stop it, she's not thinking straight." I got louder and angrier with each sentence. "Blake has her all wrapped up in love, and she misses me. She would do anything so we can live together and be in the same world again."

Tessa was lonely. Her family was rich but not really warm or caring. She always preferred my mom and spent a lot of her younger years in our house.

The silver in Lucas' eyes swirled, and some green lit up the iris. "I'll do what I can, but of course this decision does not rest with me alone. I can definitely talk to Blake though, but I cannot stop him either. Any vampire has the right to petition the council to turn a human. But rarely are they granted, so your friend should be fine. She will remain a human, and soon realize that the life of a feeder is no life for her. It is a phase many humans go through. Most come out the other side and walk away from us."

He wasn't exactly that reassuring. It wasn't the "No way, I'll totally stop Blake" I'd hoped for, but it would do for now. There was nothing more I could do except continue smashing Tessa's email inbox with my heartfelt pleas to stop being a dumbass.

We chatted for the next little while about this and that. Nothing and everything. It was nice to have someone to unload my feelings with, especially the heart-wrenching fear of seeing my best friend tied down and with a gun to his head.

"I'm not sure he's going to forgive me," I whispered to Lucas. "It's my fault he ended up like that. He could have died. Oliver could have died. I feel so guilty and responsible."

Lucas moved around my side of the bench then, sliding in next to me and wrapping an arm around my shoulders. "None of this is your fault, Charlie. You have a big heart. You care too much and you love too deeply. Our world, it's harsh. It's kill or be killed much of the time. Jayden understands this. He'll forgive you, mostly because there's nothing to forgive. So come on, let's head back to your apartment."

Lucas helped me up. "Also, I have a surprise for you."

He draped his arm around me again for the walk back to my room. Oliver was probably still there, but it didn't matter. I needed to clear the air with Jayden.

Lucas left me at the door. "I'll see you tomorrow," he said as he dropped a light kiss on my cheek and left. I realized once he was gone that he'd never showed me his surprise. He'd probably forgotten.

I took a deep breath and pushed open the door, eyes fluttering as I stepped inside, hoping like hell that my best friend didn't hate me. I already had one of them ignoring me. I needed Jayden.

Shouts enveloped me, followed by strong arms that wrapped around me and lifted me up into a hard chest. "Holy shit, Charlie, why didn't you tell us Lucas had blood wine! This is the best mutha-effing thing I have ever tasted."

Oliver spun me around once, before setting me back on my shaky legs. I realized then what Lucas' surprise must have been. He'd finally come through on the cartons of wine for me surviving the culling, and Oliver and Jayden had cracked open the first bottle. Or finished it actually, judging by the inch I could see left in the bottom.

I took a second to stare at the enforcer. He looked so much better, his injuries healed up and vitality back in his face. The olive-skinned ash had been looking mighty pale when he'd first dragged himself into our room after the Sanctum took off. Now he was all drunk and happy.

I turned my attention to Jayden, who was looking his normal gorgeous black self on the couch. He sat a little straighter and held out his arms to me. I didn't hesitate running across the room and throwing myself into his arms. "Missed you, bitch," he said as his muscled arms enfolded around me. "Don't you ever do anything like that again."

I pulled back to see him better, arching one eyebrow as I did.

Jayden grinned, before leaning in and resting his forehead against mine. "I don't care who the fuck has me and how many guns are pointed at my head, if you ever try and trade yourself for me, I will kick your ass so hard it will make Sanctum look like freakin' Care Bears."

I hadn't thought anyone had noticed in the chaos, except for Ryder of course, since I'd full on shoved him across the room to get to Jayden. But my best friend had seen too.

"Kick my ass all you want," I whispered, "but nothing will stop me coming for you. No matter what."

Jayden groaned, pulled back to stare at the ceiling. "Stubborn woman, you deserve to love someone as hardassed as Ryder. He might whip you into line."

I whacked him across the back of the head for that one, even though I knew he was joking. Plus, I'd never mentioned love before. I wasn't going to delve deep enough into my Ryder emotions to put a label on them.

I settled in beside Jayden, the couch snuggling around me. Oliver dropped in on the other side of us and handed me a glass of red. I held it between my hands, warming it.

"You have to stop with this Ryder stuff," I blurted out. The not thinking about him thing was not going well. "He doesn't want me. I mean, he freakin' kissed me like I was the only woman in his world, like he couldn't live or breathe without me. The walls were down, the fire was lit between us, and then he not only doused the flames, but iced right the hell over them."

I took a sip, letting the sweet copper tones cross my tongue. It was followed by a burst of blackberry and cherry, which was tart and crisp and delicious. I would have to let Lucas know this one was a hit also.

"Give Ryder time," Oliver said. "You mean something to him. He rarely lets anyone new into his world, but you somehow snaked your way in there almost from that first night in the club when you were just some human he ran into. He'll come around."

I shrugged, even though a part of me jumped with joy to think that it hadn't just been me who noticed the connection between us. Even from that very first night. Still, I wasn't sure I had the time or energy to wait around any longer. Ryder and I were friends, and that was where it would stay. This time I was almost certain of it.

THE NEXT MORNING I woke up dry-mouthed, with the slightest of hangovers. Luckily, Lucas had provided more than twenty bottles, because the boys and I had polished off at least ten of them – with a little help from Kyle and Markus, who had joined us later in the night. Ryder and Sam were no-shows, and I couldn't say I was surprised about that.

Breaking the silence, there was a loud knock on the door. It sent a pounding pain through my head, and for a second there I thought I might throw up. I closed my eyes for a second, gripping the thick blanket in hope of regaining my equilibrium. Thankfully, the dizziness and pain passed, enough so that I could drop my leg over the bed and stumble my way to the fridge for some blood.

O-negative, not tainted by alcohol. My fangs had descended and the bottle was already in my mouth when I wrenched open the front door. I was not in the mood for visitors today. The second I saw who it was, I instantly regretted not at least brushing my hair, or my teeth for that matter.

Ryder's eyes were light, the black swirling with silver as he stared. "Rough night?" he finally asked, his lips curling up as if he was fighting a smile. I narrowed my eyes and pulled the bottle of blood from my lips before sticking out my tongue and slamming the door in his face. I was totes not in the mood for Ryder. I sank back against the door, my body sagging as I fought the urge to tear the barrier open and throw myself at him. *Don't be pathetic, Charlie.* Not even for the hottest man that ever lived. I finished my blood before throwing the bottle into the trash.

"Charlie, open the door." His low words penetrated through to me, and I had to squeeze my eyes tightly shut, my nails cutting into my palms as if the pain would somehow make me stronger. "Charlie ... please."

My knees pretty much collapsed under me as he uttered those words. I had never heard that tone from him before, that level of low anguish and need. I bit my lip as tears rimmed my eyes. The pressure in my chest was sharp and biting as the force of my emotions slammed into me. I couldn't ignore him when he spoke like that, I needed to know what he was here for. This Ryder seemed different.

I wrenched the door open again. Ryder was still in the same position, his eyes almost purely silver now. We stared for a few long moments, and he didn't speak as the energy stretched between us. Finally, he held out a hand, asking me to take it, and jerked his head to the hallway, asking me to trust him, to follow him.

I swallowed roughly, before nodding in a jerky moment. "Just give me a second."

I dashed away from him into the bathroom, where I brushed my teeth in record time. I managed to tame the rat's nest hair I had going on, and even threw on a clean shirt. Mine had a few blood wine stains on it.

When I stepped back into the living area, Ryder was still in the same spot, just standing there waiting for me, as if he had not even moved an inch while I was gone. I couldn't stop my feet from crossing to him. My hand slipped into his like it had been made to fit. He led me from the room, silent, his body heat and spicy scent enveloping me as we walked side by side.

I had a lot of things to say and so many things to ask, but for now I was content to just be by his side, holding his hand. Ryder ended up leading me to the elevator, and we descended to the ground level. Stepping through the rubble of the entrance hall, most of the damage from our "car crash distraction" had been repaired, but not all of it.

Once we were outside I recognized the place he was taking me. It was that same green area Jayden and I had sat long ago, before the culling, where the ash had attacked us. Ryder and his men had stepped in.

"I never thanked you properly for that day," I said, breaking the silence. We were outside, standing together in the sun, the thick forest surrounding us. I loved the feel of the warmth on my face, the breeze as it ruffled my hair.

Ryder shifted his head to stare into my eyes, and then he graced me with a full-on grin. My heart sort of stopped, or stuttered at least. Ryder so rarely smiled like that, a true smile. It was all kinds of sexy and beautiful. Who was this new Ryder and could I keep him?

"That first night I saw you in the club, I knew you were trouble." He turned away again to stare off into the trees. "The days before the culling only cemented my view."

I barely heard his words over the sound of my heart pounding in my ears.

"You were so stubborn and willful, fighting me every step of the way. Resisting training, resisting killing, even though it was to save your own life. Like I said to you before, watching you fight was torture. Every single second. Knowing you could be culled before I had a chance to discover more of the hidden fire that fills you. Charlie, I have been emotionally dead for a lot of years, doing my duty, fighting the pain of who I am, of what I did. Not allowing anyone in. Well, I'm done fighting it. I can't with you."

My breath hitched at his admission.

He reached out, gently tucked a strand of hair behind my ear. "You came along out of nowhere and you completely disarmed me. You made me feel. And now I don't know what the hell to do about it. I don't know what I'm ready for..."

I leaned into him, our bodies melting together. His honesty took me completely off guard. "We don't have to make any rules now, Ryder. You have to find peace about what happened to Molly. Otherwise that is a cloud which will live over us forever."

I got all brave then, raising up on my tiptoes to press my lips to the corner of his mouth, his delicious scent and taste drawing me in. "This is enough for me, for now," I whispered against him, and with a groan he yanked me closer, our bodies slamming into each other.

"Never enough with you, Charlie."

Then he was kissing me, like the night in the karaoke club, but this time tinged with so much more desperation. We had been through a lot since then. That night in the Hive with the Sanctum had cemented the ties between us. Ryder had protected me and I would never forget it. There was a hunger in the way he kissed me, like he would never get enough.

"Is this why you were trying to keep me from coming back to save Jayden?" I asked as we pulled back for air.

His swirling eyes locked in on mine. One of his hands ran up and down my back, as if he just wanted to be touching me. "I was angry with the situation, but also with myself. I knew I should not bring you back to the Hive, but I couldn't say no to you when you needed me to say yes. I don't like that sort of weakness. I should always be able to do the right thing, even if it is the hard thing to do. I should be able to protect you and my team without giving in to you just because you flash those gorgeous silver-black eyes at me."

I smiled, dropping to my feet, my heart still rapid as I tried to adjust to this sudden change in Ryder. He was so open. So free with his words. I wanted more of this. I wanted all of it. But I also understood what he was trying to say.

"You did the right thing, Ryder. Any relationship works two ways. You have to trust I'm strong enough to handle the bad as well as the good. I would rather walk into battle by your side than cower in the car while my best friend is killed."

He smiled again. "I'm starting to see that, and having you by my side feels right."

A shadowy figure stepped out of the trees then, and Ryder tensed for a moment before he realized it was a friend, not foe.

"Hey, bro, unicorn, I've been looking for you guys." Kyle loped across to us, all happy and casual-like. He was out of enforcer black, wearing dark blue slacks and a button shirt. It was the most formal I'd seen from Kyle. Even his unruly dirty-blond hair was brushed back, emphasizing the defined cheeks and broad features in his handsome face. "Everyone is gathering in the stadium. It's time to say farewell to our fallen soldiers."

Ryder didn't say anything more, but as we turned and followed Kyle, things felt right between us. We still had a long way to go. I had no idea what Ryder wanted in the long term from us, but this felt like a positive step in the right direction.

THE QUORUM WERE DRESSED in their finest attire. It seemed nearly all of the Hive was assembled. The stadium that held the culling was now completely transformed into a clean and peaceful ceremonial hall. White and blue silk draped the walls. The bloodstained fighting mats that had covered the ground had been pulled up to reveal polished wood floors. A large chandelier hung in the middle of the room, giving an elegant ambiance that had been missing from my days in this room. Before us all lay ten gold urns. Odd that the place these men fought for their lives would also become the place they were laid to rest. A podium with a microphone stood empty, and Ryder squeezed my hand before approaching it. I stayed behind, leaning against the wall, next to Kyle and the other enforcers. My eyes remained locked on Ryder as he sidled through and around the masses of gathered Hive members. He never even glanced at the beautiful faces of our people around him. His focus was solely on the enforcers he had lost. When he reached the podium, he stood very still for a few long moments. No one made noises or spoke. The silence felt both respectful and heavy. People had lost friends, and loved ones. After this time of silence, Ryder cleared his throat and all eyes were on him.

"For centuries the ash have laid down their lives to protect the Hive, to protect the vampires and the Quorum that govern it. These ten men died doing their jobs ... protecting all of you. They will be remembered! They will be honored!" His voice grew strong and loud toward the end. These words were met with applause. This Hive hierarchy really confused me. They made us kill ourselves for the opportunity to live with them. Then, even though the vampires were physically stronger, they made us fight to protect them. But we outnumbered them ten to one.

"These enforcers are mine to protect!" Ryder was all deadly now, his long arm pointing to all of us leaning against the wall. "And I will protect what is mine."

There was no mistaking that threat. Whomever the mole was should be shaking in their boots right now. I held a little hope, too, that since he so readily grouped me in with them, it was time to mention that I really wanted to be an enforcer. Maybe he'd actually consider it at this point. Please, God, don't make me answer phones for the rest of my life.

A group of enforcers walked out military-style in a perfect line. They picked up the vases, and as they turned to march from the stadium, golden urns cradled in their hands, they stopped only once to salute Ryder. The heaviness broke then and Ryder indicated that people could leave. The Quorum disbanded, and a few members trailed over to talk to the lead enforcer.

Kyle and I strolled within earshot, stopping in the pretense of waiting, but we were really listening in. I knew of most of the Quorum members now, but except for that lovely day where they forced me to go with them to the medical wing, I had not really met them.

The leader of the second house was a willowy female. She had dark blond curls that fell around her face. She was a lot taller than my five feet seven and looked extra cheerleader cute, even though she was most probably deadlier than cancer.

She was scolding Ryder. "You have one of my vampires in the pit who has had an unnecessarily long sentence. A month for biting an ash?" Her tone indicated that this was barely even a crime at all.

Ryder stood taller, his height giving him domination advantage over her. "A month for attacking and feeding off of a female ash."

The Quorum members looked at me quickly before turning away again.

"Let him go, he has served enough time," said the dour and jowly male leader of the third house, before turning with cheer-vamp and leaving.

As he watched their retreating backs, Ryder's face indicated that he wanted to beat the Quorum into submission, but instead he just walked over to Kyle and me.

"Well, duty calls," Ryder said.

Kyle grabbed my hand. "Wanna see the pit?"

Ryder shot him a glare, but before he could protest I nodded. I totally wanted to know what this infamous pit was.

Ryder shook his head, looking resigned. "It's not going to be pretty, and starved vampires are pretty deadly. But if you want to come along..."

Even with our talk outside, I knew it was going to take him some time to stop treating me like a delicate flower and realize I was just as tough as most of the ash. Sure, I had boobs, but that only increased my power.

We all walked to the line of elevators. I paused, expecting we would take them down into the crater of hell or something. I mean, where else would the pit be? So I was a little surprised when instead of going to the normal silver elevators, we went around the corner, and there, resting in a small alcove, was an elevator with a red door. I had never seen it before in all my time at the Hive. It was perfectly hidden away. Ryder and Kyle put their thumbs on a keypad and the elevator beeped and flared to life. Whoa, legit super-secret. My stomach knotted in anxiety and excitement.

The doors opened and we stepped inside. One button on the panel, labeled "pit." Ryder hit it and the elevator made its way down.

"So," I asked, "the pit is what exactly?"

Ryder looked at me, seemingly thinking about his answer. "It's the Hive's version of jail."

Kyle snorted. "More like a mixture of, jail, solitary confinement, and torture."

Ryder and Kyle exchanged a grin. I felt a moment of queasiness at the mental images those words provoked. I must have paled, because Ryder stepped a little closer to me, his heat warming my cool limbs.

"You can still back out," he said.

I swallowed down my fear and stood taller, squaring my shoulders. "I'm fine."

The slightest of smiles tipped up the corner of his lips. Nice to know I could amuse him.

The elevator ground to a halt and opened to reveal a long hallway. Before we even stepped out I was hit with a wall of stench. It immediately had me gagging. Since becoming an ash I'd learned to separate out various smells, and right now I was surrounded by blood, sweat, and urine – plus a completely disgusting concoction of bodily fluids. To add extra ambiance to the stink room, there were distant but drawn out screams echoing across the stone chamber.

We walked slowly down the hall to a man sitting behind a reception desk. He was a vamp, with a hard, lined face, and gray hair. Vamps didn't age, so he must have been infected at an older age. This is where the Hive stuck old people, I guessed.

"Hey, Marty."

Ryder shook his hand and the man nodded, standing swiftly, looking surprised. "You bringing her in?"

Ryder shot me a side glance before chuckling, "No, she's training. I'm here to release Vincent Crow early. Quorum's orders."

Marty nodded. "Good thing too. He's been going crazy, screaming about humans and rejecting blood."

Ryder frowned. "He hasn't been here long enough to do that much damage."

The old vampire shrugged. "Everyone's different. The pit wears us all down. He's in cell 56H." He turned to a machine and ran Ryder's card key through it. Once we had clearance, the three of us stepped further into the pit, leaving Marty behind.

We walked down a series of twists and turns before stopping at a small door marked 56H. The screaming was much louder now, coming in from all directions. It was especially strong from inside Vincent's room.

I started to differentiate the sounds out, and realized he was screaming words.

"You don't understand! I need food and ... water." His voice sounded strained, weak but still in a screaming pitch.

Ryder banged hard on the door. "Vincent Crow! Your sentence has been suspended early by order of the Quorum." Ryder plugged his keycard in the small door and it popped open with a click. The space they kept the prisoners in was tiny and I wasn't prepared for the dirty, half naked body of Vincent to come tumbling out.

We all gasped at what we saw. Vincent was little more than skin and bones. He looked like a victim from a wartime concentration camp. As he rolled over, I could see bloody infected cuts along his back and side. Why wasn't he healing? Did the pit stop that somehow?

As his face came into view, my hand flew to my

mouth. The once beautiful vampire was gone. Stress and wrinkles marred his eyes. He had frizzy hair, blotchy skin. He looked ... human.

His eyes flew open as he focused on me, recognition lighting them up. He pointed a bony arm at me. "She's ... the cure," he rasped.

Holy Fuck. My hand flew to my neck as the memory of that night assaulted me. How long ago was it? A week? Two? He bit me and then ... and now ... the man before me was a frail human, starved of food and water, given blood when he clearly had no need for it.

Ryder took a step closer and made a few out of character gestures. "Fuck," he said, which was also out of character.

Before I could speak, or even think about what the hell was going on here, Ryder whipped out his gun and shot the man right between the eyes.

To a vampire that would have done nothing but hurt and piss him off, but this man was human. It was more than enough to end his life. I jumped, a scream ripped from my throat. Ryder had just killed a man, just like that without thought or consideration.

Shit ... I knew Ryder. He only acted like that when he was protecting his men or me – it had been to protect me. I was in so much trouble.

Ryder ignored me for the moment, looking at Kyle. "We need to hide the body."

Kyle looked shaken, but nodded.

I dropped back against the wall, my breathing ragged,

my heart seeming to skip a few beats as it tried to keep up with my racing pulse. It was finally penetrating my brain now, the prisoner's words. The reason Ryder had lost his shit and killed a frail human.

To keep this secret. To keep me safe. Because I was the motherfucking cure for vampirism.

THE NEXT FEW days passed in a blur of stress and panic. I basically hid in my room, expecting at any moment the Quorum were going to arrive and haul me off to my public execution. Of course, I probably should have trusted Ryder when he'd pulled me aside right after we left the pit area and promised that he would take care of it all. That he and Kyle would wrap everything up so that no one found out about the vampire I'd cured.

Because we all knew what would happen if the vamps figured out I could cure them. I was as a good as dead.

"You need to get that lovely ass out of bed and shower or something," Jayden yelled through my door, about to leave for his shift in the feeder floor. I hadn't been at my job for a few days, but since no one had smashed in my apartment looking for me, I guessed Ryder had that covered also.

I sighed into the silence. Jayden was right. I needed to get out of here. Staring at the walls was driving me insane, and it didn't answer a single question I had. I just needed to stay busy until Ryder returned.

I dragged myself up, threw on some sweats and took

the elevator up to the roof. A run was what I needed, some sun, some fresh air. Some time without vamps who maybe didn't yet know there was a ticking time bomb under their roof. No wonder the Sanctum had been hired to find me. Someone knew there was something strange in my blood. Maybe they didn't know exactly what it was yet, but how long before they figured it out? What would the humans do if they found out? Did my blood do anything to ash? Oh God, I was in deep shit.

My feet slapped against the track, my body falling into its old running patterns, my muscles enjoying the stretch and burn after so many days of inactivity. Just as I was rounding up for my tenth lap, a blur caught my attention. I spun to the left, paranoid as usual, but didn't see anything. Turning back to the track, I gave a little shriek at the mountain of man standing right in my path.

As I skidded to a halt, I tripped over my feet and tumbled straight at him. He opened his arms and caught me with ease, and in that moment I felt a sense of peace which had been missing the past few days.

"Ryder," I said, my voice low and muffled against his shirt. "Is everything okay?"

He pulled me closer, his strong arms lifting me further into his body. He lowered his head right next to my ear. "I promised you I would take care of it, at the moment no one knows of you being the cure, and I plan on keeping it that way for as long as possible."

I pulled my head back so I could stare into his eyes. "So what do we do now? What do I do now?"

As the slight breeze tousled his dark hair, a rakish grin crossed his features, and I realized how badly I'd been missing him. Even when we fought our feelings, he'd still always been around.

"Have dinner with me, Charlie?"

It took me a moment to realize what he'd just said. *Holy shit!* Ryder had just asked me on a date. I blinked a few times, trying to conceal my excitement. Getting up on my tiptoes, I pressed my lips against his. The kiss was brief but electrifying. I loved that even with everything hanging over our heads – the Sanctum, my vampire cure blood – Ryder still wanted to take me on a date. He couldn't have said a more perfect thing to me right then, and I knew we would deal with the rest when it came. I pulled back slightly, our eyes still locked on each other.

"Yes," I said. "A thousand times yes, Ryder."

Acknowledgments from Jaymin:

As always, thank you to my family for being perfect. You love me even when I'm a cranky, stressed out writer, and show me every day that I am blessed in a million ways just to have you in my life. Thank you to my beta's Andi and Marice for taking the time to read and comment on Ash. I appreciate you more than you know. Lastly a huge thanks to my BAFF Leia, writing this book with you was beyond awesome. Even though we're both strong willed and have definite ideas of how to write our characters, it was pretty much seamless writing Ash together. We make a wicked team and I can't wait to do it all over again. Love you girl!

P.S Extra huge thanks to all of you amazing readers. We love you guys. <3

ACKNOWLEDGMENTS

Acknowledgments from Leia:

I'm so thankful to my fans who suggested I read one of Jaymin's books. It started a friendship that I have no doubt will be lifelong, BAFF forever. Ash started as an idea which grew over 2,000 Facebook messages and then emails and finally this finished project. I'm grateful to my family for supporting my writing which means watching my kids, helping with dinner and a hundred other things. To my betas Bridgett Zaidi and Priscilla Whitenight for your super-fast reading and awesome insight. Jaymin, we make one hell of a team! Bring on book 2.

BOOKS FROM LEIA STONE

Matefinder Trilogy (Optioned for film)
Matefinder: Book 1
Devi: Book 2
Balance: Book 3

Hive Trilogy
Ash: Book 1
Anarchy: Book 2
Annihilate: Book 3

Dragons and Druids Series
Skyborn
Earthbound
Magictorn

Stay in touch with Leia: www.amazon.com/
author/leiastone

Email list for exclusive stuff! **https://
tinyurl.com/y88nx5bw**
Facebook: www.facebook.com/leia.stone/

BOOKS FROM JAYMIN EVE

Stay in touch with Jaymin: www.Amazon.com/
author/jaymineve
Facebook: www.facebook.com/JayminEve.Author

Made in the USA
Columbia, SC
13 February 2020